AMULET BOOKS * NEW YORK

# THE
# GRACES

## LAURE EVE

Cataloging-in-Publication Data has been applied for and may be obtained
from the Library of Congress.

ISBN: 978-1-4197-2123-6

Text copyright © 2016 Laure Eve
Jacket and title page illustrations copyright © 2016 Spencer Charles
Book design by Maria T. Middleton

Printed and bound in U.S.A.

10 9 8 7 6 5 4 3 2 1

Amulet Books are available at special discounts when purchased in quantity
for premiums and promotions as well as fundraising or educational
use. Special editions can also be created to specification. For
details, contact specialsales@abramsbooks.com or the
address below.

**ABRAMS** The Art of Books
115 West 18th Street, New York, NY 10011
abramsbooks.com

PART
ONE

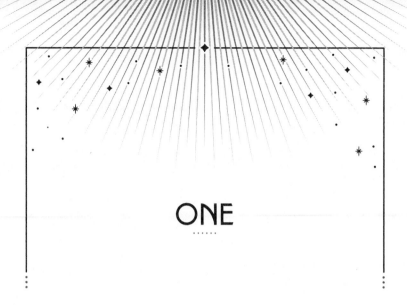

# ONE

EVERYONE SAID THEY WERE WITCHES.

I desperately wanted to believe it. I'd only been at this school a couple of months, but I saw how it was. They moved through the corridors like sleek fish, ripples in their wake, stares following their backs and their hair. Their peers had grown used to it by now, or at least pretended they had, and tried their hardest to look bored by it all. But the younger kids hadn't yet learned how to hide their silly dog eyes, their glamoured, naked expressions.

Summer Grace, the youngest, was fifteen and in my year. She backchatted the teachers no one else dared to, her voice drawling with just the right amount of rude to make it clear she was rebelling, but not enough to get her into serious trouble. Her light Grace hair was dyed jet black and her eyes were always ringed in black kohl and masses of eye shadow. She wore skinny jeans and boots with buckles or Victorian laces. Her fingers were covered in thick silver rings and she always had on at least two necklaces. She thought pop music was "the devil's work"—always said with a sarcastic smile—and if she caught you talking about boy bands, she'd slay you for it. The worst thing was, everyone else joined in, even the people you'd been excitedly discussing the band with not three seconds before. Because she was a Grace.

Thalia and Fenrin Grace, at seventeen, were the eldest. Non-identical twins, though you could see the family resemblance. Thalia was slim and limber and willowed, her fine-boned wrists accentuated by fistfuls of tinkling bangles. She had a tight coil of coarse, caramel-colored strands permanently woven around a thick lock of her honey hair. She wore her hair loose, rippling across her shoulders, or pulled carelessly into a topknot from which tendrils always slid out to wisp around her neck. She wore long skirts with delicate beadwork and rows of tiny mirrors sewn onto the hem, thin open-necked tops that floated against her skin, fringed scarves with metallic threading slung around her hips. Some of the girls tried to copy her, but they always looked as if they were wearing a gypsy costume to school, which got them no end of grief, and then they never wore them again. Even I hadn't been able to resist trying something like it, just once, when I first came here. I'd looked like an idiot. Thalia just seemed like she was born in those clothes.

And then there was Fenrin.

Fenrin.

Fenrin Grace. Even his name sounded mythical, like he was more creature than boy. He was the school Pan. Blonder than his twin, Thalia, he let his hair grow loose and floppy over his forehead. He wore white muslin shirts a lot and leather cords wrapped around his wrists. A varnished turret shell dangled from a leather thong around his neck every day. He never seemed to take it off. The weight of it rested against his chest, a perfect V. He was lean, lean. His smile was arrogant and lazy.

And I was completely and utterly in love with him.

It was the stupidest, most obvious thing I could have done, and I hated myself for it. Every girl with eyes loved Fenrin. But I was not like those prattling, chattering things with their careful head tosses and thick, cloying lip gloss. Inside, buried down deep where no one could see it, was the core of me, burning endlessly, coal black and coal bright.

The Graces had friends, but then they didn't. Once in a while, they would descend on someone they'd never hung out with before, making them theirs for a time, but a time was usually all it was. They changed friends like some people changed hairstyles, as if perpetually waiting for someone better to come along. They never went out drinking in the pubs on the weekends, never went to the Wednesday student night in the local club like everyone else. The rumor was that they were barely allowed to leave their house, except to come to school. No one had real details of their personal lives—except for whoever Fenrin was sleeping with in any given week, as he never hid it. He'd tour the girl around school for however long it lasted, one arm slung over her shoulders in a lazy fashion, and she would drip off him, giggling madly. They were nothing, just distractions. He was waiting for someone special, someone different who would catch his attention so suddenly and so completely, he'd wonder how he had survived all this time without them. They all were, all three of them. I could see it.

All I had to do was find a way to show them it was me they'd been waiting for.

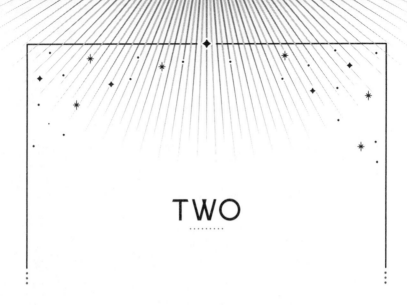

# TWO

AT FIRST, I'D THOUGHT MOVING TO THIS TOWN WAS punishment for what I'd done.

It was miles from where I'd grown up, and I'd never even heard of it before we came here. My mother had spent a couple of holidays here as a child and had somehow decided that this tiny, old coastal town caught between the sea and acres of wilds was exactly the right kind of place to move on with our lives after the last few awful months. Dunes, woods, and moors peppered with standing stones crawled across the landscape, surrounding the place like a barrier. I'd come from a cement suburb rammed with cornershops, furniture warehouses, and hairdressers. The closest thing to nature we'd had there was the council-maintained flowerbeds in the high street. Here, it was hard to forget what really birthed you. Nature was the thing you walked on and breathed in.

Before the Graces noticed me, I was the quiet one who stuck to the back corners of places and tried not to draw attention. A couple of other people had been friendly enough when I'd first arrived—we'd hung out a little and they'd given me a crash course in how things ran here. But they got tired of the way I wrapped myself up tight so no one could see inside me, and I got tired of the way they all talked about things I couldn't even muster up fake enthusiasm for, like getting laid and partying and TV shows about people getting laid and partying.

The Graces were different.

When I'd been told they were witches, I'd laughed in disbelief, thinking it was time for a round of "lie to the new girl, see if she'll swallow it." But although some people rolled their eyes, you could see that everyone, underneath the cynicism, thought it could be true. There was something about the Graces. They were one step removed from the rest of the school, minor celebrities with mystery wrapped around them like fur stoles, an ethereal air to their presence that whispered tantalizingly of magic.

But I needed to know for sure.

* * * * *

I'd spent some time trying to work out their angle, the one thing I could do that would get me on their radar. I could be unusually pretty, which I wasn't. I could be friends with their friends, which I wasn't—no one I'd met so far was in their inner circle. I could be into surfing, the top preoccupation of anyone remotely cool around here, but I'd never even tried it before and would likely be embarrassingly bad. I could be loud, but loud people burned out quickly—everyone got bored of them. So when I first arrived, I did nothing and tried to get by. My problem was that I tended to really think things through. Sometimes they'd paralyze me, the "what ifs" of action, and I didn't do anything at all because it was safer. I was afraid of what could happen if I let it.

But on the day they noticed me, I was acting on pure instinct, which was how I knew afterward that it was right. See, real witches would be tuned in to the secret rhythm of the universe. They wouldn't mathematically weigh and counterweigh every possible option because creatures of magic don't do that. They weren't afraid of surrendering themselves. They had the courage to be different, and they never cared what people thought. It just wasn't important to them.

I wanted so much to be like that.

It was lunch break, and a rare slice of spring warmth had driven everyone outdoors. The field was still wet from last night's rain, so we were all squeezed onto the hard courts. The boys played soccer. The girls sat on the low wall at one end, or stretched their bare legs out on the tarmac and leaned their backs against the chain-link fence, talking and squealing and texting.

Fenrin's current crowd was kicking a ball about, and he joined in halfheartedly, stopping every so often to talk to a girl who had run up to him, his grin wide and easy. He shone in the crowd like a beacon, among them all but separated, willingly. He played with them and hung out with them and laughed with them just fine, but something about his manner told me that he held the true part of himself back.

That was the part that interested me the most.

I got to the wall early and opened my book, hoping I looked self-sufficiently cool and reserved, rather than sad and alone. I didn't know if he'd seen me. I didn't look up. Looking up would make it obvious I was faking.

Twenty minutes in and one of the soccer guys, whose name was Danny but who everyone called Dannyboy like it was one name, was flirting with an especially loud, giggly girl called Niral by booting the ball at her section of the wall and making her scream every time it bounced past. The more he did it, the more I saw his friends roll their eyes behind his back.

Niral didn't like me. Which was strange because everyone else left me alone once they'd established that I was dull. But I'd caught her staring at me a few times, as if something about my face offended her. I wondered what it was she saw. We'd never even exchanged a word.

I'd looked up the meaning of her name once. It meant "calm." Life was full of little ironies. She wore big, fake, gold hoop earrings and tiny skirts, and her voice had a rattling screech to it, like a magpie's. I'd seen her with her parents in town before. Her plump little mother wore beautiful saris and wove her long hair in a plait. Niral cut her hair short and shaved it on one side. She didn't like what she was from.

Niral also didn't like this timid girl called Anna, who looked like a doll with her tight black curls and big dark eyes. Niral enjoyed teasing people, and her voice always got this vicious sneer to it when she did. Anna, her favorite target, sat on the wall a little way down from me. Niral had come out to the hard courts with a friend, looked around a moment, and then chose to sit right next to Anna, whose tiny child body had tensed up while she hunched even closer to her phone.

I had English and math with Niral, and she seemed pretty ordinary. Maybe she was loud because part of her knew this. She didn't seem to like people she couldn't immediately understand. Anna was quiet and childlike, a natural target. Niral liked to tell people that Anna was a lesbian. She never said "gay" but "lesbian" in a drawling voice that emphasized each syllable. Anna must have had skin made of glue because she couldn't take any little jibes. They didn't roll off her—they stuck to her in thick, glowing folds. Niral was whispering and pointing, and Anna was curling over as if she wanted to crawl into her own stomach.

Then Dannyboy joined in, hoping to impress Niral. He booted the soccer ball over to Anna with admirable precision, smacking into her hands and knocking her phone from them. It smashed to the ground with a flat crack sound.

Dannyboy ambled over. "Sorry," he said, offhand, but his eyes were on Niral.

Anna ducked her head down. Her black curls dangled next to her cheeks. She didn't know what to do. If she went for the phone, they might carry on at her. If she stayed there, they might take her phone and try to continue the game.

I watched all this over the top of my book.

I really hated that kind of casual bullying that people ignored because it was just easier—I'd been on the end of it before. I watched the ball as it rolled slowly to me, banging against my foot. I stood, clutching it, and instead of pitching it back to him, I threw it the opposite way, onto the field. It bounced off along the wet grass.

"What did you do that for?" said another boy, angrily. I didn't know his name—he didn't hang out with Fenrin. Dannyboy and Niral looked at me as one.

Fenrin was watching. I saw his golden silhouette stop out of the corner of my eye.

"God, I'm sorry," I said. "I kind of thought those two might want to be alone for a while instead of nauseating the rest of us."

There was a crushing silence.

Then the angry boy started to laugh. "Dannyboy, take your girlfriend and get the ball, man. And we'll see you in, like, a couple of hours."

Dannyboy shuffled uncomfortably.

"There's the thicket at the back of the field," I commented. "Nice and secluded."

"You stupid bitch," said Niral to me.

"Maybe don't give it out," I replied quietly, "if you can't take it."

"New girl's got a point," said the angry boy.

Niral sat still for a moment, trying to decide what to do. The tide had turned against her.

"Come on," she said to her friend. They gathered their bags and their makeup and their phones and walked off.

Dannyboy didn't dare look after her—the angry guy was still ribbing him. He went back to playing soccer. Anna retrieved her phone and pretended to text, her fingers tapping a nonsensical rhythm. I nearly missed her almost-whisper. "Thought the screen was cracked right through. Looked broke."

She didn't thank me or even look up. I was glad. I was at least as awkward as she was, and both of us awkwarding at each other would have been too much for me. I sat back down next to her, buried my face in my book, and waited for my pulse to stop its erratic drumming.

When the bell rang, I shouldered my bag, and then and there made my bold ploy. Without thinking about it I walked up to Fenrin, as if I were going to talk to him. I felt his eyes on me as I approached, his curiosity. Instead of following it up with words, though, I kept walking past. At the last moment my eyes lifted to his, and before my face could start its tragic burn, I gave him an eyebrow raise. It meant, *what can you do?* It meant, *yeah I see you, and so?* It meant, *I'm not too bothered about talking to you, but I'm not ignoring you either because that would be just a little bit too studied.*

I lowered my gaze and carried on.

"Hey," he called behind me.

I stopped. My heart beat its fists furiously against my ribs. He was a few feet away.

"Defender of the weak," he said with a grin. His first ever words to me.

"I just don't like bullies so much," I replied.

"You can be our resident superhero. Save the innocent. Wear a cape."

I offered him a smile, a wry twist of the mouth. "I'm not nice enough to be a superhero."

"No? Are you trying to tell me you're the villain?"

I paused, wondering how to answer. "I don't think anyone is as black and white as that. Including you."

His grin widened. "Me?"

"Yeah. I think sometimes you must get bored of how much everyone worships you, when maybe they don't even know the real you. Maybe the real you is darker than the one you show the world."

The set of his mouth froze. Another me from another time recoiled in horror at my recklessness. People didn't like it when I said things like this.

"Huh," he said, thoughtfully. "Not out to make friends, are you?"

Inside, I shriveled. I'd blown it. "I guess . . . I'm just looking for the right ones," I said. "The ones who feel like I do. That's all."

I'd told myself I wouldn't do this anymore. They didn't know me here—I could be a new me, the 2.0 version, now with improved social skills.

*Stop talking. Stop talking. Walk away before you make it worse.*

"And how *do* you feel?" he asked me. His voice wasn't teasing. He seemed curious.

Well, I might as well go out with a bang.

"Like I need to find the truth of the world," I said. "Like there's more than this." I raised a hand helplessly to the gray school building looming over us. "More than just . . . *this*, this life, every day, on and on, until I'm dead. There's got to be. I want to find it. I *need* to find it."

His eyes had clouded over. I thought I knew that look—it was the careful face you made around crazy people.

I sighed. "I have to go. Sorry if I offended you."

He said nothing as I walked away.

I'd just exposed my soul to the most popular boy in school, and in return he'd given me silence.

Maybe I could persuade my mother to move towns again.

\* \* \* \* \*

It was raining the next day, so I ate my lunch in the library. I was alone—the friendly girls I'd hung out with when I'd first arrived never asked me to sit with them in the cafeteria anymore, and I was glad to have the time to read more of my book before class. It was too cold to go outside, and Mr. Jarvis, the librarian, was nowhere to be seen, so I put my bag on the table and opened my

Tupperware behind it. Cold beans on toast with melted cheese on top. A bit slimy, but cheap to buy and easy to make, two important factors in my house. I took out my lunch fork, the only one in our cutlery drawer that didn't look as though it came from a plastic picnic set. It was a thick kind of creamy-colored silver and had this flattened plate of scrollwork on the handle bottom. I washed it every night and took it back to school with me every day. It made me feel a bit more special when I used it, like I wasn't just some scruff, and my mother never noticed it was missing.

I'd worried about my conversation with Fenrin that whole day and well into the night, turning my words over again and again, wondering what I could have done better. In my mind, my voice was even and measured, a beautiful cadence that positioned itself perfectly between drawling and musical. But in reality, I had an awkward town accent I couldn't quite shift, all hard edges and soft, dopey burrs. I wondered if he'd heard it. I wondered if he'd judged me because of it.

I ate and read my book, this particular kind of fantasy novel that I secretly loved. It was my favorite thing to do—eat and read. The world just shut up for a while. I'd just got to the bit where Princess Mar'a'tha had shot an arrow into one of the demon horde attacking the royal hunting camp, and then I felt it.

Him. I felt him.

I looked up into his face, which was tilted down at my shit, embarrassing book and my shit, embarrassing lunch.

"Am I interrupting?" said Fenrin. A long wave of his sun-gold-tipped hair had slipped from behind his ear and hung by his cheekbone. I actually caught a waft of him. He smelled like a thicker, manlier kind of vanilla. His skin was lightly tanned.

I hadn't lowered my fork; I just looked at him dumbly over it.

*It worked. I told him the truth and it worked.*

"Eating in the library again, when the rest of the school uses the cafeteria," he mused. "You must enjoy being alone."

"Yes," I said. But I had misjudged it because his eyebrow rose.

"Er, okay. Sorry for disturbing you," he said, and turned away. I lowered my fork.

*NO, WAIT!* I wanted to shout. You were supposed to say something self-deprecatingly witty at this point, weren't you, and get a laugh, and then you'd see it in his eyes—he'd think you were cool. And like that, you'd be in.

But nothing came out of my mouth, and my chance was slipping away.

The only other person in the library was this guy Marcus from Fenrin's year (always Mar*cus*, never just Marc, I'd heard someone say with a sneer). He had the kind of presence that folded inward, as if he couldn't bear to be noticed. I understood that and gave him a wide berth.

So I found it interesting when Fenrin turned to Marcus and locked eyes with him instead of ignoring him. And instead of trying to be invisible, Marcus held his gaze. Fenrin's mouth drew into a thin, tight line. Marcus didn't move.

After a moment more of this strangeness that wasn't quite aggression and wasn't quite anything easy to read, Fenrin snorted, turned, and caught me watching. I tried to smile, giving him an opening.

It seemed to work. He folded his arms, rocked on his feet.

"So, at the risk of looking like an idiot coming back for another serving," he said to me, "why *do* you enjoy being alone?"

My mouth opened and shut and I gave him a truth, because truth had got me this far, and truth seemed like it would endear him to me more than anything else ever could.

I forced myself to look straight into his eyes. "I can stop pretending when I'm alone."

Fenrin smiled.

Bingo, as my mother often said.

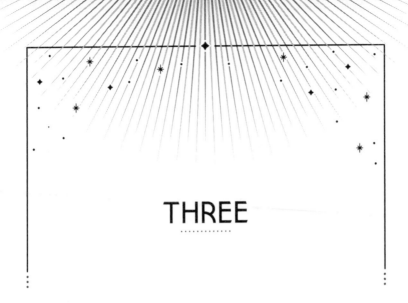

# THREE

THERE WAS A STORY ABOUT THE GRACES, A STORY SO woven into the fabric of the town that even my mother had already heard about it from someone at work. It was about Thalia and Fenrin's eighth birthday party.

Grace birthday parties had been legendary up until then. Most of the mothers around town would pray that their child would get an invitation, so they could come, too, and lounge in Esther Grace's spacious French country kitchen, drinking cocktails in slender flutes and stealing glances at her pretty husband, Gwydion, as he passed by with his easy, loping stride.

The party had been fairly standard all afternoon. The mothers had put on their most carefully chosen outfits, their most vibrant shades of lipstick, and had lingered in the kitchen drinking freshly made mojitos with mint from Esther's sprawling herb garden. Their tinkling laughter had grown stronger as the day wore on, and they had stopped checking on the children so often, who had had their fill of food and party games and were congregating in the parlor. The Graces had the kind of house with a parlor.

No one knew for sure who suggested the Ouija board, but most of the children thought it was Fenrin. He was a show-off, after all. They'd been strictly forbidden to touch it, but that didn't stop him from producing the key to the cabinet it was stored in and balancing carefully on a chair to reach the highest shelf. Down it came, a solid shape wrapped in a rust-colored velvet cloth and bound with loops of black ribbon. When the ribbon was undone and the velvet unraveled, there sat a sandalwood box that gave off a creamy wood smell when you put your nose right up to it.

Half the children felt their hearts quicken in fear. Because what if? But Fenrin just laughed at them and said there was no such thing as ghosts, and did they want to play or did they want to be sissies for the rest of their lives?

So they played—every last one of them.

For the truth of what happened next, you'd have to talk to the parlor walls. Accounts varied so wildly from child to child, no one ever did know for sure exactly how it had played out.

When the adults heard screaming, they rushed into the parlor and found Matthew Feldspar on the floor, his eyes shut and his breathing shallow. No matter how violently his mother shook him, he wouldn't wake up.

He was rushed to the hospital.

By the time they arrived he had come to, and the doctor who examined him assured his mother that he exhibited no signs of physical abuse. Tests turned up nothing unusual, and the eventual conclusion was that he had suffered a fainting fit of some kind. Perhaps he hadn't eaten enough that day. Perhaps it was a reaction to all the excitement a birthday party could bring.

Mrs. Feldspar, however, was not having any of that. She was adamant that Matthew was not a weak boy, and had never fainted in his life. She much preferred the idea that something had been done to him, something that a doctor wouldn't be able to see. Something only the child of a witch could inflict. Accusations flew around for weeks afterward. Some said it was revenge— Matthew had a reputation for spreading rumors, as well as for goosing other kids to make them cry. He'd apparently done it to Fenrin only a couple of weeks before, and then told everyone Fenrin had enjoyed it just a bit too much. Fenrin had tried to punch him in gym class and earned detention for it. After that, things seemed to have died down. Until the birthday party.

Mrs. Feldspar said that Matthew was a playful boy, that was all. She tried to press criminal charges, but the police laughed at her. She tried to sue the Graces, but lawyers told her there was no evidence of any kind of assault on her son, and without evidence she didn't have a case.

The Feldspars left town not long after that.

No one was allowed to go to Fenrin and Thalia's ninth birthday party; but instead of feeling snubbed, the Graces went right ahead with it, inviting a whole swathe of people from out of town. For days before, you could see them arriving at the house. Some of them looked like rock stars and some of them like American Psycho, a few were as coolly bohemian as the Graces, and all of them were striking, in one way or another.

The twins' birthday was August 1, and if you went past the top of their lane on that day, you could hear music and laughter coming from the garden, and smell ginger carrot cakes with cream cheese frosting, sausages in mustard sauce, and freshly made lemonade.

Every year Thalia and Fenrin had their birthday party, but no one from school ever got another invitation. Two or three days before, the town was flooded with Grace strangers, and two or three days afterward they were gone again. The most popular rumor was that they were witches from around the country gathering for some kind of debauched ritual. The birthday was an excuse, the town whispered—after the children went to bed, the adults held their own, darker kind of party.

For a long time after that unpleasant eighth birthday, anything that went wrong was blamed on August 1. It started as a joke between the town adults: "Stubbed your toe? Must be the Graces' fault." This was taken on by their children and woven into scary fact. For instance, one year, old Mrs. Galloway had fallen down *for no reason* and died the next day, not a week after August 1. Another year, a fire in the school gym happened August 2. And how would a gym just catch fire like that? Another year, four separate kids came back to school in September with their parents' recent decisions to divorce hanging over their heads like leprosy. Something bad happened every single year after Fenrin and Thalia's birthday, without fail.

It was the town's own Friday the 13th. It was their punishment for judging them.

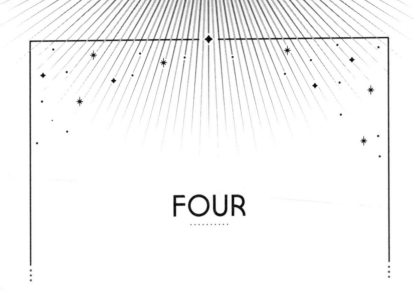

# FOUR

THAT ENTIRE WEEK I ATE MY LUNCH IN THE LIBRARY.

Every time someone came in, my heart skipped, and I waited to see a shadow fall over my desk. But the only other person who was there as much as me was Marcus. I wondered why he was in the library every lunchtime. I wondered most of all what that look between him and Fenrin had meant. There was history there, but the town's rumor mill on the Graces hadn't supplied that particular story, and I could hardly ask either of them myself. Not yet.

Fenrin never showed up, but Summer did.

The next Friday, the library's double doors swung violently open, slamming back against the walls. Marcus, sitting two desks away from me, jumped. Summer strode in, looking around with undisguised disgust. She paused just inside, as if striking a pose. If anyone else had done that, I'd have choked on my own disdain. But Summer looked like she would forever not give two shits what you thought because what you thought wasn't worth giving two shits over. And it just worked.

She slowly folded her arms over her chest, scanning the room. Her long black hair had been wound into a coil at the nape of her neck and her lace-up knee boots creaked very slightly in the silence as she shifted her weight. All this I saw in the instant before her eyes fell on me, and one brow rose.

She walked over to my desk.

"Hey, new girl."

"Hi," I said, startled.

"You've been here a couple of months, right?"

"Yeah."

"It's March. How come you transferred in the middle of the school year?"

The official reason was that we had to move because of my mother's new job.

The unofficial reason would die with me.

She rolled her eyes at my silence, put her back to me, and turned her head so it was silhouetted above her shoulder. I tried to commit the movement to memory.

"Are you coming?" she said.

"Where?"

"One-time-only invitation."

One time only.

This was it.

*Don't screw it up*, whispered the voice in my head.

I didn't intend to. I shoved my empty Tupperware box into my bag, the fork rattling around inside, as well as the dog-eared paperback I'd been reading. Summer had already moved to the doors, not even looking back to see if I was following. I had better keep up.

She strode through the corridors ahead. Most people were in the cafeteria, but the few milling about watched her surreptitiously as she passed them. I walked a couple of paces behind—not enough to crowd her, but enough to signal to others that I was allowed to be there.

We reached the locker corridor, and as we passed Jase Worthington, he said, "Stupid goth bitch."

Summer stopped.

His friend Tom, whom I had briefly fancied when I first got here, hissed, "Dude, *don't*."

They were both popular surfer types, Tom much shorter than the rest of them and constantly irritated by it. That meant they naturally fit in with Fenrin, who was in the same year as them, and I had thought they were all friends. A friend of Fenrin's would never dare to start on any of his family like that.

Especially not Summer.

"Oh, Jase-ington," she said, with a fluttery sigh in her voice. "I simply don't have time for you today."

I began breathing again. Summer started to walk off.

"Ooh, what are you going to do?" Jase jeered. "Put a spell on me?"

She threw him an impatient look over her shoulder. "Of course."

Silence.

It wasn't until we'd reached the double doors at the far end that Jase suddenly yelled, "I'm not afraid of you! You're just a faker! Your whole family is a bunch of stupid carny fakers!"

"What a superlative vocabulary," Summer muttered. "What an intellect. What a—" She stopped herself.

Someone else would try to comfort her or suck up. I said nothing.

We moved across the outdoor hard courts, where a couple of other boys from Fenrin's year were kicking a ball about. It was starting to drizzle, and their game looked dismal in the half-light.

"Hey, Summer," said one of them. She stuck her tongue out at him as she passed, but there was a little smile on her face.

I felt her gaze light on me.

"What?" she said, challenging me to comment.

I shrugged.

"Wow, you really are the silent type, aren't you? Cards close to your chest, right?"

Was that bad? Was I treading too carefully with her? I couldn't tell.

We were making for the thicket at the end of the field, where a huddle of trees and low bushes gave people some shielding from prying teacher eyes.

"I was kind of seeing him," Summer said, as if we had been talking about it already. "Jase. He may be hot, but my god he's dull. It's a 'smoke weed and surf a lot' kind of life. I mean, there is literally nothing else that interests him. Plus he's bad in bed. He's all loud groaning, like a crap zombie."

I disliked these kinds of conversations. There wasn't an obvious response. I didn't know him, so I couldn't exactly agree.

"Oh right," I tried.

We reached the thicket. There was a lookout, this sullen girl called Macy who was good at making herself useful to popular people. She eyed me up and down.

"Is everyone there?" Summer asked.

"Everyone who was invited."

The last was directed at me, but Summer didn't even appear to notice.

"Come on," she said. My shoes slid over a squelching carpet of leaves as we walked farther in. It was pretty useful, this place. The clearing beyond was hidden from view by an array of tall bushes. No one could approach from any other way than the field, as the thicket backed onto a wall, marking the boundaries of school property. One lookout on watch and you could do what you liked here without being seen.

In the clearing, sitting in a ragged circle on their coats, were a few girls from our year. I knew two of them were particular friends of Summer's right now. They had at least ten piercings each and always wore band T-shirts with snakes or insects or rivers of blood splashed across them. The one with jagged, pillar-box red hair, Gemma, was the perky kind of girl who everyone liked. I'd never really hung out with her, but I'd been paired with her in math a couple of times—she was unfailingly nice. The other girl, Lou, had jet-black hair like Summer, two nose piercings that she had to take out before school every day, and a low, wicked laugh.

There were three others, and when I saw who one of them was my heart dropped.

It was Niral.

What was she doing here? She didn't hang out with Summer. Was she trying to get to Fenrin? Our last meeting came back to me in full Technicolor glory.

*There's the thicket at the back of the field. Nice and secluded.*

Summer sat in a gap in the circle, and Gemma obligingly wiggled sideways to make room for me. I watched Summer clap her hands together once, in a weirdly formal gesture. The others stopped talking and looked up at her expectantly. I could feel their eyes flickering over me. I knew what their eyes meant. I wasn't supposed to be here.

"Did you bring what I asked?" said Summer.

Each girl started rummaging in pockets or bags at their feet. Lou took out a black velvet cloth and spread it out on the ground, smoothing it down. Onto the cloth each girl placed an item. Red tea light candles. A deep, crimson-colored cooking pot. Little glass herb bottles from the supermarket. Scissors.

Niral burst out laughing, pointing at the cooking pot. "What is *that*?"

Another girl flushed. I always confused her with at least two other girls in our year because they had the exact same long blond hair and wore similar clothes. "She said bring a red container, so I did!"

"You make, like, *stew* in that, you dope."

"It's exactly what we need," Summer said, with an unusual calm to her voice. "Did you all bring an item?"

No one moved. I hadn't brought anything, but then I hadn't exactly had any notice.

"I take it that's a yes. Don't worry, we'll all have our eyes closed when you drop it in the pot. No one else will see it."

Summer took out a book of matches and lit each tea light, placing them into a rough circle around the red pot. She then took up a glass bottle—basil, I caught on the side of it—and sprinkled the contents around the pot, letting them flutter down onto the tea lights, which sputtered and burned the dried herbs, giving off a wispy smell.

I should have been happy. This was it—the confirmation I'd needed that the rumors about the Graces were true.

It was just that I'd thought this kind of thing was done with a bit more . . . style.

Supermarket herbs and red tea lights?

"Summer," I muttered. Everyone was watching her.

"Yes," she said, in the same calm voice. She was starting to unnerve me, and I wasn't the only one. The world had gone strangely quiet. There were only the sure movements of Summer and the coiled silence of the group.

"I don't have an item," I said.

She straightened, raising her voice for the rest of the circle.

"It doesn't matter. The item is significant to you, but it's just a channel." She shrugged. "If you're powerful enough, you don't need any kind of item at all. Or even any candles, or any of this. You do it by will alone. But I don't think we're quite there yet."

One or two of the girls snickered nervously.

"This is how it will go," said Summer, and no one doubted her one bit right then. "We will start the chant. The chant raises energy inside each of us. We'll do it with our eyes closed. We'll do it until enough energy has been raised. If it takes an hour, it takes an hour."

"But lunch is over in like twenty minutes," said someone.

"Why do you care? What's more important: this or some class? You guys *asked* me to do this. You badgered me for weeks. So now we get to it, you're all running scared?"

The circle was silent.

"This is only going to work if you put everything you have, everything you *are*, into it." Summer sat back on her haunches. "No holding back. No thinking about other things. This is magic, and it's hard. If you break concentration, you lose energy. Lose energy and the spell won't work. You've got to be here, with me, right now, for as long as I need you. As long as it takes. Are you in or are you out?"

I felt a knotted thrill blossom deep inside my guts. I was wrong. This was real. She was the real deal.

"Commit," Summer stated in a cold voice. "Each of you say, 'I'm in all the way. I'll give everything I have.' Say it now. Lou."

Lou replied without hesitation, her voice eager. I'd have felt embarrassed for her if I didn't also feel the way she sounded. "I'm in all the way. I'll give everything I have."

Summer made each of us say it. A couple stumbled, awkward. When it came to me, I wondered at how steady and clear my voice was. It's surprising what you can get yourself to do when you want something badly enough.

"The chant is this," she said. "*Bring them to me. Make them see.*" She paused. "Substitute *them* with *him*. Or *her*." She flashed a wicked smile, the first I'd seen since we'd reached the thicket.

Niral snorted, nervous and irritable. "It's just a rhyme. How's that a spell?"

"Words have power. But the words are meaningless without your intent behind them, driving them. The rhyming is just to help even idiots remember what to say. Now shut up and join in, or leave. If you bring doubt, you wreck it for the rest of us."

A couple of the others threw Niral irritated looks. I dared to join in, and Niral saw it.

"I'm not bringing doubt," she said, narrowing her eyes at me. "I'm in."

"Then let's start. Close your eyes."

I watched them all do it. Then I closed mine.

Instantly, I felt vulnerable and embarrassed.

This was stupid. This was really stupid. What if a teacher came?

"Bring him to me. Make him see," said Summer, her voice soft. "Bring him to me. Make him see."

No one joined in at first. I felt like laughing. I swallowed it.

"Bring him to me. Make him see," I said, my voice mismatching hers. But I kept on until we were in time with each other. More voices joined in. Muttering, stumbling at first. But the more we said it, the less it made sense, and the more we fell into one another's sounds, like a flock of birds turning together.

I don't know how long we chanted. I don't honestly know. It could have been forever. I never lost it, like a dream where time has lost all meaning because you no longer feel it, and it just kept rippling out from us, *bring him to me, make him see,* and I started to drown in the rhythm because there was nothing else.

"Lou," Summer said. "Open your eyes, and put your object into the pot. The rest of you, don't you dare stop chanting."

It registered, barely. I heard a little clink. I couldn't have stopped chanting. My voice was being pulled out of me.

Summer said something in a low voice. Rustling.

I didn't stop. None of us stopped. Whispering sounds, rolling around me, again and again.

"Lou, close your eyes, keep chanting. Gemma, open your eyes, and put your object into the pot."

Summer went round the circle. It seemed to take years to get to me. I was the last.

"Open your eyes," she breathed into my ear.

I did, but it was hard, like they were stuck together with honey. I blinked and looked around. Somehow, I expected it to be dark.

"Cut a piece of your hair," Summer said, and offered me the scissors. She held something tightly in her other hand, and I couldn't see what it was. "Put the hair into the pot. As you do, visualize the one you want. Visualize them right in front of you, as if you could lean forward and kiss them. Don't let go of their face."

I took the scissors. My muscles were liquid. My head was buzzing with the noise of the chant. I cut a long strand and held it up between my fingers. I looked beyond it, and I saw his face. His antique gold hair flopping down, brushing his cheekbones. His grin. His eyes on mine.

I leaned forward and put my hair into the pot.

*Fenrin*, I thought, as my lips kept moving.

Rustling, the sound of footsteps.

And then a sharp, angry, "What the hell d'you think you're doing?"

Our chanting faltered, stumbled, and we fell over the broken words. The velvet cloth was embarrassing. The pot was ludicrous. Niral had been right—the herb bottles made it seem like we were making a stew. I looked up, cheeks blooming.

It was Thalia. Spring wet was still in the air; she was wearing brown leather boots and a long-sleeved beaded top that draped over her skin in all the right places. Her hair was knotted high on her head in a floppy bun, the ends trailing down her neck.

My relief that it wasn't a teacher was short lived, because Thalia looked furious.

"Well?" she demanded, scanning the group.

"I'd have thought that it's pretty obvious," Summer said coolly.

"Clean this stuff up and get back into school."

Summer didn't move. The rest of us were caught, squirming.

"You're such a drama queen, Thalia," said Summer finally. "It's just a bit of fun."

"That's not what you said earlier," Niral interjected, her voice hot with embarrassment. "You said we had to put everything we had into it!"

I raised my eyes heavenward at the mistake. *God, don't do that. Don't try and make Summer look stupid in front of her sister. Thalia won't like you for it, and then you'll lose Summer, too.*

Thalia's toffee-colored eyes narrowed at Niral. "Get back into school," she repeated. "I'm sure you're missing a class. Go now or I'll report you. Go on, all of you."

Summer still hadn't moved. Unsure, cheeks burning, the other girls started to get up, dust their coats off, and leave the thicket. No one dared take the pot or anything else.

I stayed where I was. If this was a test, I would pass with flying colors. The answer was too easy: loyalty. They had all failed it, but I would not.

Thalia was peering into the pot and wrinkling her nose. "Did you know you could hear it all the way back to the hard courts? You're lucky it was me who caught you. Fen would have popped a vein."

At the mention of his name, my heart sped up.

Summer scoffed. "He doesn't care what I get up to."

"Please. He hates this stuff, you know that," Thalia snapped.

"That's his problem. Not ours."

Thalia sighed, hackles lowering. "Look, I know. But still." She shifted her gaze away from the pot. "And it's not just Fen who'd lose his rag, is it? If Esther ever finds out, she'll go completely insane."

It took a second to work out who she meant by Esther, but then I remembered that it was their mother. Did they always call her by her first name? That was strange.

"So don't tell her," Summer said.

"So don't *do it.*"

"This whole town knows about us, Thalia."

Thalia half turned, looking distracted. "I'm not having this conversation yet again. Take this crap with you when you leave. Teachers will ask questions, and then we'll all be in a world of pain."

She whirled off.

When she had disappeared from sight, Summer let out a breath. She seemed a little twitchy. I hadn't noticed it when Thalia was there; she was good at hiding it.

"Are you okay?" I said carefully, expecting her to snap at me. "Yeah."

"Will Thalia tell on you?"

"No."

"How do you know? She didn't say she wouldn't."

"If I'd asked her not to, she'd have done it out of spite. This way she thinks I don't care about it, so she won't bother."

Summer's other hand uncurled as she talked, and I risked a quick look at the object she'd been clutching this whole time. It was a figurine, made of polished stone, streaked with swirling orange-brown colors and shaped like a bird. The light caught on the deeply carved ridges of its wings. I stared at it surreptitiously, wondering what it meant.

"So the rumors are true." I tried a teasing tone. "You really are witches."

"Is that why you came along today?"

I tried to think of the right thing to say. "I guess I was curious. How come you asked me along?"

"Same reason." She gave me a playful smile and then looked off into the trees. I felt safe enough to push just a little more.

"Why doesn't your family like people to know?"

"Well, let's just say they really enjoy having their little secrets. I'm the only one who's up front about it. Why hide? Esther makes her living from it, after all."

Their mother, Esther Grace, ran a health and beauty shop in town, all-natural and organic products. Tinctures for headaches, salves made of plants I'd never heard of, face masks that smelled like earth and rainwater. Some of her creations got sold at the higher-end pharmacies and department stores in the city.

"You're telling me her face cream is magical?" I said dubiously.

Summer laughed. "The price tag might make you think so." She got up from the ground, brushing off her slim flanks. "Come on. I'd better give Emily her pot back."

I didn't move. "We haven't finished the spell. I mean, it doesn't look like we have."

Summer regarded me. I tried not to squirm. I had no idea what she was thinking.

"Nope," she said, after a moment. "Want to?"

I said nothing. She dropped back to her knees and picked up the matchbook, striking one.

"Don't we need the chanting?"

"A lot of energy still here," said Summer. "Especially with Thalia's little outburst. Might still work."

She dropped the lit match into the pot. I didn't look. Only she knew the objects they had all thrown in. The smell of burning hair crept past us. I stared hard at the ground, pouring myself into the moment, conjuring his face as it all went up in flames.

I didn't care if it was wrong. I couldn't afford to, if I wanted to make him mine.

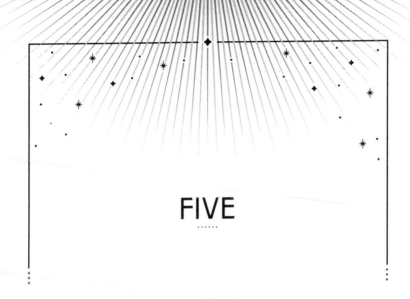

# FIVE

TWO WEEKS AGO, I STARTED MY OWN BOOK OF SHADOWS.

Since I'd found out about the Graces, I'd been reading up on witchcraft. According to my research, a Book of Shadows was a diary that witches kept all their spells and knowledge and observations in, building it up into a kind of working manual. I carefully wrote down ideas from books by authors with names like Elisia Storm, books I bought with money saved up from an old weekend job I'd had doing the dishes in a dime-a-dozen burger restaurant. I'd never owned books like these before. The only kind of magic I'd ever read about was the "hurling fire bolts" kind in fantasy books. The only kind of friends I'd ever had would have thought there was something wrong with me if I'd talked about witchcraft with them. I didn't even know there were people who had conversations about it as if it might actually exist.

I was usually cautious with money, but I wanted those books so desperately. I needed them. I knew they weren't going to solve all my problems at once—I mean, if it were as easy as reading about it, everyone would be doing it—but maybe they could help. The rest would be up to me. That was where the Graces came in.

I didn't want my mother to know about the books, but it didn't matter in the end because she found them anyway. I knew she had—I'd put a circle of salt as protection around the box I kept them in under my bed. Last week, when I got home from school, a section of the circle was broken and scuffed, and they were stacked in a different order to how I'd left them.

My parents had always acted overly twitchy toward anything remotely abnormal, so it was ironic that they had birthed a kid who craved the strange like other people craved drugs. The moment I saw that my mother had been in my box, my stomach churned and turned over, and I waited for her to come storming up to me, demanding to know just what the hell I thought I was doing, just where had I got the money from, just *how* did I think being like this was going to sort out my life?

She had to know why I had those books.

She had to know that it was to try and bring Dad back.

To try and fix things.

But she hadn't said a word.

"I'm the best mother anyone could ask for," she liked to announce decisively nowadays. "I let you do whatever you want. I let you be independent. Anyone else would love to have me as their mom."

She was right. And she was wrong. If I were on fire, would she douse me with water or push past me and go down to the pub instead, leaving me to burn to the ground? Sometimes you need boundaries. Boundaries tell you that you're loved.

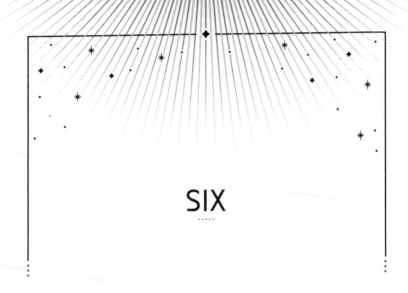

# SIX

WE PASSED NOTES TO EACH OTHER IN CLASS, CHATTED during breaks, and she grinned at me in the corridors, but Summer hadn't yet asked me to sit with her at lunch. Every day I hoped for it, but part of me dreaded it, too. I still hadn't found a weekend job, so I could never afford to eat in the cafeteria. We lived in different worlds—the food I brought in would be a window into mine that I didn't want her looking through.

In homeroom one morning, a neatly folded note landed on my desk. We could use cell phones until the first class, but the Graces, unbelievably, didn't even own phones.

The paper had that off-white rough recycled thickness to it that made me feel more special just touching it. I wished I could buy some, in a beautifully bound notebook, and write my Book of Shadows on that paper, but I had to make do with a set of lined ones with shiny black covers from the dollar store.

I opened up the note.

*Is it working yet? any tingles? — S*

She meant the spell. And no. But then again, I hadn't even seen Fenrin since we'd done it. I had been half-hoping he'd come over to me the next day, mumbling something about not being able to help himself, he just *had* to know if I was free that evening. But that only happened in movies. I was glad it hadn't happened that way. It would have felt fake, and I wanted real—so real it was painful.

I got out my thin purple nib pen, the one that made my writing look delicate and creatively loopy, and scribbled back.

*I don't think so. Maybe it takes some time?*

She was five desks away from me on the diagonal, but people always passed her notes along without opening them. I watched her read it and then scribble something back in tiny letters at the bottom.

*Lunch?*

My heart leapt. I'd just eat the fish fingers I'd brought during afternoon break instead, and if she commented on my lack of food, I'd say I'd had too much breakfast. But when we both came out of physics, and she glanced at me in the hallway to make sure I was following, we didn't go to the cafeteria. We went back to the thicket.

It wasn't raining, but the wind still had an edge to it, and I wished I'd brought my striped scarf. It made me look five, but it was the only thick one I had. We traipsed across the field in silence. Summer never seemed to expect me to ask questions. I guess no one ever did, they just followed her around. Did I want to be one of those, too? Or should I try to impress her by challenging her?

We reached the thicket clearing and sat down. Summer still

hadn't looked at me. She rooted in her bag—a hippy patchwork thing, totally at odds with the rest of her style—and pulled out a massive Tupperware box. I watched her, safe for a few seconds to stare. Her legs were so willowy. I'd have killed for legs like that.

"Where's your lunch?" she said as she opened up her box. It was full to the brim with colorful-looking food.

I thought of my sad little bundle of fish fingers wrapped up in foil and a plastic bag at the bottom of my backpack. "I didn't bring any."

"Huh? Why not?" Summer's mouth twisted. "You're not one of those who's always on some diet, are you?"

Judgment oozed from every syllable. Summer could get very impatient with anything she deemed stupid, which crossed a pretty wide range of behavior. I needed to remind her of the reason she'd taken an interest in me, that I wasn't like other girls—but not everyone was as naturally slim and beautiful and well off and lucky as her.

"No," I said. "I don't do diets. I'm just not very hungry, that's all."

"You want to try this?" she said, offering me her box. "It's pretty good. Esther is actually a great cook."

"Um, I'm not going to eat your lunch," I said, still stung. Did I really look that pathetically starved?

Summer was taken aback. "Wow. I'm not diseased."

"No, I didn't mean it like that. I just . . . I'm a really fussy eater."

"Just try it. If you don't like it, don't eat it. Simple as that."

I peered into the box.

"It's just meatballs with a lentil and vegetable salad. But she does have a wicked way with spices," Summer commented.

I picked up a meatball with my fingers and tasted it gingerly. It was good.

It was *so* good. Springy meat edged with something sharp, like lemon, with onion and garlic and something else I didn't know, something wild and fruity. I ate three of them before I even realized what I was doing.

"Sorry," I said, pulling my fingers back. "Christ, I'm shoveling your lunch in like a hog."

"I'm not hungry," Summer said with a shrug, and she tossed me a fork wrapped carefully in a roll of cloth. The salad was even better. Lentils were something I boiled until they were this bitter slushy mush, and then I threw a couple of sausages in to make a greasy kind of stew. They'd always been cheap, stodgy winter filler. Never these little buttons of crunchy spice.

"Your mom is a genius," I said, my mouth full.

Summer's lips, stained with a deep plum color, curled up at the edges in a cold smile. "No, she's not."

"Well, my mom's idea of cooking is to collect takeaway menus and decorate the kitchen with them, so in comparison."

Summer didn't respond. Mothers seemed like a sore subject for her, and I wouldn't push anymore, but I found myself wondering if I'd ever get to meet fearsome matriarch Esther Grace.

I tried to change the subject. "Why aren't you eating in the cafeteria today?"

"Didn't feel like the crowds."

"But you always meet at least Lou and Gemma in there on

Tuesdays," I said, and then stopped, annoyed at my slipup. My guard came down around her too easily.

Summer didn't seem to notice that I'd just confessed to semi-stalking her. "Ditched 'em," she said, looking up at the treetops.

I ducked my head down to hide the grin I could feel threatening to break out.

She'd ditched them to have lunch with me. On our own.

The hour we spent together that day was the first time I ever really talked to Summer properly. I was half-afraid she'd ask me about my house, or my family, or my life before this town, like everyone else had, as if existence could only ever be about those things and nothing more.

Instead we talked about dreams we'd had, the ones that felt more real than being awake; we talked about reincarnation and ghosts and whether we'd try to kill Hitler if time travel was real; about how intoxicating it was to lose yourself in another world so completely that you forgot your own reality. It was books for me. Music for her.

I'd never met anyone who wound her way through conversations like this, as naturally as dancing, as if there were no other way to talk. She told me that for her music was the closest to the concept of the divine as she'd ever get. I told her that the music she liked sounded more like demons mating in hell, and she roared with laughter, obviously pleased.

I was sitting next to a wild creature, sharing my innermost thoughts with a Grace who had turned her attention to me; it was terrifying and a thrill. It was the start of something.

We had lunch like that together three times before I finally worked out that Summer was feeding me on purpose. I didn't understand why at first. But then I remembered Fenrin seeing my slimy beans and cheese on toast, and for days afterward I could only feel the hot flash of shame whenever she was near.

If she noticed, she never said anything.

* * * * *

My name changed the next week.

I'd never told anyone my secret name before. I'd written it in my Book of Shadows on the inside cover.

### This being the journal of the workings of the craft By River Page

It had always been River, my secret name, as long as I could remember. That was how I knew it was the right one. It had unfurled itself in my mind, grown its roots right down into my spine. I couldn't be anything else, ever. Page because turning over to a blank page always gave me a sickly-sweet feeling in my guts. Blank pages could be transformed. They were new lives, over and over.

But I'd never told anyone about that name, and I thought I never would.

"I don't really like my name," I said to Summer one lunchtime. We were sitting in the cafeteria—the rain was pelting outside. She'd given me her lunch as usual, after having two bites and declaring herself full.

Instead of churning out the usual platitudes people liked to do, like one of her other friends would to her, Summer said, "Of course not. It's a boring name."

I liked her for that. But it still stung, until she followed it up with, "It doesn't suit you. It's not your real name, is it?"

I got exactly what she meant. And she said it because she knew that I would. And in that moment we connected, hard, and I felt something grateful and happy and fierce stirring inside me. My coal-black insides flared in recognition of a soul like mine.

"Nope," I said. "Not even close."

"So what is your real name?"

I didn't even think about it. I should have, but I didn't. Lou and Gemma were sitting with us, but they were screeching at each other about some TV show and paying no attention to our conversation.

"River," I said. "River Page."

"Way better," she commented, and that was that. "I'm going to call you River from now on."

No big deal. Done.

"So what are you doing this weekend?" she said to me.

"Summer," Lou murmured urgently, before I could reply. Her eyes were fixed across the room. "Look. He's totally *stalking* her."

I followed her gaze. Thalia had entered the cafeteria and was joining the queue for food. As I watched, Marcus detached himself from the wall he'd been leaning against and slipped in behind her.

"Jesus, that's creepy," said Gemma.

I watched him tap her on the shoulder, and her face dropped like a stone when she saw who it was. They exchanged a few words, but it was clear she wanted nothing more than to get away from him.

Sweet, friendly Gemma was full of fascinated disdain. "Why is he even in here? He never comes to the cafeteria."

"What's the deal with him and Thalia?" I dared to ask.

Lou shrugged. "Marcus is totally obsessed with Thalia, ever since forever. It's kind of sad, really. I mean, she'd obviously never go near him. But he just doesn't get it. He needs professional help."

I glanced at Summer. She was silent, watching them across the cafeteria.

"I'm going to go and rescue her," Gemma said.

Summer snorted. "She doesn't need rescuing."

Gemma obediently relaxed back down.

"She should get a restraining order," muttered Lou.

"They used to be friends, didn't they?" said Gemma.

"Yeah, but not anymore. Anyway, you can't be friends with someone like that."

"Someone like what?" I asked.

Lou tossed me an appraising glance. I was too new. I didn't get to have an opinion. I tried my hardest to look bland.

"Someone with mental problems," said Lou shortly.

Gemma nudged her. "He's gone."

"Thank the lord."

I glanced at Summer. She was toying with her necklace, turning the little piece of curved jet over and over in her fingers, and appeared not to be listening.

Fenrin's glaring match with Marcus made more sense now—Fenrin had a problem with him because of Thalia, and everyone knew about it. I'd seen Marcus interact with precisely no one around school. He was a pariah because that was what happened to people who messed with the Graces.

He was a lesson for me.

"Sum, stop playing with your jewelry and eat some food," said a voice.

Summer smiled sweetly. "That's rich, bitch."

Thalia shot her a look and slid into the free seat next to me, her hips curling forward to slip herself into the gap without moving the chair out. She had two thin scarves looped around her neck, long dangling feather earrings, and a deep pine-needle-green top that wrapped around her tiny torso and had ties that circled her waist twice, the ends trailing down one thigh. The caramel-colored hair wrap dangled loose from her topknot, resting against her shoulder. Summer had told me that the wrap was made from the hair of a mustang tail.

It was impossible not to stare. I tried my best. Thalia was only two years older than us, but in every other way she seemed miles ahead. It was curious how close the Graces were to one another because I knew it wasn't done for older people to hang out with younger people, especially if they were related. But the Graces gave no sign they'd ever noticed that rule.

"Hey, are you okay?" said Gemma, her voice carefully concerned. "What did he say to you?"

Thalia paused. "It's fine," she said. "Nothing." She started rearranging the objects on her tray with quick, precise movements, bracelets jangling and dangling off her wrists.

Lou shook her head. "What a prick."

Thalia's shoulders were stiff. Couldn't they see how much she hated them right now for bringing it up?

"Boring," said Summer loudly. "You'd be far more interested in the conversation we've just been having." She nodded to me.

"Why, what was it about?"

"People's real names," said Summer. "Sometimes, you know, you get given the wrong one."

Thalia raised a brow, leaning her chin on her hand in rapt attention. Out of the corner of my eye, I saw Lou start talking quietly into Gemma's ear.

"And," Summer continued, "sometimes you just know what the right one is."

I listened in sinking horror. Was she really going to tell her sister, the sun goddess, about it?

"So," concluded Summer. "Her real name, we've ascertained, is River."

"Oh no," I said. "I mean, we were just messing about."

Thalia shrugged. "If it's your real name, you should go by it, right?"

I swallowed, trying not to think about the fact that Thalia Grace was talking to me, casually, as if we did this every day.

"Yeah," I said, "but I can't just . . . change my name."

"Of course you can. Your name is simply what everyone collectively chooses to call you. So we'll just call you River."

"Sure," I muttered uneasily.

But inside, I felt myself start to unfurl with a secret kind of excitement. What if I really became River?

"So River," said Summer, and it came out of her naturally as if it had always been so. "As per our previously interrupted conversation, what are you doing this weekend?"

"Nothing much," I said. Everyone else would probably be going to the Wader, the late-open bar where all the surfers apparently hung out. It was all anybody could talk about in English on Friday afternoons. What they were wearing. Who they'd be seeing.

My extraordinary plans involved hitting up Luigi's, the Italian chain restaurant next to the cinema, to see if they needed any weekend kitchen staff. The rest of the time I'd bury myself in movies. Read some more of my witchcraft books. Write in my Book of Shadows.

Wonder what the Graces were doing.

"We're having a thing on the beach," said Summer vaguely. "Just a few of us. You should come."

"It's April. Isn't it, like, freezing right now?"

"Oh, we always have a massive bonfire. It'll be cool. We'll have food. BYOB."

I looked blank.

"Bring your own booze," said Thalia helpfully. "We bring food. You bring drink. And a gift."

"A gift?" I echoed, mystified. Was this some kind of strange local custom?

Thalia was coolly amused. "Well, it *is* considered polite when attending a birthday party to bring a gift. Or do you not do that where you come from?"

"Whose birthday party is it?"

Summer rolled her eyes. "It's not like a big thing."

I rounded on her. "Yours? You never said anything!"

"Really, because it's just not a major deal."

"Not a major deal?" drawled Lou, cutting in. "Are you serious? It's basically the party of the year. Last time everyone got completely naked and did these chants—"

"Don't be ridiculous," said Thalia. "I was there, nothing like that happened."

"It was after you fell asleep." Summer grinned wickedly at her.

I couldn't tell if it was all a joke. Naked chanting? I'd never be able to do that, no matter how drunk I got. But back then I didn't know just how far I would go.

Thalia must have noticed my dismayed expression. She leaned closer to me as the rest of the table discussed the highlights of the year before.

"What's up?" she said softly, underneath the cafeteria noise.

"It's just . . . I need to get her a gift."

"I have to get her something from Fenrin, on Saturday. He never sorts it out in time. You want to come with me?"

Fenrin's name made my nerve endings sizzle.

"If you don't mind, that would be great," I said, without letting myself think about it. "Because I have *no* idea what to get."

I still had a little bit of money stashed in the box under my bed—I could use some for a gift. Though these days I often had to dip into it for food shopping when we were tight. We'd never exactly been a yacht-owning family, but with Dad gone, there was no second income to hide my mother's love of slot machines. We had a silent pact I never remembered making—she wouldn't remind me of the reasons why he wasn't around anymore, and I wouldn't remind her that gambling wasn't the best way to try and solve our money issues.

Thalia's voice was casually sly. "Fenrin's not coming with us, though," she said. "He always surfs all day Saturdays. It'll just be you and me."

"Oookay," I drawled. My heartbeat skipped. His beautiful face flashed in my head.

Thalia peered at me, then glanced at Summer and laughed. "You were right. There's nothing."

Summer shrugged. "Told you. It's a miracle."

"So she's gay."

I frowned. "She? I'm right here, you guys."

"Are you gay?" Summer said, leaning back in her chair.

I suddenly noticed that Lou and Gemma were listening in.

"What are you talking about?" I said.

"You don't like Fenrin," said Thalia, her soft doe eyes narrowed in amusement.

"I mean, I don't know him. I'm sure he's really nice."

"But you don't lust after him. Hence, you must be gay."

Lou laughed. Even Gemma was grinning at me. I wanted to strangle them both.

"Um, okay." I held my hands up. "I'm not gay."

"There's nothing wrong with being gay," Summer said, her expression cold. "Are you, like, *ashamed*?"

The wolves were circling. Think fast.

"No way," I replied firmly. "I read an article once that said there was no such thing as gay or straight, that sexuality was fluid. I mean, maybe if you're totally straight, you're kind of boring. No offense."

Summer smirked at Thalia, who shook her head and said, "No *offense*, but girls don't have what I need."

"The cock?" said Summer, delighted.

"Shut up. Gay, bi, straight, whatever she might be, River and I will be going shopping for your present on Saturday, so get your requests in now, 'cos you totally dropped the poor girl in it by not telling her it was your birthday in *three days*."

"Who's River?" asked Gemma.

They both ignored her.

Summer shrugged. "You know the kind of thing I like. Get me a band T-shirt."

"I will not," Thalia said. "The last one you bought had a picture of two skulls that sat right on your boobs. Esther pitched a fit, and I don't really feel like making her mad at me."

"Whatever," Summer said airily, and started talking to Lou on her left.

"So I was thinking of going around noon," Thalia said to me.

"Cool. I can meet you there. You're going to the Four Bells, right?"

The Four Bells was the shopping center in the middle of town. It was a strange name to call a shopping center, so I'd done a little research. Apparently, the council had named it after an old town myth, maybe thinking to root it into the community somehow, make it part of the local history. As if a man-made building full of gold-plated jewelry and plastic burger smells could be anything near as cool as that story.

Thalia scoffed. "That dive? No way. We're going to the Mews."

The Mews area was full of twisting alleys, away from the sea and close to the train station. I'd been told it was weirdo central.

"Don't look so worried. It's okay around there," said Thalia, offhand. "Well, during the day, anyway. We won't be hassled."

I shrugged. "I'm not worried. So, we should meet at noon outside the train station?"

"Yup."

Inside, I was whirling.

I was going out with Thalia on Saturday.

She called me River.

They'd both called me River, as if it was my name.

Thalia threw a dangling scarf end back over one shoulder, picked up her fork, and started to eat. But she didn't just eat. She *shoveled*, forking it in like she'd die if she didn't consume every last scrap within a minute, jaw furiously working, cheeks puffed with food.

I think my mouth fell open.

Summer was watching me sympathetically.

"Yeah," she said. "Everyone gets the same look on their face the first time they see that dainty bitch eat."

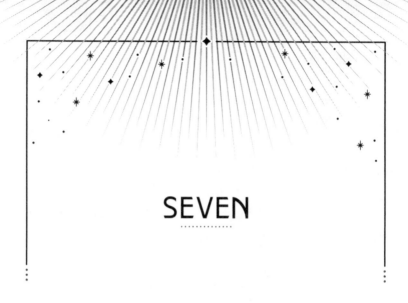

# SEVEN

I HAD ALREADY BEGUN TRYING TO CAREFULLY PIECE together the exact construction of a Grace life. Maybe if I knew their formula, the combination of elements that made them what they were, I could understand them. Understanding something was one step closer to becoming it. So I noted it all down, all the little snatches of story and character they threw my way, and I asked them questions whenever I thought they might least mind.

* * * * *

I'd found the website early on.

As well as the no cell phones rule, according to Summer they didn't have Internet at their house, so maybe they weren't aware of its existence. It was buried as a link on some strange forum with only a couple of hundred members.

It was kind of a crap, basic site, the images misaligned, with white text on a black background that hurt your eyes after a while. But what it lacked in design, it more than made up for in information.

A biography section gave a brief rundown of each Grace family member, including the parents, Esther and Gwydion. Esther's shop, Nature's Way, was listed there, with a couple of photos of the inside. Gwydion Grace went on business trips a lot. He was an advisor. The site wasn't sure what he advised on, but his clients were important people. The parents were both lovely to look at. Fenrin looked a lot more like his mother than his father. There were uncles and aunts, grandparents, cousins. Everyone seemed to be a lawyer, or a CEO, or in government. An uncle was a record label head. An artist cousin sold his creations for ridiculous amounts of money. It seemed that whatever a Grace did, they'd make a success of it.

The website was adamant that they were witches. There was a rundown of every incident in town for the last nine years that people blamed on August 1. This was in a submission section, so it wasn't just one person speculating—a lot of people had posted their own stories in the comments.

The website said that their family had been in the area forever. That the Grace name was as old as the ancient standing stones that sat on the moors outside town; they were a part of the landscape as much as any cliff edge or knotted tree. Officially, they were a wealthy, well-respected extended family, and a lot of them seemed to hold positions of power.

It made total sense. If you were a witch, you'd use magic to make sure you got ahead in life. It was human nature.

The site said there were four main types of Grace witch:

*Water:* They were restless, creative, flighty, and persuasive. Like water, they eroded people's wills away. If you knew a water witch, chances were they'd be the ones that everyone tended to agree with. They were deeply charming and could change people's minds. Their symbol was Bilios, the world tree, which sat in a circle representing the universe.

*Fire:* They protected people. They were strength. Confidence. Power. They could usually fight. They were natural leaders. Their symbol was a thick cross with tapered ends inside a circle.

*Air:* The seers. They told the future and could see the truth of the present. They were the ones most used as consultants by powerful people, and that was how they made their living and their money. The site speculated that Gwydion was an air witch. They were very susceptible to mental attack and tended to be extremely sensitive individuals. Their symbol was a three-pronged rod inside a circle.

*Earth:* They were the practical witches, well-versed in herb lore. They took care of the everyday necessities of the witch, such as health products and medicines, home protection, magicked food. They got none of the glory, but they were the most essential of all witches; often the head of the family. They were grounded, patient, loving, and forthright. Their symbol was a five-pointed star, representing the five senses, usually with a gem studded in the middle to symbolize themselves, at the calm center of all things.

I spent some time trying to work out which one each Grace was. Summer I had down as air. She had a thing for birds and enjoyed telling the truth. Fenrin was fire, maybe, a natural leader. But then again he surfed and loved the sea and was the most charming creature I'd ever met. So maybe more water. Thalia was earth, through and through. She looked like a dryad, something born of trees and sunlight. I let myself think about which one

I would be if I were a witch, but none of them seemed to fit me exactly right.

There was no clue as to the website's creator. It had to be someone in town, but I couldn't even begin to guess who it was. Was it secretly one of the Graces who had set it up? How else would anyone know any of this stuff? I read everything on there obsessively, but I wondered if the website writer was some kind of crackpot and everything I read was a lie.

I couldn't deny the tingle inside me, though: an insistent rush that said "what if?"

Just because it sounded unbelievable didn't mean it couldn't also be true.

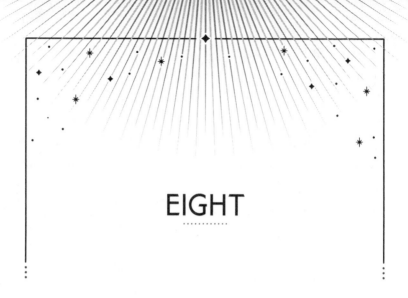

# EIGHT

THALIA WAS ALREADY WAITING FOR ME OUTSIDE THE train station.

I was only two minutes late, but it was kind of ridiculous I was late at all considering what time I'd gotten up. It had taken me longer than I'd thought to settle on an outfit to wear—something that said everything I wanted to say so that I didn't have to say it.

Her expression was of vague impatience, like she was already regretting the whole thing. Her hair was loose, sticking on her shoulders in shining folds, and around her hips she wore a thin belt chain with little burnished flat disc charms hanging off it, making her tinkle faintly when she moved.

"I thought we could start in Summer's favorite shop," she said, as soon as I was close enough to hear her.

I cocked my head, nervous. "Um, hi? Yeah, that sounds good."

She led the way and I skittered alongside her. We cut through the back of the station, down a rough set of steps with an iron handrail that looked as if it had been battered straight into the rock. The steps ended in a cobbled alley, the stones all mismatched sizes, tripping the careless. There was nothing down here but the back of some pokey shop, its doorway crammed with split garbage bags.

Thalia's stride was confident. I tried to match it. Something caught the edge of my gaze, and I looked up at the wall we passed.

There was a carving of a face sticking out of the slabby rock.

"What is that?" I said, stopping in my surprise.

"Hoffy Man," said Thalia.

"What?"

"The Hoffy Man," she repeated, coming to stand beside me. "You don't know about that? Oh, you're new here, aren't you? I forgot. The Hoffy Man. He's just a local nature god."

I stared at the carving. The face was soft and round with big, pursed lips and hollow eyes, its forehead crowned with hair that looked more like bunches of leaves. Was it a real being I could talk to? Did it appear to people if they said the right incantations, or if they knew its real name? What did it think about humans? What did it know?

"What's it doing here?" I said. The face stared across the alleyway, seeing nothing.

"The Mews is the oldest bit of town. Normality doesn't intrude so much around here. The old stuff hangs around, you know?"

She tugged gently on my elbow. "We should go," she said.

I dropped my gaze quickly. I didn't want to alert them so soon to my obsession with things like this. The friends they had were attracted to the implication of magic that hung over them like mist as much as the glamour they talked and breathed. I was different. I wanted to see beyond the glamour to the real them.

Thalia moved us out of the alley and into a more normal high street, though it was cramped and dirty in comparison to the main part of town. This was the kind of place that never got any council-funded Christmas lights.

She didn't say much as we walked. I'd expected her to be more like Summer, who seemed to talk until you gave her what she wanted from you. Thalia didn't seem to want anything.

We came to a door. A painted wooden sign dangling from a bracket fixed into the wall read TROVE. The little bell above the lintel tinkled sweetly. Steps led down to another door, which was pulled shut.

"It looks closed," I said.

"It's not." Thalia pushed the door open and I followed.

Inside we were greeted with a claustrophobic jumble of insanity. If you were tall, you'd bang your head on the odd musical instruments strung across the ceiling, and people of all heights had to navigate around the glass globes hanging almost all the way to the floor. Objects were piled on tables and stools, dark wood cabinets full of trinkets lined every wall and corner. Roiling, buzzing tribal music played faintly in the background. The air smelled musty and old.

"We're bound to find something in here," said Thalia over her shoulder.

She wandered past a tall, ancient-looking desk, and a man suddenly popped up from behind it.

"Oh," he said, looking at Thalia. "You're her sister."

"Hi, Mr. Tulsent," said Thalia. "You mean Summer?"

The man pushed his glasses up his nose with a nervy move-ment. He was thin, all angles, an oversize cardigan hanging off his frame and graying wispy hair sticking out from his head.

"Well, yes," he said. "Is she not with you?"

Thalia smiled. "Not today."

We rounded a wall and stood together in a pokey corner, hidden from view. Thalia picked up a huge glass marble with a strange, dusky splash caught in its core.

"He's so into Summer," said Thalia in a whisper. "And he's pretty weird, like he doesn't quite know how social rituals work. I've never once heard him say 'hello.' It's almost like he's not from around here, but he's not exactly foreign either, you know? Summer's in here all the time, though, and she says she talks to him sometimes."

"Really? Why?" I said, matching Thalia's disdain.

She laughed. "No idea. You know Summer."

I didn't, actually. Superficially, maybe, but not enough to know what Thalia meant. That was another Grace thing, I was starting to notice—when you were in their crowd, they assumed you'd always been there and you knew everything they did. It was somehow isolating and comforting at the same time.

I wandered over to a cabinet and peered through the glass. It was packed full of jewelry—thick bracelets, rings, necklaces with twisting silver chunks, everything studded with polished, colored stones as big as my fingernails. I wanted to touch them all, run my fingers over them, slip them over my skin. You could spend hours in this place, just peering at everything Mr. Tulsent had to offer. We were in there a while, giggling over fertility idols and staring at instruments I couldn't even guess how to play. Eventually, I saw a wooden bowl with one side raised into a carved bird, its wings hugging the rim.

"This is pretty cool," I ventured.

It was too small for a serving dish and too pointless for anything else, but it looked mysterious and elegant.

Thalia took it from me and turned it over in her hands. "Nice. An incense burner. How come you picked that out?"

I shrugged. "Summer likes birds, right?"

"How do you know that?"

"She's mentioned it before. And she carries that orangey brown bird everywhere with her," I said. "What is that?"

"It's amber," said Thalia shortly. "Come on. Let's get the incense burner."

She turned away before I had a chance to say a word and took the bowl to the register. It was twice as much money as I'd scraped together from my box that morning. Before I'd even protested, Thalia paid the other half without so much as a word. I didn't know how to thank her, so I didn't—I just promised to pay her back next week—and I had to watch her shrug and laugh and say I shouldn't ever bother because she had too much money as it was. I'd often wondered what it would be like to have too much money. I'd thought it was an affliction only professional athletes and celebrities suffered from, but apparently you could be rich in a quiet way, too.

After that, we went to a tiny music shop, and Thalia bought an album of some obscure band from the grinning guy behind the register, who clearly thought she was the most delicious thing he'd ever seen. I felt like smacking him. I felt protective. Everyone in this town was in love with a Grace.

I was hoping we'd have coffee together, sit with our gifts nestled on the table between us and sip foamy cappuccinos and talk and laugh and other people would look over and envy us. But Thalia said she had a lot to do, so only a couple of hours later, I found myself standing at the train station again, watching her move away from me, sunshine on her hair. She told me to come down to the beach that evening at around six. I waited until she disappeared from sight and then went home, my mind already full of potential outfits.

By five o'clock I was ready, but there was no way I was turning up that early. The bus to the beach only took ten minutes from my place, so I sat in the living room and watched TV, trying to ignore the nervous curdling in my belly.

At quarter to six, my mom poked her head through the door and glanced at my clothes. "Going out, are we?"

"There's this party down the beach—"

"I'll be back late," she interrupted, and disappeared again.

That was the most I tended to get out of her these days. She had always been the expressive one, equally quick with a joke or a shouting match. But now that Dad wasn't around, she'd all but gone silent, like it was better she never said anything to me again. I missed that. I even missed the shouting.

I suddenly realized Summer's gift and the bottle of vodka I'd taken from the cupboard were on display at my feet, but she hadn't even looked at them.

* * * * *

I arrived about half past six. The party was in a cove secluded from the main beach by a row of tall, slippery rocks. I slid and picked and wobbled my way down there, and I saw a surprisingly small crowd busily setting up. I stood awkwardly for a moment before spotting Thalia and making my way to her.

"Hi," I said. "I'm not late, am I?"

Thalia looked at me in surprise. "No, you're kind of early, actually. No one else is here yet."

"Oh, sure," I said casually. "I came early to help you guys set up."

Thalia paused, like she was assessing me. The risk of seeming uncool was worth it if I got to hang out with the family before anyone else.

"Okay," she said. "There's a big table over there. Dump your alcohol with the rest, and Summer's gift can go on the pile next to it. I've got all this food to unwrap from the cooler. Come find me."

She floated off.

I kept my head down as I moved, fixing my neck firmly in place so I didn't look around for Fenrin. I put my gift and vodka bottle on the table and went to join Thalia in arranging the amazing array of food she'd brought.

"Are those your parents?" I said, even though I knew they were. A man and a woman were standing next to a half-built bonfire in the center of the cove. The woman, Esther Grace, was throwing handfuls of something into the heart of it, and her lips were moving.

"Yeah. Don't worry. They'll leave soon after people start arriving."

I watched their mother stretch her slender arm out again, and I couldn't help myself.

"What's she doing?" I said, turning back to Thalia—and then

freezing. Fenrin had suddenly appeared in front of us. He was helping himself to a thick hunk of walnut bread.

"She's 'witching' it so that it burns all night for us," he said, making sarcastic air quotes, his mouth full.

"Shut up, Fen. Don't start. And don't hog all the food already. Go away." Thalia flapped at him. "And please wait until after she's gone to start drinking."

Fenrin gave her a bulging grin, still chewing. Even with his mouth stuffed, he was flawless. Like all of them. He swallowed and shifted his gaze to me.

"So we finally get to see you out of your natural habitat," he said.

"You mean school? That's not my natural habitat."

"Oh, I think it is. You love the library, all that brooding quiet and rustling paper. You hear the call of the books, like the far-off howling of wolves." His voice was teasing.

"Books are knowledge. Knowledge is power," I said archly.

"And power is your goal? Curiouser and curiouser, Alice."

"Power is everyone's goal, isn't it? It's just not something most people are brave enough to admit to."

"I'll admit to it." He spread his hands grandly. "I *love* power."

I laughed. I liked watching him peacock. He did it knowingly, which helped him get away with it.

"We're the brave ones," he said, leaning toward me with a soft smile.

Flirting.

I was sure we were flirting.

I searched for a quippy reply, and then saw that Thalia had glazed over. I suddenly realized why—Fenrin flirted with every female he came across. It was probably as natural as breathing to him.

I was nothing special. Not yet.

"Sure," I said. Then I turned back to Thalia. "There's more food to sort, right?" Her eyebrows rose.

"Um . . . yeah. Salads. They just need to be emptied into those bowls."

"Cool." I busied myself at the food table. I wondered what they were thinking.

It got pretty busy after that.

Half the school was there, and I was sure most of them hadn't been invited—they were tagalongs, attracted like moths to candlelight. Word about the party had gotten around. When I asked Summer about it, she just laughed and said she didn't care who came as long as the most interesting people were there. I dared to think that just maybe she'd directed that at me.

Thalia had been right—Summer loved her gift and gave a very un-Summer squeal when she unwrapped it.

"Where did you find this?" she said, her eyes round.

"Trove."

"Oh my god, I love that place. Oh my god, it's perfect. Thank you."

Her eyes sparkled. I felt a warm glow I'd been missing start to spread its wings inside my chest. I'd made her happy. It was worth owing money to Thalia to feel that, even though Thalia had waved away my promises to pay her back.

"I'm glad you like it," I said. My face was a glowing beacon of pleasure, but for once I didn't care about showing what I felt.

Summer carefully wrapped the bowl back up and put it with her other gifts. She leaned back on her hands as we sat together on a blanket, looking up at the swirling black sky. The bonfire roared steadily nearby.

"So how come you're into birds?" I asked.

"I like hawks the most," she said. "But anything that flies, really."

"Why?"

"Because they're free. They can go anywhere they like. No one controls them."

She looked at me for a moment, and the moment stretched out, growing a little too long, and then longer, and I couldn't look away.

"Did you have fun with Thalia?" she said, with a knowing little smile.

"She's great. Kind of scary at first, but it's a front, right?"

Summer said nothing.

I backed up quickly, feeling the misstep. "I mean," I said. "Well, everyone has their reasons."

"We all hide our true selves," Summer agreed, and my heart gave an excited, frightened lurch.

But it was too soon to play that hand.

Music shuddered against the rocks and mingled with the cracks of the bonfire. We watched as Thalia laughed and twirled underneath a boy's arm, flamelight licking up the side of her.

"She's more fragile than she looks," said Summer, unexpectedly. The offer of an opening sanctioning my next question.

"Marcus isn't going to show up here, right?" I said.

"Nah, he wouldn't."

"He's not dangerous, though, is he? I mean, he's just a bit obsessed."

Summer sighed, upending her drink into her mouth.

I spoke as she drank, my voice dismissive. "Let's not talk about it. It's her business."

"Marcus . . ." Summer paused. "It's more complicated than that."

She glanced around, but the low roar of the fire and the rolling of the sea and the noise of the crowd kept our conversation private.

"They were kind of together, briefly," she said to me.

My eyebrows crawled up into my hairline.

"It wasn't public knowledge. And now, people . . . they think what they want about the whole thing." She shrugged, as if to say "what are you going to do?" Then she tossed me a glance as sharp as knives. "Don't go telling anyone about this. It's her business, like you said."

"No way." I shook my head. I meant it, too. Another test of loyalty. I could be trusted with secrets.

"But then they broke up, and he wouldn't leave her alone," Summer was saying. "He's everywhere she is. He follows her around constantly, trying to get back with her. She hides it, but it's making her miserable."

I glanced at Thalia, dancing, giggling. You never knew what went on underneath the surface of things. You wouldn't look at that gorgeous girl and think she had anything bad in her life.

"Well, maybe someone should do something about it," I offered.

Summer shrugged. "Like what?"

But her face said she knew what I meant.

Lou and Gemma came bouncing up just then, shoving their gifts into Summer's hands and talking over each other. They'd both bought her music. The three of them shrieked about bands I didn't know for a while, and my cup was empty, so I got up to refill it.

I'd managed to get one vodka mixed with orange juice out of my bottle, but now it was empty, so instead I had some of the fruity punch Thalia had made. It tasted the way spring flowers smell, and before I knew it, I'd had two cups and suddenly realized I was drunk floating, that strange dislocation of feeling half outside of myself. Like my soul had detached its head from mine and I was watching everything with two sets of eyes, one of them under a time lag, as if someone kept accidentally pressing the pause button.

The adults were long gone, and I was talking to someone whose name I couldn't even remember, and it was later but who knew by how much. The bonfire drew everyone to it, and there was music, and girls screaming and dancing. I kept losing jumps of time, floating back down into the present every so often. Drunk. I remembered I was drunk. There was a call for skinny-dipping. Girls shrieking like gulls. Running.

"You gonna come?" said the girl I'd apparently been talking to.

"It's freezing."

"So?" She laughed. "We're young and fucked up." And she was off, skating across the sand, pulling off her sweater to the sound of whoops at the surf's edge.

"Christ," I muttered, but I must have said it louder than I

thought. I heard a laugh across from me, and there was Fenrin, glowing through the haze in my eyes. We were almost alone; most of the party had gone to watch the stripping, shrieking girls or to join them.

"You don't care about impressing people, do you?" he said to me.

"Oh, if only that were true. Then I could be all cool, like you," I said wryly and grinned, then I worried that the drink had slurred my words.

He made his way over to my blanket and sat next to me, leaning back on his hands with a sigh. Our fingers rested close alongside each other.

"I'm not cool," he said to the stars.

"Ah," I replied, wagging a finger. "Now it comes out. I've been waiting for this."

"I like you drunk." He smiled.

"I'm not that drunk."

"You are. I can tell."

"How?"

"You're more relaxed. Not so walled up."

"Huh. Should I be offended or flattered?"

"Oh," he said through a wide smile. "It's a compliment."

There might have been a pause then, but I couldn't tell; I kept losing those leaps of time. Fenrin. Fenrin was talking to me. My body hadn't yet caught up with the situation, and I felt no sickly flutterings. I felt funny and in control.

"Summer's been telling me all about you," he said.

"Oh, really?" I replied, nervous and pleased.

"Really."

"What terrible lies has she told you?"

He laughed. "Summer never lies. She makes a point of it."

"What about you?" I asked, with what I hoped was just the right amount of tease.

"Oh, I lie all the time. Doesn't everyone?"

"Yes."

"You do, too, don't you?"

I didn't reply. I watched his fingers creep up and touch the winding turret shell dangling from his throat.

"Why do you always wear that?" I said.

He ran his fingertips over it, the kind of gesture that looked like he'd done it a thousand times. "It's just a thing. Like a family thing. Each of us has an object. We chose them when we were kids."

"Like Summer's amber bird," I said.

"She told you about that?"

"I guessed."

"Aren't you the observant one."

"Is it like a magical thing, then? She was talking about channeling energy through objects, once. Is that your magical object?"

But my eyes finally caught up with my brain and I saw his expression. I'd gone wrong, somewhere.

"You don't actually believe all that stuff, do you?" he said, with what was, I think, meant to be an easy smile. "You know magic isn't real, right? Like unicorns and Father Christmas."

I remembered what Summer had said about the rest of her family wanting to hide the truth about what they really were.

"Oh, I know," I joined in, offhand. "Except fairies. They're still real, right? Don't go ruining my childhood, now."

He laughed.

"Fairies *are* real," said a girl called Clementine on the next blanket over, who had been making her way through a giant joint and looked almost asleep. "You just have to look hard enough. They don't show themselves to impatient people."

"You're both delusional," said Fenrin affably, and gulped his drink.

"If it were real, though," I continued. "Magic. What would you do with it? I mean, say you could make anything happen. What would you make happen?"

He shrugged. "God, I don't know. I'd make myself King of the Universe."

"It has to be realistic."

He looked amused. "Oh, *realistic* magic. Well, why didn't you say? I'd probably wish to be a shape changer, or something stupid like that. So I could spend as much time as I wanted being a dolphin or a whale or something, out in the sea. Leave all this behind."

I glanced sidelong at him. He was the second Grace to talk about freedom to me tonight. Curiouser and curiouser.

"How about you?" he said to me.

Well, if we were going for truths between us . . .

"I think I'd use it for vengeance," I said.

His eyebrows rose, and he laughed. "Christ, that's dark."

"To help people who'd been wronged," I insisted.

"I don't know if you're aware of this, but there's a whole legal system for that."

"I'm not talking about, like, major crimes. I'm talking about the things people do to others on a daily basis, just because they can. The things they get away with. If you could use magic to stop people being hurt, turn it back on the bad guys . . ."

"You're talking about vigilantism. An eye for an eye."

I shrugged. "Wouldn't you ever be tempted?"

"To go down the dark path? Black magic?" he teased. "Nah. It would have to be a pretty bad situation for me to think that was a good idea. Those kinds of things always have consequences, and they're almost never worth it." He paused. "But I can see why Summer likes you now."

He grinned at me, and I shoved him.

Soon after that, Summer found us. She stood over us in nothing but soaking black jeans and a velveteen crop top that clung to her in heavy wet wrinkles, dripping onto the blanket, hands on her hips and her shoulders jerking with the cold. I was cracking up at something Fenrin had said when she spoke.

"Don't sleep with her," she said to Fenrin suspiciously. "She's my friend."

My laugh turned into a choking noise.

"Try not to be crass, Summer," Fenrin said airily. "That's more like something *you'd* do, not me."

"Jase was a mistake," she snapped. "I really don't get why you hang out with him."

"Well, it doesn't matter now," Fenrin replied. "He's ignoring me."

Summer deflated. "Sorry," she managed.

Fenrin shrugged, kicked her shin. She yowled and threw herself on him, her long hair showering us with freezing droplets. Jase didn't matter, not really. Nothing came between the Graces, and you'd be stupid to try. Would I succeed where Jase had screwed up? Could I?

Maybe I could, because even Summer now thought Fenrin was into me.

Fenrin. Into *me*.

The spell was working.

# NINE

IT WAS EDGING INTO MAY, THE WEATHER WAS THAT PER-
petual rain-shine, rain-shine that made the outdoor courts steam,
and Summer and I had now been friends for well over a month.
People's jealousy followed us around the school corridors like
a bad smell, and I was getting more unsubtle attention than I
could stand. It turned out that being under the wing of a Grace
still didn't make you invulnerable.

It started in homeroom, while the teacher, Miss Franks, called
attendance. She said my name. Before I could reply, Niral stuck
her hand up.

"Miss," she said. "She's not here."

Miss Franks peered at me, trying to work out the game.

"She's right in front of me, Niral. I can see her."

I was mute. I should have just come out with something quick
and slick and wry, and it would have broken Niral's attack before
it could really begin. But my throat closed up on me, betraying

my body's fundamental cowardice, its life mantra: better to be silent than stupid.

Niral's eyebrows rose in surprise. "Oh," she said. "You mean River?"

She looked at me.

The whole class was silent, soaking it up.

Miss Franks waited for me to say something, then cleared her throat. "Her name is not River, Niral."

"Well, that's not what *I've* been told. I think she's changed it."

She. Her. They were talking about me and I still couldn't speak.

Silence.

Everyone waited for me to defend myself. But I knew if I opened my mouth, it would all come out wrong, or not at all.

Summer would have sighed, lounging on her chair. "You're just jealous, sweetheart," she would have said. "I mean, your name means 'calm' and you're, like, a screaming clown. Your whole existence is one big irony."

Laughter. Niral somehow smaller than before.

This scenario ran through my head while the room stared at me. I ducked my head down.

Miss Franks sighed. "Well, thank you for your delightful input, Niral, but I think I'll stick with her given name."

She moved on down the list.

I heard giggling.

I heard someone whisper *"pretentious bitch."*

\* \* \* \* \*

I sat outside in the last dregs of the afternoon light and read through the instructions again.

The chant was stupid. I'd flicked through my books for help, but I couldn't find anything that wouldn't make me feel like an idiot saying it out loud. One book said you could make up your own chant, which fit in with what Summer had said about magic—it wasn't the words, it was the intent. The words just helped you form your intent. So I'd written my own, and in the dark of my bedroom at three in the morning, it had sounded shivery good. In daylight it was all wrong.

I picked through the objects I'd brought—a coil of black satin ribbon, a black clove-scented candle, and the picture of Niral I'd printed out from the array of photographs she had put online.

"Boo."

Startled, I dropped Niral's picture, and caught by the wind, it skipped across the ground. Summer's biker boot clamped it down with a jangle.

I clutched my stupid spell toys. Summer planted herself down beside me. She was dressed head to toe in black, and her legs looked endless in the skin-tight jeans she was wearing. I'd chosen a scrubby spot on the riverbank, a ten-minute walk from school. We were shielded by a few spindly trees, but right opposite was a supermarket parking lot, filled with people going to and fro with their shopping bags.

"Why'd you pick this spot?" said Summer.

"You need a river, to carry the ashes away from you. But this was the only part of the bank I could find that was easy to get to. It's stupid, isn't it? Someone's going to see."

"Even if they did, they wouldn't know what you're doing."

"Bet they would," I said. "This whole town is obsessed with witches."

With Graces, I wanted to say.

"Come on, then," said Summer. "Get on with it."

I frowned at her.

"Oh please, you can do it in front of me. Why did you even ask me to come down here?"

"So you could check I was doing it right. I don't want to mess it up."

Summer crossed her ankles, leaning back on her hands. Her hair was loose and the ends blew around her arms. "It doesn't matter *how* you do it, or what with. It's your will that drives it. Remember?"

"So if I used, like, a neon pink ribbon instead of a black one and vanilla instead of clove, it wouldn't make a difference?" I was trying to be sarcastic.

"It makes a difference in the beginning, I guess. Certain things amplify certain other things. And you make those associations in your mind, you know? So: Red for love. Black for restraint. First comes ritual magic, with specific objects and tools to help you focus. Then channel magic, where you don't use anything except one object to channel your will through. Then thought magic. Thought magic is just you. You change things with just yourself, your presence in the universe like a weight on a piece of string, bending it to your will."

My heart began to thrum painfully in my chest.

This was the kind of knowledge I needed. How it worked. How to control it. How to actually *do* it. She spoke the language of the possible and it gave me hope.

"So now I get why you wouldn't tell me who the binding spell was actually for. It's not polite to cast spells on your friends, you know," Summer remarked.

I looked down at the printout of Niral.

"Are you joking?" I said, coldly. "We're not friends. She hates me."

"She's just jealous. She doesn't hate you."

"What could she possibly have to be jealous about?"

Summer grinned at me, but it was all jagged at the edges with apology. "I guess because we're friends now."

"She didn't like me before that, either." I held the picture up, rolled it into a scroll and started to wind the black ribbon around it with deliberate slowness, making sure each strip was touching the one before. No gaps. Screw the chant—I didn't need it, did I? As I wound the ribbon, I silently asked the universe to shut Niral up so she couldn't say one more nasty word about me.

*Careful,* said a voice in me. *Just be careful. What if something really does happen to her?*

*Go away,* I told the voice. *She deserves it.*

When the ribbon was knotted and secure, I placed the clove candle in front of me. A lighter appeared before my hand.

"Thanks," I muttered. I lit the candle and held the dangling end of the ribbon over the flame until it caught. I let go of the whole thing, dropping it into the tin can balanced on the ground before me, watching the ribbon burn and fizzle, the paper curl to ashes.

When it was burned through, I took the tin can, slid down the incline of the riverbank, and crouched precariously, stretching out one hand to tip the ashes into the water. I would not look up. I would not see the puzzled open mouths of the shoppers opposite as they wondered what on earth I was doing.

"Do you even know why Niral goes after you like that?" Summer said from behind me. She hadn't moved.

The spell done, I pulled myself back from the bank and sat, copying her pose. "Who knows?"

"Because you're all impervious. You have this shell around you like no one can touch you. Like no one is as good as you." Summer saw my face and held her hands up. "I know, I know. But until people get to know you, you can seem a bit like that. And to someone like Niral, it just feels like a 'screw you,' you know?"

"It's *not* a screw you. I don't even want her to notice me. That's why the shell."

"Don't be angry, I totally get it. But Niral doesn't because she's all surface. She only sees that far."

I sighed. "Logic or whatever."

"The truth hurts."

I felt a splat on my neck. And then another.

"Crap, it's raining," I said. "We'd better go."

But Summer's hand was on my arm. Her slender black nails.

"Wait," she said. Her face was suddenly animated, alive in that changeable way she had, flitting from emotion to emotion. "Wait."

"We'll get soaked."

She grinned. "So let's. Stay here with me."

I couldn't say no. I was beginning to wonder if I could ever say no to anything she wanted. She didn't have to come here. I was spelling one of her friends, and she didn't have to be okay with that. She didn't have to spend her time with me at all. But she did.

The rain poured down on us. All of a sudden it got violent, buckets tipping from the sky, drumming down so hard I couldn't catch my breath. I watched her kneel on the ground, her legs soaking up the wet. She still had my arm, and she shriek-laughed, and I wanted so much to be that carefree. Her face turned toward mine, and her hair was stuck to her cheeks. I was laughing, too, uneven gulps that sounded more like choking.

The rain eased.

"Hot chocolate at my house?" she gasped out, water running over her lips in rivulets.

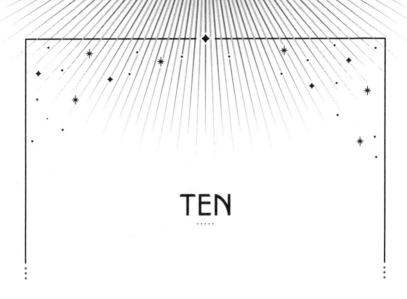

# TEN

I WALKED HOME IN THE SPARKLING AFTERMATH OF THE rain, every grass blade like green glass. It took me a good half hour to get to my housing complex from the riverbank, but somehow I couldn't stand the thought of being cooped up on a bus. I wanted to grin stupidly into the air, where no one could see me.

Because Summer had said she wanted me to bring overnight stuff.

"Overnight stuff?" I'd repeated, puzzled.

"Yeah. You know, dolt. To stay over? I want to watch some movies, and it'll probably get pretty late, so you should just stay. We'll feed you. It'll be fun."

Overnight.

No one that I knew of ever got to go to their house, least of all for the night.

"Check with your parents that you can stay over, right?" she yelled over her shoulder as she left. "Don't be ages. I want hot chocolate."

I turned in to my housing complex, the smell of wet concrete crawling up my nose. Two kids were nudging a ball about, trying to boot it into puddles, squealing with laughter whenever either of them got sprayed.

I'd insisted on Summer letting me go home first to change, and when I finally looked in a mirror, I was glad I had. My hair had separated into scruffy rattails and clung to my skull. My makeup tracked down my cheeks. I did not pull off wet chic.

The house had that special quiet that meant I was alone. My mother was on a crazy shift pattern again at the warehouse where she worked. I sent her a text that just said, "staying overnight with some friends, back in the morning." I wondered if she'd reply this time, but my mood was too good for that kind of thinking, so I pushed on the thought carefully until it scuttled away. I let thoughts of Summer and movies and food and pretending to be a Grace, just for a night, grow and grow in my head until there was no room for anything else.

As I packed my backpack, I pictured Niral's face when she found out.

Overnight in the same house as Fenrin.

I hopped on the public bus that took me toward school, and then I skirted around the back of the sports field and walked onward for a while longer as instructed, until roads turned into potholed lanes, and buildings dwindled out into spartan landscape.

Summer was waiting for me at the top of the rocky track that ran to her house. I was glad to see her familiar shape against the lowering sky—I was beginning to think I'd gone the wrong way and the wilderness would simply swallow me up. The smell of clean, wet plants filled the air as I followed her back down. I breathed it in, and then stopped abruptly as we reached the bottom.

"It's not going to bite you," said Summer, her voice teasing.

I stood, my backpack dangling from my shoulder, looking up at the house.

It was beautiful, a fairy-tale place. It was everything my life was not.

Summer led me up the drive, and I tipped my head farther and farther back as we neared, trying to keep the whole place framed in my gaze. Three stories of pale stone and dark wood. Windows with shutters that were neatly pinned back against the walls. Ivy and a purple climber plant, which Summer called virgin's bower, snaked across the front brick, its leaves wagging in the wind.

I saw winking aquamarine stones in the white stone pots that lined the paved path to the front door. I saw a wooden wind chime hanging from a black iron handle set into one wall. A fat silver horseshoe nailed over the lintel. Gardens stretching around the side of the house, hedges tangled with blooming creepers, white flowers like little lilies. I saw everything; all the little details they'd probably been taking for granted their entire lives.

Inside, the hallway had an airy coolness to it. Summer led me to the bottom of the stairs, but I hesitated.

"Come on," she said. "We'll go to my room, dump your stuff. Are you hungry?"

"I could eat." I could always eat.

The staircase creaked as I put my foot on it. It felt like the house was warning me, like it was alive. We passed a windowsill housing a thin, hammered metal bowl full of strips of bark and shiny chestnuts. Dangling from the top frame was a bunch of dried herbs, hanging upside down from a wrap of thin leather that reminded me of the kind Fenrin always wore on his wrists.

Then we were on the second floor. Summer pushed open her door, and we went inside her room.

My first shocked thought was that it was messy and imperfect. I'd expected lots of black, and heavy textures like velvet and oak. What I got was a jumble of colors and clothes everywhere. Mismatched chairs and posters for art house–looking films next to prints of cartoons I watched when I was a kid. Beaded lamps. A purple-and-pink rug.

"The inner sanctum," said Summer, spreading her arms wide, but underneath the dry tone I thought she looked nervous, like she might fail a test. That was all wrong. I was the one taking tests here. Every minute I spent in their company was loaded with my concentration, my constant study in how to make them like me.

"It's great," I ventured, and her shoulders relaxed. Her desk was underneath the window, scattered with notebooks and pens and hair clips and bottles of nail varnish. It was all so jarringly normal, until I caught sight of what looked like thick parchment fastened to one wall, with two long columns of tiny gems that jutted out from its surface. I moved closer. The gems had holes bored through their centers and were sewn straight onto the parchment. Next to each one was a description in carefully printed handwriting.

"Rose quartz" read the description for a dusky pink-colored stone. "Love, both romantic and platonic. Intimacy and friendship."

"Yeah," said Summer. "It's this handmade gift we all got from our parents when we were, like, ten. It's just this family tradition. Different gems supposedly have specific attributes."

I tried to imagine the gem parchment on Fenrin's wall. I tried to imagine Fenrin's room.

We went down to the kitchen. It was cavernous, tiled in warm colors, every wall taken up by white painted cabinets with pretty glass panels. The thick wooden countertops were covered in boxes, tubs, pie dishes with cloths draped over them, fat vegetables stacked into corners, wooden bowls of nuts and shiny round fruit.

"This is like a food *palace*," I said. I don't think I managed to hide my envy.

"Well, with the ravenous pack of animals in this house, it never stays that way for long," said a rich voice behind me. I turned.

Standing next to Summer was her mother, Esther Grace, and around her all the light seemed to gather. Up close, she was Thalia but to an almost unbearable degree. Her blond hair hung around her body in untamed rivulets, and every part of her was *flow* and *ripple*, and yes, *grace*.

She smiled. "Summer never brings friends home, so I made sure she told me all about you."

It was said to be flattering, but Summer had an odd look on her face, and I thought maybe there was an undercurrent to the sentence; something I couldn't see.

"Thank you for having me," I said.

"Oh, anytime. We've always got friends or family staying, so we're quite used to it," she said, waving one arm absently. She wore jangling bangles like Thalia, or maybe it was that Thalia wore bangles like her. Just for a moment, I tried to imagine what it would be like to have her as a mother.

Intense, I decided. How could you ever measure up to someone so seemingly flawless?

"Help yourself to anything," said Esther, indicating the countertops. "I've got to make a load more food anyway, for when the Grigorovs arrive—"

"This house is just *full* of gorgeous women." Fenrin sauntered past us all, dressed in a steel gray T-shirt that hugged his arms. I watched as his long golden fingers selected a peach from a bowl. I tried to look completely unaffected by the fact that he was there.

"Well?" he said. "What are we all hanging around for? Isn't this movie night, in honor of our guest?" He bit into the peach and winked at me while chewing. Juice ran down his chin. It was simultaneously the sexiest and most embarrassing thing I'd ever seen. Did he just have that Grace trait of seeming as if it hadn't occurred to him to care what he looked like?

Was he flirting with me?

"Don't you have an elsewhere to be?" Summer teased.

"Nope."

"Well, you're not invited to movie night."

"Oh, really? Aren't you totally planning to use my room?"

"Of course. It's the biggest, and you're the only one with a TV."

"So never mind being invited, I'm the goddamn host."

"He shouldn't even *have* a TV in his room," said Esther mildly. She'd crossed to the huge double fridge and was fishing inside it. "And I had no idea you were going to be wasting the evening glued to that idiot box."

I caught a glance between Fenrin and Summer.

"Gwydion okayed the TV," Fenrin protested. "And I barely switch it on." They seemed like they were only mock fighting, but Fenrin's eyes were alarmed.

"Your father has the potential to be wrong about things," came Esther's voice from the fridge.

"That's true," Summer said. Fenrin shot her a deadly look. She gave him the finger.

"Come on," he said, impatiently. "Films to choose. Plans to make."

"Where's Thalia?"

"Already upstairs."

Summer danced off, and I followed. Fenrin was behind us. I had a feeling he was grinning at my back. Was he looking at me? I tried to walk normally. Then I tried to sway a little more than usual. Then I panicked at how that might look and stopped. He caught up with me halfway to the second-floor landing.

"You call your father Gwydion and your mother Esther," I said, for conversation.

"Those are their names."

"Yes, but. You don't call them 'Dad' or 'Mom' or anything?"

"It's reductive and twee," called Summer over her shoulder. "Parents have names. Being a mother or father is not their sole occupation."

Fenrin shrugged. "They never liked it. We're just used to it now."

We went up the next flight of stairs to the top floor. Summer opened a door and disappeared inside. I followed.

Fenrin's room.

The first thing I said was, "Christ, you have your own fridge up here."

"Fen's the darling child, the only son," said Thalia, who was sitting on his bed, leafing through a book. "He gets whatever he wants." Her feet were bare, with tiny silver toe rings and soft plaited bracelets around her ankles.

"Don't listen to her," said Fenrin.

His room had a sloping ceiling lined with dark wooden beams, sitting snug under the eaves of the house. He called it the aerie. In contrast to Summer's room, it was clean and bright. There were discs of polished stone propped carefully up against surfaces, and shells scattered on his windowsill. Thick, sea-blue curtains were held back with rope. The same gem parchment was up on his wall. I went to it and ran my fingers over the little gemstones, reading the descriptions, trying to commit them to memory.

Summer hauled me over to look through their horror movie collection, while Thalia and Fenrin went back downstairs for the food. There was some dark stuff in that collection, and I've never had a stomach for horror, but I wanted to please Summer, so I asked her which were her favorites, and she talked through them animatedly. We chose three, and then Summer put on some music she'd just bought. I tried to like it.

"What about this one?" she bellowed over the noise.

I gave her a weak thumbs up.

"STOP THE RACKET," roared Fenrin as he came back into the room, arms laden with plates and bowls. He put everything down and leapt on Summer, who was defending the stereo with her life. I watched them as Thalia started spreading food out on the floor. I watched Thalia. I watched them all and felt an ache for something I couldn't name.

Thalia opened the fridge, brought out a bottle of wine, and started pouring.

"Oh, thank god," said Fenrin. "Let's get trashed." He swiped the glass from her and perched on his bed, sipping.

"Your parents let you keep alcohol in your room?" I said, surprised.

Thalia looked up from her pouring. "We've been drinking at family parties since we were, like, fourteen. And we have wine with dinner, sometimes. They're not as narrow-minded as some people."

Her voice had a mildly superior air to it. This was a semiregular occurrence with Thalia.

"I think they figured a long time ago that if we were going to drink, we might as well do it openly rather than secretly," Summer said. "Only in the house, though."

"You guys don't go out to bars or clubs or anything?"

There was a short pause.

Fenrin tried to grin. "We have, how do I put it, control-freak parents? They don't enjoy letting us range too far out of their sight."

"Oh, what's the point of bars and clubs, anyway?" Summer

interrupted. "They never play the music I like. I want to be comfortable. I want to surround myself with people who actually interest me."

Thalia handed me a glass. I sniffed it cautiously.

"You don't smell it, you drink it," said Summer.

Thalia grinned. "She's being a connoisseur. You know, smell, swirl, taste, spit."

"I don't know anything about wine," I protested. "I've drunk it, like, once before."

"Seriously? What do you usually drink?" said Thalia.

"Vodka."

Fenrin laughed. "The girl takes her alcohol seriously."

"Wine is a better buzz," said Thalia. "Spirits are just . . . bleurgh."

*Common*, I think she wanted to say.

Fenrin put on some different music. I turned to him in surprise. "I love this band."

"Oh god, you pop conformists," Summer groaned.

Fenrin snorted. "Whatever. *She* knows good music when she hears it." He nodded to me.

"Don't blame her for your bad taste."

Thalia interrupted. "Have you chosen the movies then, or what?"

Summer put the first one on. And we drank.

I had settled at the foot of the bed. Fenrin was draped on top of it, farthest away. Every time the mattress rustled, I wanted to look around. They were like yowling cats throughout, lounging and shifting and eating and talking over the movie. I missed half of it, but I didn't care. This was what it was like to be one of them. This was what they must do all the time.

I didn't even realize when the movie ended—Summer had an uncanny knack for voices and had us in stitches re-creating the villain's lines. We were drunk. We were drunk together, and it was the best feeling in the world.

"Food break!" Thalia announced, standing up. "I'm going to get the cookies."

"And I need the . . . well, you know." I made my way out.

"To the left!" Summer shouted cheerily behind me. "To the left, to the left!"

I waved my hand behind my back. It had gone so dark outside, and there were no hallway lights on. Thalia slipped past me and raced down the stairs like a ghost in the dimness, her feet almost noiseless on the wood. I crept along and found two empty bedrooms. The third was a toilet.

I locked the door firmly and stared at myself in the mirror.

I looked all right.

It was going well.

I repeated this to myself several times until I could almost believe it. I ran my fingers underneath my eyes, cleaning up the makeup that had smeared. I washed my hands twice with this odd, lumpy bar of soap that smelled of the sea. Maybe it was from Esther's shop.

I couldn't face going back into that room, not quite yet, so I crept down the stairs to the second floor. I just wanted to explore a little. It was a big house. How could I ever know it if I didn't look at everything in it?

Summer's bedroom was on the far left. The next door along hid a bathroom dominated by a sunken plunge bath tiled in foggy blue glass. Another bedroom after that—it was grown-up and beautiful, filled with thick woven throws and rough-textured furnishings in natural colors. A spindly desk had open books scattered across it, and herbs in little clay pots perched on every available surface. The same gem parchment was on the wall.

Thalia's room.

Next to hers was an emptier guest bedroom and then a study. I went inside, not daring to turn on a light in case someone saw. The light from the hallway would be enough to see by.

It smelled old, warm, and spicy. The study walls were covered in black lacquered glass-fronted cabinets. I itched to see and touch the objects inside. Reams of cardboard files jostled for space with pieces of crystal, a clock with glass balls that constantly rotated, trunks no bigger than shoe boxes with ornate iron hinges and tantalizing keyholes. What secrets did they have locked inside them?

"What are you doing in here?" said a voice.

I jumped. "I'm sorry," I said into the dark, while my heart climbed up my throat and buzzed in my mouth. "I'm really sorry."

A desk lamp came on. There, sitting in the chair, was Gwydion Grace.

I hadn't even noticed his shape when I'd come in. He was sat on his own in the dark.

Was he going to kick me out? Would he tell everyone? Drag me upstairs and out me?

"I was just looking around," I said. "Your . . . your house is really beautiful, Mr. Grace."

He blinked at that, and his eyes shifted away. It gave me

space to look at him properly. He was pretty. Not handsome—pretty. High cheekbones, long slim nose. Summer looked like him. They had that curve to the mouth, that arrangement of face. His chestnut-brown hair curled past his shoulders and was pulled back into a ponytail. His eyes were big and glassy.

He looked up at me. Sad. His eyes were sad.

"You're Summer's friend," he said.

I waited. It hadn't seemed like a question. He had gone silent, watching me.

"I didn't mean to disturb you," I tried.

"You didn't know I was here."

"Well, you were sitting in the dark."

That had been too much like a challenge. He leaned forward. "I think we both know who's in the wrong here."

I didn't feel like squirming, though. Maybe it was the wine. I was drunk. "What's the matter?" I said.

He looked startled. "What?"

"You're here in the dark, alone. I thought maybe you were upset."

He stood up. I felt like stepping back. I made myself stay still.

"Why are you *here?*" he asked.

"Summer. Summer invited me."

He seemed to consider this. "I'm surprised Esther allowed it." I kept silent.

He started toward the door.

"Stick to the top floor, and drink your wine, and watch your movies," he said at the doorway. "It's nice to be young, isn't it?"

I felt my held breath slowly hissing through my lips.

*You have no idea what it's like,* I thought. *How hard it is.*

I think he knew that, too. The way he said it hadn't seemed to indicate "nice."

A part of me wanted to tell him that. He looked like he needed to talk to someone. Maybe I'd imagined it, though. No, I would give nothing away.

He left.

I gave it a minute. Then, cautiously, I slipped back upstairs. He had disappeared, and I heard a burst of laughter from behind the bedroom door, signaling safety. His eyes were in my head one final time, before I opened the door and the sight of Fenrin sprawled out on his bed slapped everything else away.

I wanted to run over, launch myself next to him, pretend to be a child, carefully uncaring of who else was there. Accidentally brush his leg with mine.

I didn't.

They had just started the second movie. Thalia was back and arguing with Summer over an actor's name. I realized I was hungry and placed myself on the floor next to Thalia, reaching for the bowl of popcorn. At some point, my glass was full again, and I didn't know where all the wine was coming from, and I forgot to care.

We kept laughing, and I kept noticing how I tilted my head back so far I thought my neck would snap, and how much my stomach hurt. It felt so good. I knew if I were on the outside looking in at this night, I would ache so much to be part of it.

The second movie finished. We'd switched all the lights off. Summer and Fenrin had changed places—she was now sprawled on his bed with sleepy eyes. He was on the floor, Thalia in between us.

I willed Thalia away with everything I had. *Please,* I thought silently. *Please go away.* A few minutes later, I got my wish. Thalia clutched her stomach, sitting bolt upright.

"I think I need the bathroom," she announced and didn't even wait for a response. Once she'd bolted out of the door, Fenrin and I looked at each other. He laughed, and I followed suit.

"Some people can't hold their drink," he said, tossing a salted almond into his mouth.

"Will she be okay?"

"Oh yeah. She'll chuck it all up and feel right as rain. Don't worry, she's used to it."

"Really? I didn't think she was a big drinker."

Fenrin paused, as if only just aware of what he'd said. He shrugged.

I leaned closer to him, using the bowl of nuts as my excuse. He stretched his head up to look over the bed.

"Summer is out," he said as he relaxed back down and sighed. "Guess I'll be sleeping in her room tonight. That place looks like a bomb hit it."

"We could carry her," I suggested, flushed with my new role as coconspirator.

"You try moving her. She weighs a ton when she's asleep. And she does *not* wake up until she's had her ten hours or whatever."

"Wow. I wish I could sleep like that."

"So do I."

I kept my voice light. "Bad dreams?"

"Sometimes," he said absently, staring at the wall. "Or, you know. I suppose I just . . . think about things too much."

"What kinds of things do you think about?" I asked him.

"You know. Life. The world. The human race." Fenrin propped himself up on one elbow. We were close now.

Close enough to kiss, if he stretched.

"The thing is," he said softly, "we're all going to die."

"Yes."

"But the first time you really realize it . . . how do you get over that?"

"Get wasted."

We laughed.

"You don't, I think," I said, finally. "You never get over it. The rest of your life is spent knowing it, over your shoulder."

"Are you okay with it?"

"No. But sometimes yes. And then no, again. Sometimes it's okay. Like now. We're drunk. We feel good. But tomorrow . . . life crowds in again. And then you find another way to block out the truth, just so you can get through the day. If we let ourselves see too much truth, it scares us. You have to block it out, or you'd never get anything done. You'd just wander around being perpetually depressed or amazed." I paused. "That doesn't mean we shouldn't want to see the truth. It's just that maybe we have to see it in stages to be able to understand it."

Fenrin gave me a side glance. "Truth stages. I like that. I like the way you think. The way you talk. You're not afraid of the truth. So many people are afraid of the truth."

His eyes were glistening at me in the light of the television. He leaned back against the side of the bed, and I copied him. As we spoke in low voices, life seemed to expand before us, the endless universe, filled with questions and dark mystery.

At one point, and he did it so smoothly—lots of practice,

though I shoved that thought away as soon as it came—he put his arm around my shoulders, pulling my back into his chest, my head resting against his shoulder. His fingers dangled, brushing my skin, my collarbone. He did it as if it were the most natural thing in the world. My lower belly squirmed.

"What about your family?" he said. We'd been talking about his sisters.

I tried not to tense. "What about them?"

"You never talk about them. What are they like?"

"Boring."

"It's just you and your mother, right?"

"Yeah."

"Where's your father?"

I hesitated. "He's . . . he's not around," I said. I couldn't face talking about that, not with Fenrin Grace.

*Block it out. Push it down into nothing.*

"Any brothers or sisters?"

"Nope. Only child."

"That's tough."

"Is it?" I said, though I agreed with him. "Some people might say it's easier."

"No. You might get what you want more than others, but it's lonelier."

In my belly, something turned and dug its claws into me, sharp. It was. It *was*.

"Do you get on with your mother?" he asked.

"God, no. She can't even stand to be in the same room as me." I laughed, trying to lighten my tone. "Not like you guys."

"Oh, sure." His voice was sharp.

"No?"

"What you see is not necessarily what you get with the Graces, my River."

I smiled into the dark. Just two words. *My* and *River.* Amazing how just two words could change so much.

Silence. I wanted to ask more, but he came out with it first.

"Ready for a truth stage?" he said in an overly casual tone.

I felt him underneath me, his voice vibrating through my skull. I felt the weight of his arm and the conversation.

"Yes," I said.

"It's about why I never stick with one girl for long."

"Tell me."

"You'll laugh."

"Only if it's funny."

"Oh it is," he agreed, his voice a comfortable purr. "See, my family has this superstition. They say that if a Grace has a relationship with someone 'normal,' then something bad will happen. It's a curse."

"Someone 'normal'?"

He said nothing.

*Someone who isn't a witch.*

"You've had lots of relationships," I tried.

"You couldn't call anything I've had such a long word. I've had fun. It has to be more serious and long-term than that, or it's not a curse."

His words were gently slurred around the edges.

"They have these stories. These bullshit stories they've fed us ever since we were little. Great Aunt Lydia hanged herself because her 'normal' husband went mad. A Grace back in Victorian times eloped with a farmer's daughter—she ended up shooting him dead. My mother's cousin, her husband killed himself the day after the wedding. A curse. You see?"

The drink fog had lifted slightly. "Those are true stories?" I said.

"Completely. Of course, whether they're because of a curse or not is another matter. And those stories work on you. We believed them without question when we were kids. Then we grew up and derided them as overblown crap. But they left their stain on us. There's always a little part of your mind, right at the back there, the bit you keep locked up, that wonders *what if?*"

Silence descended. I didn't know what to say. A curse. It sounded impossibly tragic, something that belonged to myth and legend rather than real life.

Fenrin laughed, a noise that cut the quiet. "It's become so bad that my sister breaks up with a guy she's known her whole life because of it, and then he goes psycho anyway, so now of course she believes in the curse implicitly because look, there's the evidence. Never mind that maybe he's just naturally unstable. Never mind he's always had issues. Which she knows."

Marcus. He was talking about Marcus.

Curiouser and curiouser.

"Maybe that's how it works," I said softly. "It makes you attract people who are already dangerous."

"That's a pleasant thought," he replied, and his voice was just a little sharper than before.

I kicked myself, wondering how I could repair the damage. I felt him shift underneath me, and I reluctantly pulled away from his chest, my whole body shrinking crossly when the heat of him left it. I thought it was all over, that I'd ruined it, but then he spoke again.

"Well, maybe you should tell my mother your theory. Then she might stop having affairs."

I raised my eyes to his. His features were unreadable in the dark.

"She's having an affair?" I said, astonished. "With who?"

"Take your pick. At least three that I know of. They never last long. She makes sure they don't." His voice was bitter. "Guess why."

"She's afraid of the curse?"

He gave me a sardonic thumbs up. Had he drawn the parallel between Esther's behavior and his own? Of course he had. He was waiting for someone. Someone special—a witch who could withstand the curse.

"Your dad—you think he knows?"

He shrugged, expansive in his false, drunk bravado. "He knows."

I thought of their father sitting in the dark, alone. His pretty, sad eyes.

"Why don't they just divorce?"

Fenrin snorted. "Because then they'd have to admit that there's something wrong. And we're never wrong, darling." His voice trailed off dreamily. "Never never."

I thought about Esther. Beautiful Esther who drew all eyes to her. She could have anyone she wanted. If I was like that, would I be able to stick to just one person for the rest of my life? Could I ever love anyone that much?

She had power. Of course she used it.

Fenrin's eyes were half-closed as he leaned his head back against the bed.

"River, River," he said, his voice just above a whisper. I felt my skin prickle with slow delight.

"Fenrin, Fenrin," I replied, smiling. Dropping my face just a little closer.

His eyes were closed now. The corners of his mouth curled up.

I let myself imagine how it could go, for just a moment. Maybe later, when we were all in bed. Maybe he'd slip into my room. Say he couldn't sleep. Lean toward me in the dark. He'd try and brush it off afterward, of course, just like Thalia had done with Marcus, afraid I'd go crazy on him. I would have to earn him back by proving myself as one of them.

We'd keep it secret, of course, just in the beginning. Everyone at school would find a reason to hate me where before they'd barely even known me. But it wouldn't matter if I had the Graces as a shield. My best friend's brother. The thought of it made my heart swell until it threatened to pop out of my chest.

The bedroom door flew open.

I turned, startled, guilty. It was Thalia. She stood in the doorway and she said, "Wolf's here."

Amazing how just two words could wreck so much.

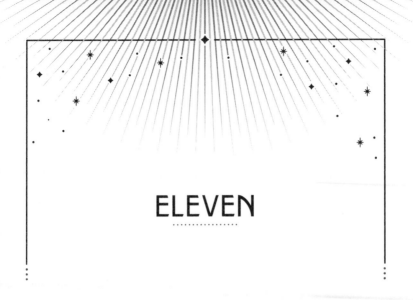

# ELEVEN

WOLF'S REAL NAME WAS VALKO GRIGOROV, AND HE WAS Bulgarian.

As far as I could tell, the Grigorovs were friends of the family from a long time back, and Wolf had been coming to the Grace house every summer holiday since he was a kid. He and his parents had recently moved here permanently from Sofia, so now he came over much more often than just once a year—a weekend here and there, a week or more on school breaks. He was a year older than Fenrin and Thalia, and now that he was out of school, he'd started to apprentice in his father's international law firm based in the city.

He had dark curly hair and olive skin, and he was attractive in a hawkish kind of way, I guess, although he was too short for me, and his expression was always blank, as if he didn't want anyone to know him. He didn't talk much, either, although when he did his curtly accented English was perfect.

Thalia brought him into the bedroom to hang out with us,

but the evening was over, and we went to bed soon after that. His arrival broke whatever ephemeral magic had been holding us together in that room, and a kind of desolation washed over me. Fenrin especially seemed to resent Wolf's arrival—he stared at him a lot, his expression an angry kind of cool. I hoped it was because he'd interrupted us. I thought it could be.

I spent the night in the spare bedroom down the hall from Summer's and Thalia's rooms. The room was a plain, pure white with dark oak beams running down the walls. A small bowl of polished black stones sat on the bedside table. I picked one up. It fit perfectly into the hollow of my palm. It had a neat, round hole through the middle like a fat doughnut. I couldn't tell if it was a natural or man-made thing. A dark olive rag rug perched on the floorboards. I ran the bottoms of my feet over it, tickling my soles, swaying my legs as I contemplated, too keyed up to go to sleep. I wondered if Fenrin would come in. If he came down and saw the light on, he might risk it.

But he never did, and eventually I fell asleep.

In the morning, my head had the raspy furriness of a hangover. I lay in bed for a while, hoping to hear telltale noises of the family stirring. But there was nothing, so I got up and crept into the en suite bathroom.

I started to get the distinct feeling that the house wanted me out. Every move I made was an intrusion. I had a hasty wash, too nervous to take a proper shower, and tried to make my hair look perfectly messy, but it just looked messy, and I gave up.

When I went down to the kitchen, Thalia, Summer, and Wolf were there, but there was no Fenrin, and my heart sank. Wolf was slouching against a countertop and stirring coffee, his feet bare.

Summer's long dark hair was loose against her pale skin, dripping over her arms. She looked tired in a glowering, rock-music-photo-shoot kind of way. I wanted to brush her hair back, take it in my fingers. I wanted to be allowed to do that. She wasn't good in the mornings, anyway, but with a hangover she barely raised her voice over a grunt. Thalia looked impossibly fresh and luminous, which was pure sorcery—maybe one day she would admit to me what she was and then give me the spell that made her look like that.

Breakfast was all business. They barely looked up as I came in. Wolf wasn't a Grace. Wolf was an outsider, too, surely—but I was the one who felt like I shouldn't be here.

The dining table was piled with different breads and pastries. Melon slices. Bowls of freshly cut herbs scenting the air. Expensive-looking muesli with ingredients I'd barely heard of in sleek packages from health food shops. I grabbed a piece of melon and sat awkwardly, eking out the minutes until Fenrin came down.

But he didn't show, and he didn't show.

I'd finished my melon, and then a pastry.

The house seemed to shift, bearing down on me.

I cleared my throat.

"I think I have to go soon," I said into the quiet. "My mother's expecting me. We're going shopping today."

"See ya later," said Thalia absently. She was reading a book, her hands wrapped around a mug. As I watched, she reached out to a bowl and took a handful of green leaves, dropping them into her mug. Wolf was staring out of the window. Summer was making more coffee, her back to me.

What had happened since last night?

Had I done something wrong?

Was this it, now? Were they dropping me?

I stood up and left the kitchen, fumbling in my haste to make it look like I couldn't care less about staying. I'd left my bag by the foot of the stairs, and I picked it up. Their parents were nowhere to be seen. After the encounter with Gwydion in his study, and everything Fenrin had told me, I wasn't exactly anxious to seek them out, even though I knew it would be rude not to say thank you—but just then I heard voices from another room down the corridor and a tinkling laugh.

"Hey," said a voice behind me.

I turned. Summer had appeared, one foot resting on top of the other, her hand wrapped around a staircase post.

"Hey," I said.

We stood. She seemed awkward.

A sudden need to tell her about Fenrin, about our conversation and our closeness, pushed at me. I resisted it. I couldn't risk being that obvious—not yet.

"It was fun last night." Her tone was more like a question.

"Yeah," I said. I tried to reassure her. "It really was." It was the most fun I'd ever had, but that was something I'd never admit to. Needy people didn't keep friends like the Graces.

"Next time let's just you and me hang out," she said. "We can do anything you like."

"Okay," I said. Maybe I was too eager because it seemed to take her by surprise.

"Okay?" she repeated.

I was grinning. "Yes, idiot."

The corner of her mouth was tugged into a half smile.

"You don't have to go right away, you know," she said. "You could stay—"

"Are you heading off, River?" came a voice behind us. I turned.

Esther and Gwydion Grace, together at last.

She was like an elf queen; he a fairy king. Of course, this was a family of witches—you just had to look at them. Gwydion had his arm around Esther's waist, and she nestled back into his shoulder.

It didn't seem like she was having a string of affairs. It definitely didn't seem like he knew about it. Had Fenrin been messing with me? But I remembered his face and his voice. No. They were good at secrets, this family. Good at glamour, hiding the cracks underneath.

"My mother's waiting," I managed, stammering in the face of them. Why was it so hard to talk to beautiful people?

"Will you be able to get back all right? Is she coming to pick you up?"

"Oh no, it's fine. We're going to meet in town, so I'll get the bus."

Esther frowned at that, but Gwydion squeezed her side.

"All right then," she said. "It was lovely to meet you."

"Thank you . . . thank you for having me."

Esther's eyes slid over Summer. "Feel like hanging out with your mother after breakfast?"

Summer folded her arms tightly. "Yeah," she said. She'd been smiling just a second ago.

Esther and Gwydion walked off.

"Um," I began, unsure how to ask her what was wrong. "Are you okay?"

"Yeah, of course. She just wants a report on last night, that's all. Make sure I didn't say anything to you that she wouldn't want me to," said Summer, and then she turned abruptly. "See you Monday, then."

She went into the kitchen, leaving me alone. I waited for a long moment, but she didn't come back.

I took a key dangling off a carved set of wooden pegs on the wall next to the front door, opened it, shouldered my bag, locked the door, posted the key back through the mail slot, and walked away as softly as I could.

* * * * *

I went home to a heavy quiet. I knew I shouldn't, but it was all too easy to compare my duplex to the Graces' home. Theirs was a warm, deep place, each room seemingly designed to evoke a cascade of memories. A place to get lost in. Ours was blank, beige, tiny, and cramped. Dim and dusty. Plastic chairs in the kitchen. Sagging couch. A temporary box to hide away in.

The ceiling creaked as I stood in the hallway. Mom was walking around in her bedroom. Even in a new house, the sound of her tread was so familiar to me. It was the only thing I had left of our old life, apart from the Giger and Matisse posters on my wall, with their curling edges I could never stick down no matter how much Blu-Tack I used.

I went upstairs and knocked on her door. She didn't answer. She never answered. I went in, anyway.

She was folding her laundry. "There's a pile on your bed," she said. "Put it away or it'll crease something chronic."

"Don't you want to know who I've been with all night?"

She shrugged. Her hair crinkled as it met her shoulders. "I

thought you said you were at a friend's house. Why, are you trying to tell me you were out all night clubbing?" Her grin was hopeful.

"No."

"It's fine if you were, you know."

"Seriously. When was the last time I went out clubbing?"

"You might do it all the time, for all I know," she said. "You've got some new friends, have you? Well, that's good, isn't it? Things seem to be going better here. You're different."

"Different?"

"You just seem happier the last few weeks, I don't know," she said. "You know how you get all worked up, sometimes. But you've been out of the house a lot recently. It's good. It's a good thing! We moved here to make a fresh start, didn't we? What's that face for?"

"Moving towns doesn't make everything magically okay."

She sighed, a here-we-go-again kind of noise. "Why are you spoiling for a fight? I'm not in the mood."

*Why won't you just tell me that you think it's my fault?*

I took in a deep breath, testing the waters. "Have you spoken to Dad since we moved?"

Her face turned hard. "You know I haven't. He's gone. So get it out of your head, okay?"

"He can't just disappear like that and never even talk to us again."

She sank down onto the edge of her bed. "Well, he did." She was unusually quiet instead of angry, so I felt safe to push.

"Maybe you could give me his number," I tried.

"Love—why are we going backward? I thought we'd moved on

from this the last couple of months. I thought you were better."

"I just want to talk to him. I just want to know he's still . . . he's still around."

She raised her arms and her voice. "Well, he's not! He's not hiding under the stairs, is he?! I just . . . look. If it's going to be like this again, maybe we need to have a talk about that medication you were on before we moved. Maybe it was too soon to stop taking it."

"Oh yes, mom, lovely. Dope me up and shut me up!" I said, suddenly furious, at myself most of all. This was her favorite distraction tactic—get me focused on the hated pills she'd guilted me into taking after he'd gone.

"That's not the point of them at all," she protested. "Just . . . you're not so up and down all the time on them, you're more—"

"More normal," I said bitterly. "Yeah. I know. Just like you always wanted."

She didn't even try to deny it. Her silence followed me all the way back to my room, until I slammed the door on it.

The thing was, six months ago, my father disappeared off the face of the earth.

No explanation, nothing. Police not interested. Another missing persons report.

Mom closed off the whole thing for good just before we moved. She said he'd suddenly been in contact. He said he was up north somewhere, and he didn't want to talk to us—he just wanted us to move on without him.

I needed to believe her. I really, desperately did, and just one phone call would do the trick, but she said she didn't have any contact details for him. He'd called her from a private landline while I was at school, and the number hadn't shown up on the phone. He'd only talked to her for as long as it took to reassure her that he was all right. He had a new girlfriend and a new life. He was happy. And he wasn't coming back.

I hadn't heard his voice or seen his face since the night he supposedly walked out. I say *supposedly* because he didn't even pack a suitcase. His razor was still on the side of the sink, wiry chin hairs caught in its blades. Not one item of his was missing. Who decides to walk out of their house, walk out on their family, without even taking a change of underwear?

No one. That was who. One day, Dad was in our lives. The next, he wasn't. And I'd been the last person to talk to him. To drive him away. Mom kept saying I'd heal on my own, but you couldn't heal from that kind of guilt. It was my fault he was gone.

It was because of what I did.

# TWELVE

I LEANED AGAINST THE RAILING, THE WIND ROLLING OFF the sea and streaming my hair back from my face.

My gaze jumped between the three surfers, each one popping up out of the waves every so often. They had a small crowd watching them, mostly girls, calling cheerfully to one another, fit to compete with the cries of the seagulls circling overhead. It was late afternoon on a Sunday, a pretty strange time to pick considering the tide timetable, but coincidentally perfect for drawing bystanders to the seafront, a rare tourist or two in the mix, shading their eyes and pointing them out with grins, clapping when they rode a wave even for just a couple of seconds.

I'd gone for a walk, hoping to accidentally run into a Grace. I'd caught sight of the surf crowd and wondered if Fenrin would be among them. He wasn't, not today, but my house was empty, and it made me itch restlessly inside, so I lingered to watch them.

It was Jase Worthington and two of his friends. His new girlfriend, Seela, was among the crowd on the beach, waving and laughing. She had shorts on to show off her tanned legs, as if the cold didn't even give her a moment's pause. I watched Jase emerge, gasping, from underneath the water. Seela blew him a kiss.

I remembered him calling Summer a stupid goth bitch.

His friend Tom managed to crawl up onto his board and stood for several seconds, howling to the beach crowd, who responded with claps. A tourist not too far from me leaned against the railing and joined in, indulgent and eager for a show. Tom wobbled, and then dove neatly back into the sea to prevent an embarrassing tumble off.

There was a time before moving here, a time I would have watched that crowd on the beach and hated them. Hated them because I didn't want to admit that I'd have given anything to be down there with them, so carelessly accepted. Belonging. I couldn't seem to get on with people who wanted so much to belong, but underneath that, I knew that I wanted it, too. Now, though, the hate was gone. Envying a group like that seemed pointless when you had the Graces.

Stupid carny fakers, Jase had called them, hadn't he?

I'd grown tired of the whole parade, and I watched Jase come up again, bobbing and shouting, until something about the shredded note in his voice and the stillness rippling through the group on the beach caught me.

He wasn't shouting anymore. He was screeching.

Seela went down to the water's edge.

The wind turned and I heard her. "Tom!" she screamed into the sea. "Go get Jase! Something's wrong!"

Tom turned, his head slick as a seal, catching sight of his

thrashing friend. He dove for him, their other friend reaching them both a moment later.

Sea spray and confusion for long, long seconds. Heads bobbing up and diving down.

I watched them drag Jase out of the surf and onto the beach. As soon as his foot touched down on the sand, he squealed, piercing and sharp. Nearby gulls lurched out of the way and took off clumsily, panicking.

"Shit," I breathed. "He's broken his leg."

"It could be a shark, or something," said a voice beside me, tinged with nervous fascination.

I glanced around.

It was Marcus.

He was gazing at the scene, his hands braced on the railing. The wind in my ears had covered his approach.

"It's not," I said. "Round here?"

"Has someone called an ambulance?"

I pointed to the crowd. Several of them had phones in their hands. Jase was sobbing now, wobbling wails drifting across the sand.

"Poor guy," said Marcus with a frown. "That's bad luck."

"Yeah."

He cupped his hands around his mouth. "Do you need any help?" he yelled to the crowd.

Only one of them looked up, and when she saw who was shouting, she quickly glanced away again. Jase had disappeared beneath a knot of bodies. I felt Marcus watching me.

"You look like you think I'm planning to stab you," he said. "I guess you've heard all the rumors about me."

"I'm pretty new," I replied. "I don't know anyone well enough to make assumptions about them."

"And yet."

This nettled me.

"What do you want?" I said.

"Can I talk to you a second?"

"What about?"

His voice was quiet. "Maybe stop acting like whatever I have is catching and just have a conversation with me?"

I shifted, awkward. "Sorry."

"Don't worry, I get why. It's what happens." His face was open. It bothered him, but he didn't try to hide it. That was brave. I hid everything I could.

*You have good reasons,* whispered my coal-black voice.

Sirens floated to us from the distance. An ambulance was on its way. The crowd at the seafront had swelled, and I felt suddenly uncomfortable with so many people around, so many gawping vultures, and me standing there like I was part of them, watching the show.

"Come on," I said. "Let's get out of here. The cavalry's arrived."

＊ ＊ ＊ ＊ ＊

We walked away, back into town.

I resisted the urge to look at him as he moved beside me. Marcus inspired curiosity. Everything I'd heard implied he was crazy or dangerous, but he didn't seem it, and I enjoyed that. More importantly he'd managed to catch a Grace, and I wondered how he'd done it. I wondered if he could help me.

I skirted past the entrance to the Mews and moved us into the rest of the town center—what I now thought of as the normal, boring bit—wandering aimlessly along the tiny cobbled streets. I always tried to wear the thinnest, flattest shoes I had when I went into town because I loved the feel of the smooth rounded stones against my feet. They felt ancient and immovable, fixed points in time. People would flit over them, people would come and go, come and go. The stones would remain the same.

"I heard you changed your name," said Marcus, as we walked.

I didn't reply.

"It's cool," he said quickly. "I mean, people can call themselves whatever they want."

"You're two years above me in school, right?" I said, to change the conversation.

"Yeah. Same year as the golden twins. Where are you from originally?"

"City suburbs. Totally different from here."

"How come you moved away?"

I stopped. I would not be delving into my past with a stranger. "Why do you want to know?"

"It's just conversation," he said.

"Look. I feel like I should say that Summer kind of told me all about you."

Something skittered across his face—an expression I couldn't quite catch before it was gone. He glanced up and down the street. It was a gray, half-light kind of a day, and most people were holed up inside.

"What did she say?" He tried to look casual, but desperation stood stark on his face.

"That you're obsessed with Thalia."

"Yeah, yeah. That I'm a stalker." He snorted. "Oh good. How original."

"I don't think I can help you get to her."

"That's not why I'm talking to you," he said quickly.

"Then why?"

He waved his hands defensively. He was all elbows and long piano fingers. "You're new. There are things you don't know, okay? You should be warned before you get in too deep. Because trust me, I know what it's like to get in too deep with the Graces."

"Oh really? How come?"

"Because I've been best friends with them my whole life. Until recently."

His black hair was lank, his face pleasant enough. He was pale. Average. If you were feeling generous, you'd call him interesting in a consumptive, vampirish kind of way. He seemed so normal, but I knew that outsides sometimes didn't match insides. I watched him glance up and down the street again. We were next to an empty café, its horribly cheery striped awning flapping sadly in the wind. It was a primary-colors, mothers-with-strollers kind of a place. No one our age would be caught dead in it. He gestured.

"Can we just, like, sit down inside for a minute?"

He'd played me well, I'd give him that. When he pushed open the door and disappeared inside without even waiting to see if I'd follow, it was because he knew I would.

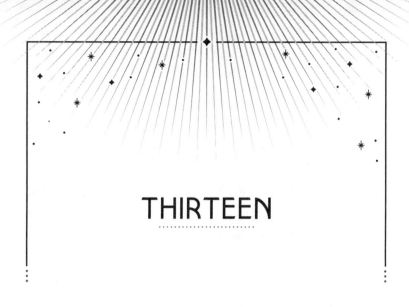

# THIRTEEN

MARCUS BOUGHT US BOTH HOT CHOCOLATES WITH marshmallows floating on their thin surfaces. We sat in the back, tucked into a corner table and away from the street view.

"You're wondering why they'd be into someone like me," he said, without preamble. "We kind of grew up together. My dad used to work with Gwydion." He smiled at my surprise. "It's not a secret. You're new, that's all."

"Were you friends with all of them?"

"Fen in particular. But you know how it is. If one adopts you, they all do."

I knew.

"So what happened?" I said.

Marcus looked away.

"Summer told me that you and Thalia were together for a while." I was trying to be kind.

His head reared. "She told *you* that?"

He seemed surprised they'd trust me with such secrets already, and I couldn't help feeling a little bit proud.

"Why don't you just say that to everyone?" I said. "They wouldn't treat you the way they do if they knew you were actually involved with her."

"It's not up to me," he muttered. "It's Thalia's business. I'm not about to stab her in the back like that."

"But—"

"Look, I don't care about the rumors," he snapped. "I don't care what anyone else thinks about me."

The unspoken hung in the air. The Graces' opinion was the only one that mattered. He remained loyal, maybe hoping it would eventually win their favor back.

*Well, good luck with that, Marcus.*

I remembered Summer maintaining a staunch silence in the cafeteria that day he tried to talk to Thalia in the lunch queue. They didn't join in everyone's mocking of him, but neither did they do a damn thing to curtail it. The power lay with them, but they didn't use it. What did that mean? Were they punishing him? Were they crueler than I wanted them to be?

"You think it's stupid," he said, softly, looking at me. "Are you going to tell everyone what Summer told you?"

"Of course not," I began.

"Why not?"

*Because I don't know you and I don't owe you anything.*

"Because you feel the same loyalty I do," he finished for me. "Because that's how they make people feel."

"They don't *make* me feel anything."

"Please. They totally manipulate everyone in this whole town."

"How on earth would they do that?"

He licked his lips nervously. "You know. The witchcraft stuff. Black magic."

"You really believe in that?" I said in my best poker voice.

"Are you saying that after hanging out with them, you really *don't*?"

I was silent.

He looked triumphant.

"So what else don't I know about them?" I asked casually.

Marcus stared at the far wall, drumming his fingers on the table. Tap tap tapping. A lot of nervous energy wrapped up in that slim frame.

"For starters," he said, "the Graces might be one of the most powerful families you'll ever meet. I'm talking about money. Old money, and fingers in every pie you can think of. Half the government has a connection to a Grace, somewhere down the line. I mean, it makes sense—the water witches are best at being charming and persuasive. Persuaders can become leaders, and make the right people change their minds about things—"

"That's kind of paranoid."

"Not really. That's life, for rich and powerful people. You have no idea what they could do with a wave of their hand."

"Come on. They're rich, so what? They don't run this town."

"Yeah, they do. You just don't see it yet." He laced his fingers together in his lap. "Fen and I used to talk about it a lot. He said being a Grace is like being in a cult. When you're in it, you can't see why anyone else would live or think or act any other way. It's only when you start to surface that you realize how screwed up it can be."

"So, what? They brainwash everyone? They're just that powerful?"

"Why not? You've seen how everyone hangs on their every word, right? And they have all sorts of strange things going on, like arranged marriages with other families, just as old and moneyed as they are. They treat their own family members like prize horses. And they treat everyone else like cattle. It's so 'keep it in the family,' and they hate anything that threatens that."

"Fenrin isn't like that. Summer's not like that. Thalia—" I hesitated.

"Fen is like that, actually, and it's something he really hates about himself. Summer's the same, for all she plays the rebel. Thalia, are you kidding? She's her mother mark II." He sighed. "Cut her in half and you'd see 'Grace' the whole way through. Like rock candy."

I was beginning to see why people didn't like Marcus. Why he had the "weird" brand stamped on his forehead. He said things other people only thought in the privacy of their own heads, and he seemed utterly fearless about looking like an idiot for it. He knew what everyone thought of him and didn't care.

I felt a grudging admiration begin to stir.

"Even if I believed in your conspiracy theories," I said, "why are you telling me all this?"

His eyes darted to mine, quick and then away. "Everyone in school's been watching you for the last few weeks. Did you know that?"

I was silent, unsettled.

"And they wouldn't have if you'd just been another friend the Graces picked up, you know the way they do." He paused. "But they don't have *best* friends. They don't ditch people in favor of someone else, the same someone else, all the time."

"So?" I managed.

"So," he said, his voice wavering with amusement. "People don't get how you did it. They don't get you. Everyone's afraid of what they don't understand. And fear turns to anger."

"And anger leads to hate, and hate leads to the dark side."

"You can take the piss all you like. That's how it works. You've stayed over at their house. Do you know how many people in school have done that?"

"A few."

"None. No one since me."

I felt a thrill scuttle down my spine.

"So I felt like I should warn you, from one Grace reject to the next, what that's actually like. Because it feels good now, but when you do something they don't like, your life is going to go very wrong. And as soon as everyone else notices you're out of favor, the rumors will start. To be shut out and rejected, when you're not even the bad guy . . . you'll see how it feels. It's not *them*. It's never them. It's everyone else. While you're friends with them, you're under their protection, but as soon as they're not into you anymore, everyone else will punish you for being in with them. It's just how it works."

"I know how bullying works," I shot back. "I'm not afraid of small, pathetic people who treat others like crap just so they can feel better about their own small, pathetic lives."

Marcus studied me keenly. "No, I guess you aren't," he said. "But these are not ordinary people you're friends with. And this is not an ordinary town because of them. It's just . . . it's hard for anyone to see straight around them."

"But you do, I guess."

"I do *now*."

Now he was on the outside.

"Does this mean you're not going to try and get back with Thalia?" I asked.

His face dropped, hard. "That's none of your business," he said flatly.

"But it seems like you still love her, despite what you say."

He had clammed up. Maybe he thought I was fishing for the Graces. I wasn't, exactly—I was curious. Was he just going to passively sit around and wait for them to like him again, or was he going to do something about it?

"Why did you guys break up?" I tried.

He was silent.

A drop of suspicion began to bloom. "What did you do?" I said.

"Still none of your business."

He'd just spent the last few minutes trying to shroud the Graces in shades of gray, but what I hadn't yet determined was just how innocent he was in all this. What if he'd done something awful? What was I supposed to think about all the bad things he'd said about them then? How could I find out more about the truth? There was that website, but . . .

Something clicked.

"Hold up," I said.

He looked at me.

"You said something about water witches. Persuaders."

"Right."

"*You* made that website."

His face changed.

I thought I was starting to understand Marcus. What a person chose to keep secret could tell you all you needed to know about them. What they showed was who they wanted to be. What they hid was who they actually were.

I leaned back, my chest growing tight. "Oh my god. That's how it has all that private stuff on there about them. I knew it must have come from someone close to the family."

"It's not private," he said. "Everyone already knows most of it."

"Including all the witch types and their symbols? All the anecdotes about family members? I'm supposed to believe they tell everyone about things like that?"

He was silent.

"Isn't that kind of like stabbing them in the back? You know, the thing you said you would never do?"

"It was right after they turned on me," he muttered. "I was angry. And I wanted to warn people."

But the website didn't read like that. It read like someone who was in love with them, their danger and their secrets. I still didn't know whether he wanted me to stay away from them or to use me to get him back in with them, but either way I wasn't interested. He didn't want to help me—he wanted to help himself. I didn't hate him for it; it was just human nature, but I wasn't prepared to be used like that. I had my own plan to worry about.

"Look, I have to go," I said.

He looked up at me with a startled rabbit face. "Wait a second."

"I'm sorry for what happened between you guys, but it's nothing to do with me, okay?" I stood, backing out of the tiny corner he'd maneuvered me into. "I can't help you, Marcus. You just have to let it go. Just leave Thalia alone. Leave them all alone. It's better that way."

His mouth opened and closed. I felt a little bad. But I wouldn't jeopardize my friendship with the Graces because he'd screwed up his.

I turned and walked fast out of the café. Away, away, breathing a sigh of relief.

He was shouting at my back.

"You think they won't fuck you over, too? They will. They *will*."

# FOURTEEN

IT WAS TOUGH BEING AT A SCHOOL WITH NO UNIFORM. It was supposed to make you feel adult, but all it did was give me anxious thrills each evening as I went back and forth through my clothes rail until the sound of squeaking metal hangers gave me a headache.

Fenrin didn't seem to discriminate between fashion types, though he'd been through his fair share of surfer girls. Anyway, I was the different one, right? He liked me because of that. I tried to smudge a load of eyeliner under my eyes to give them a smoky, glowery effect, but all it did was make me look tired, so I rubbed half of it off.

This was ridiculous. I'd never been like this about anyone before. I'd never had many friends. I wasn't good with people, and it was hard to get along in this world if you weren't. Easier to not put yourself out there, less hurt all around.

But then again, I'd never thought I'd meet anyone like the Graces. I knew now that I'd been holding out for them all along.

Were we close? I couldn't tell. I'd never had best friends before, so I wasn't sure what behavior told you that you were. But they were giving me secrets, weren't they? I needed them to like me, to trust me enough to give me their help, to teach me to be a witch so I could fix everything that was wrong.

Maybe even get my father back.

It was the first and the best chance I'd ever been given, and I had to do everything in my power to use it.

I read a book as I walked into the cafeteria at lunch, letting it dangle languorously from my hand when I looked up to find a spare seat, trying to seem like I was still too immersed in the world on its pages to pay much attention to the world around me.

There they were. All three of them, together in the middle table, surrounded by a parade of gigglers.

*Just go up to them like you're supposed to be there.*

*Go on.*

What if they ignored me?

*You just spent the night at their house. How many other people in school can say that?*

I walked through the cafeteria, Marcus's warnings crawling through my head. I passed Niral, sitting with a group at another table, and for a moment I felt panicked, like she could see the binding spell I had done on her playing like a projector movie over my head. But all that happened was that she looked up, tossed me a dirty glance, and then went back to talking with her friends.

She seemed disappointingly unspelled. I guessed that meant I wasn't a witch yet—but part of me was glad. It was a petty, angry little thing to have done. I should have risen above it, but instead I'd risked an awful lot to teach a bully a lesson. From now on I'd behave as if I was barely aware of her existence. That was the Grace thing to do.

When I got to their table, I realized my mistake: there were no spare chairs. My face started to burn. It began at my neck and ate away at each section of skin until it reached my forehead.

"Hey," I said, looking at Summer.

She had a drink to her mouth and didn't reply.

"Are you passing through on your way to the library, or will you be staying to enjoy this cafeteria's fine roast beef with us?" asked Fenrin, who had the suspect-looking meat in question skewered on his fork and a ripple of distaste across his mouth.

The face burn faded, leaving cautious relief in its wake. "I've got some time. For you, maybe even ten minutes."

"You're a generous soul, Your Majesty. Have a seat . . . wait, there's no chairs."

No one moved.

"I can stand," I said. "I'm not going to be here long."

"Dean, you were supposed to be gone already. Give River your chair."

Dean eyed me.

"Seriously," I said. "It's fine."

No one would risk making a Grace ask twice. Dean got up slowly like he didn't care. "Yeah, I'm so late," he said, stilted. "See you in biology?"

"Yeah," said Fenrin absently.

Dean shambled off. I took the chair beside Fenrin. It was warm.

"So you're going to have to tell me the ending of that last movie," I said to Summer. She was in conversation with Lou, who looked irritated when Summer broke off and turned her face to me across the table.

"You mean you guys didn't watch it?" she asked.

Thalia rolled her eyes. "What are you even talking about? You fell asleep."

"So?!"

"So we were under no obligation," Fenrin remarked, leaning back in his chair. I watched the way the curve of his shoulder moved underneath his T-shirt, and then forced my eyes back to the table. "It was your crap pick, anyway."

"Where were you guys? At the cinema?" said Lou.

Summer shrugged. "No, we just chilled out with some movies and food at the house."

I wanted there to be a stunned silence. Instead, I had to settle for a quick, shocked glance between Gemma and Lou.

Good enough. I wondered how long that piece of news would take to circulate.

"You hear about Jase?" asked Lou, rapidly changing the subject.

"Oh my god, that's bad," someone else joined in enthusiastically.

"Why, what happened?" Gemma asked.

"He broke his leg surfing. Had to go to the hospital. They said he was screaming and crying like a five-year-old having a tantrum."

"Really?" Summer said. "When was that?"

Lou gave her a pleased look, as if she was being wonderfully sly. "Yesterday."

Gemma whistled. "That must have hurt."

"Yeah, well. I'm not too sad for him, after all that shit he's been saying about Summer. So maybe he got what he deserved."

"Harsh," Gemma commented, her eager tone suggesting otherwise.

Now I understood. They thought Summer had made good on her promise to curse him.

I watched her. Her face was carefully blank, and she wasn't exactly going out of her way to correct them. Had she really done something, or was it just coincidence? The conversation faltered.

"So how's the birthday party planning going?" one of Thalia's friends asked her.

"Oh man, it's such a nightmare," Thalia moaned. "Just even organizing that many people."

"Esther's doing most of it," Summer commented.

"Not even. She's dumped a load of it on me this time." Thalia was trying to sound disgusted but she looked happy. "I think it's because Gwydion's not going to be around. She's freaking out about corralling everyone. You know what it's like getting them to turn up to anything on time."

Summer rolled her eyes. "God, our family. Remember Yule?"

Fenrin snorted. "Uncle Lleu in the bathtub?"

"The *straws*," said Thalia.

"And then all three of them at the front door, five hours late . . ."

"And he's all covered in mud, and he says . . ."

All three of them chorused, "Bloody tarot woman!"

Summer shrieked a laugh that tore into the air. The other two were convulsing. The rest of the table sat around awkwardly.

"So your whole family always comes around for it," said Thalia's friend, as soon as she judged it safe.

"Whoever's free," said Thalia. "If we had the whole family around, we'd have to have it in a castle to fit them all in."

"But it's your eighteenth."

"So?"

The friend looked nervous. She was one of those who thought dressing like Thalia made her more acceptable. Camouflage, I guessed. Look like them, be like them. She had this dramatic silver streak in her hair. "Well that's, like, special, isn't it? It's your eighteenth."

"If all you cared about was drinking in pubs, I guess it would be," said Thalia. "It's never been that big a thing in our family. It's just a number, you know?"

The girl nodded like she totally knew.

"Our family" means you're being reminded that you're excluded, I thought.

"You should invite us this year," said Lou. "Gemma makes this wicked vodka cocktail called Sex on the Beach. It's amazing. The whole party will love it." Her eyes slid briefly to Fenrin. "You could ask your parents if you could have friends there this time," she finished, hopeful.

"Well, we do," Summer replied. She seemed uncomfortable. I wondered if people tried it on like this every year. "We have family friends coming."

"Yeah, but, like, friends your age."

"Some of them are."

"It kind of seems unfair on you guys," Lou tried, glancing

at Fenrin and Thalia. "I mean, Summer gets to invite loads of friends to *her* birthday. Is it because of that thing with that kid? Because that was years ago, and it was just a stupid accident."

The Graces exchanged swift glances.

"Um," said Thalia. "Well, it's become like more of a family gathering these days. I mean, Summer's is out on the beach, but ours is always at the house, so the family can stay round—it's just easier."

The unspoken hung on the air. No one from here was going because no one from here got invited to their house anymore.

No one except me, that was.

I swallowed a burst of pure happiness before anyone could see it.

I felt a poke in my side. Fenrin was looking at me. "I'm bored," he said. "This party is all I hear about right now. What are you reading?"

I showed him.

"*The Virgin Suicides*? Yay."

"It's for English."

"Yawn."

"It's pretty good, actually," I said, giving him an arch eyebrow. "It's got interesting things to say."

"Isn't it just about a load of stupid girls killing themselves over nothing?" said another of Thalia's friends.

"Not really. It's all about how sometimes normal people can be capable of extraordinary things. Like, you'd just never know that these girls had it inside them to do the horrible things they do. We always have to find reasons to make order out of chaos, but the worst horror is when the reasons are totally banal, or when there isn't any reason at all."

When I stopped, I realized I had talked myself into a yawning cavern of silence.

The girl's forehead scrunched as she stared at me.

"You might want to calm down," she said. "I mean, suicide's not exactly something to get excited over, is it?"

"You must be into morbid stuff," remarked another. "You're one of those people who think they're vampires, right?"

"Do you have a coffin at home?"

"Do you drink blood?"

I knew what was happening. I just couldn't seem to do anything about it.

*You should be happy*, said my coal-black voice. *It means they're threatened by you.*

"I *love* that kind of weird shit," said Summer. "Why would you want to be someone who never questions anything and just lives to eat, procreate, and die? Probably in front of the television, watching some reality show about other bland people trying their hardest not to be bland?"

Beside me, Fenrin laughed. Summer blew him a kiss.

I loved them. I loved them with everything I had. How could I have doubted?

The first bell rang. As everyone started to pack up and leave, I waited until Summer was getting up, and then I copied her. We left together while Fenrin and Thalia lounged behind.

"Thought you had somewhere else to be?" she said to me.

I owed her the truth, after how nice she'd just been. "I was trying to be cool."

She laughed. "You *are* cool."

"Well, thanks, Queen of Cool."

"Hey. You're coming to the party, though, right?"

I stopped, astonished. "I am? I'm invited?"

"Of course you are."

Holy. Shit.

I didn't even mind that she hadn't said that in front of the others. It felt more personal. It existed just between us.

"Oh god," I said suddenly in realization. "I'll need to get them a gift."

Summer started to laugh.

"Don't laugh. What the hell do I get them?"

"Stop freaking out—they get enough gifts from all the people who come as it is. They will want nothing from you, I'm telling you. They just want you there."

I was blushing with happiness. It showed all over me, a neon glow, I was sure. It didn't matter.

"Well, when is it?" I said. "I'll have to check my calendar."

I knew exactly when it was. August 1.

"Trying to be cool again? You don't have a calendar. Your calendar is mine," said Summer.

"You don't own me," I sniffed, mock outraged.

"Not yet," she replied, and flashed me a wicked smile.

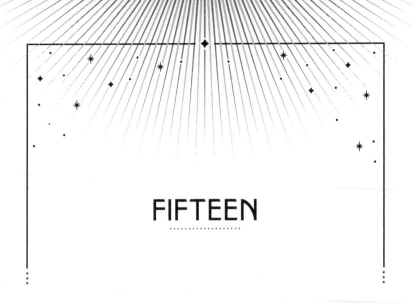

# FIFTEEN

ONE DAY IN JUNE, THALIA DIDN'T SHOW UP FOR SCHOOL.

I hadn't seen Summer all morning—we had no early classes together on Tuesdays—but I usually met her in the cafeteria if we had no other plans. At lunch I ignored my nerves and slid straight into an empty seat at the Graces' usual table, despite none of them actually being there yet. Their friends said nothing, and I let myself relax, taking out my phone and fiddling with it to look busy.

"She must be terrified," I heard someone comment, as I gazed at the screen and tapped on the keys. "To ditch school because of him."

I lost the reply in cafeteria noise.

"Has anyone seen him today?" asked someone else.

"Nah, he'll be hiding away in the library."

"Maybe we should go and pay him a visit."

"I wouldn't." That was Gemma's unmistakable squeak, and

my gaze slid up to rest on her face. "They don't like it when you interfere."

"He's *stalking* her," protested Lily, Thalia's silver-hair-streaked friend.

"I know, but they can take care of it, can't they?" Lou paused. "I mean . . . you know what I mean."

"So why haven't they?"

"I don't know, but—"

"Come on, you guys." Lily looked around the table for support. "Thalia skipped school today because of him. He's officially terrorizing her. We can't just let him get away with it."

Marcus was a little obsessive, okay. But terrorizing?

"What did he do?" I said.

There was the briefest of pauses as the table adjusted, weighing whether to include me or not.

"You don't know?" said Lily.

I shrugged.

Gemma sighed. "He showed up at the Graces' last night, asking for Thalia. They told him to leave, but an hour later they found him *inside* the house. He'd opened the back door somehow and was on his way to her room."

Oh, Marcus. I felt sorry for him, but breaking into their house? Whatever made him think that was a good idea?

"Did they call the police?" I asked.

"No."

"Why not?"

"My point exactly," said Lily, slumping back into her seat.

"That would scare him off properly, wouldn't it?" I ventured.

"Considering what he's done before, I seriously doubt it," Lou sniffed.

"Why, what's he done before?"

Silence.

Gemma shrugged. "She's new, remember? It happened before she got here."

"I can't believe they haven't told you about that," Lou said.

"Oh come on," Gemma said reasonably. "It's not something they'd want to talk about with strangers, is it?"

*Except I'm not a stranger. I'm their best friend.*

I waited, looking between them. I wanted to know what Marcus wouldn't tell me too much to play the fake apathy game.

* * * * *

"It happened during Christmas break," said Gemma, and then stopped. "How do I put this? Marcus kind of attacked Thalia."

"*Attacked* her? How?"

"Their parents walked in on him, like, forcing her down on her bed," Lou said, her voice flat and hard with anger. "Apparently, he'd flipped and kept telling her they were meant to be together. When she said she wasn't interested, he basically leapt on her like a predator. Who knows what would have happened if he hadn't been interrupted?"

My stomach twisted in slimy, sickened knots. "Oh my god."

Their voices fluttered on. I couldn't believe it.

Thank god I hadn't tried to help him.

I sat at the table for the rest of lunch, but neither Summer nor Fenrin showed up. When I reached my next class, Summer was already there. She gave me a tight smile, but passed me no notes, and when I tried to talk to her afterward, she practically sprinted out the door.

She had no phone to text and ask what the matter was, no opening to her. I couldn't ask anyone else, and I couldn't do anything about what might be going on without me. I just had to drift along like the ghost I was before, no Summer to anchor me, feeling like the last three months had never happened, and how fragile my existence was without her even for one afternoon.

I got through the last class by distracting myself with day-dreams. It was warm outside and the teachers couldn't be bothered, either. Everyone was just waiting palpably for the end of term, that rush of cut grass and sun through the open classroom windows turning their heads.

The last bell rang. I walked through school to the front gate, moving past the stragglers and the after-school clubbers. My face said I was going out into the sunshine, nothing bothering me. I hung around outside, pretending to wait for a pick up. Friends of theirs slid past me, their faces that strange mix of half-glee and half-grim seriousness that always accompanied bad gossip, but I saw no sign of the Graces.

There was nothing else to do. It took about twenty minutes to walk to the Grace house from school, and by the time I reached their shaded lane I could feel a thick line of sweat running a groove down to my stomach. The windows stared down disapprovingly at me as I rapped the knocker three times and stepped back.

Nothing.

I couldn't go home without knowing. I brushed past tangled vines on the brick wall, making my way to the wooden gate that led down the side of the house and into the gardens beyond. The bell chimes hanging from the gate's top frame tinkled sweetly as I walked through, skirting the herb garden before arriving at the back door that opened into the echoing cool of the hallway.

It was unlocked.

"Hello?" I called, my voice strangled with nerves.

Nothing.

Someone had to be home—they'd never leave a door unlocked like that, particularly after what had happened with Marcus. But if no one was around . . . I longed to look through the glass jars in the cabinets of Esther's conservatory, the base oils and pastes she kept in the fridge, the dried herbs and droppers and mixers and the pretty lavender velvet cloths. I wanted to flip through the books on her shelves, the ones with the thick leather bindings, run my fingers over the words and symbols inside them as if I could absorb them by touch alone. I came to the bottom of the stairs, wondering what to do next, when Wolf appeared next to me.

I flinched. "Jesus, you scared me."

"Why are you here?" he said, his dark eyes probing. His accent glotted up his throat like chocolate, deep and rich.

"Thalia wasn't at school today, and there's all these rumors floating around, so I just wanted to know if everyone was all right."

I started to feel stupid. They were all fine.

But then Wolf said, "Keep your voice down. They're in the kitchen."

He moved toward it, glancing back over his shoulder to me as if I should follow. So I did.

The Grace family sat around the huge oak table. Thalia was noticeably absent. I wanted to ask where she was, but the air around them was heavy and damp with something just past—or just beginning—and I felt like an intruder.

Wolf slipped silently into the kitchen and leaned against the nearest wall, but I hung back in the doorway, uneasy. Esther and Gwydion had their backs to us—I didn't think they even knew we were there. Fenrin and Summer were opposite them. I saw Summer's eyes slide up and catch on mine briefly before falling away.

"Don't be ridiculous." Gwydion's normally melodious voice was honed sharp. "We don't need the police interfering in our business. We will handle it ourselves."

"He was in the house," Esther shot back. "He got into the *house*. What kind of protection does that afford us?"

Gwydion snorted. "He isn't some stranger, Esther. He spent half his childhood here. The house knows him."

Silence.

Esther folded her arms with a gentle clicking of bangles. "Then it must be Thalia. She must still be seeing him, talking to him, to aggravate it like this."

"She's not," Fenrin snapped. "She's done everything you asked her to do. That's the problem. God, it's got nothing to do with the curse—*you* created this mess. She's being crushed under the weight of all your expectations of her, and he's mentally unstable. What did you think was going to happen?"

His mother shot him a glance that could have cut stone. She had a delicate and fragile air, but underneath that, there was something I'm not sure I would have dared cross.

Gwydion leaned forward. "It'll be dealt with, Fenrin. And you'll say no more about it."

"Dealt with how? What are you going to do?" Fenrin's voice rose and rose, a car heading straight toward a cliff. "Nothing. Because that's how we deal with problems in our family. We ignore them and hope they go away. We freak out over curses and secretly screw a string of people instead of admitting we're miserable, waving our hands and chanting instead of doing anything *practical* about—"

"Stop," said Summer, her voice sharp. "Fen, stop—"

Gwydion stood. He pointed toward the door. "Get out."

No one moved.

"Get out, go to your room, and calm down. Your mother and I will deal with this. It doesn't concern you. None of this concerns you. Leave."

I tried to shrink into the wall. It was then that Gwydion turned his head and caught sight of me.

His eyes were no longer sad. They were furious.

"*All* of you, please," he said.

Esther started to turn in her seat. I backed out of the kitchen fast.

Wolf came out after me. Fenrin brushed past him as if he wanted to shove him out of the way and marched to the stairs without so much as a glance in my direction.

"She's here because she's supposed to be." I heard Summer's voice in the kitchen. "We have an assignment due together, so I asked her to come round after school. It's not her fault, is it?"

Shit.

Wolf stood by me. I was grateful for the solid weight of him there—he could have abandoned me. In that moment, we were outsiders together.

Summer came out of the kitchen.

"I'm sorry," I started to say, but she shook her head.

"Don't worry," she said. "Just give me a minute."

I watched her catch up to Fenrin on the second-floor landing.

"Fen," she said. "Wait."

He rounded on her and held out a finger, pointing it straight at her face. She shrank from it.

"You. You could have said something. But for all that you play at the rebel, Summer, you're just a fucking daddy's girl. You'll do everything they tell you. You'll suffocate and wither away here, just like everyone else."

His eyes were alive and his body shook. He raced up the stairs. We heard the slam of a bedroom door.

Summer stood for a moment, her back to us. She went into her bedroom without looking back.

I turned around, unsure of what to do with myself. Wolf's eyes were on me as he tilted his chin up to the back door.

"Come on," he said. "We'll go in the garden, out of the way."

I followed him out.

# SIXTEEN

WE WENT DOWN TO THE VERY BOTTOM OF THE GARDEN where the pond sat, shaded by an enormous apple tree that stood like a sentry at the start of the fruit grove.

Wolf sank to the grass and then, without any warning, stripped off his shirt. I looked at his back, his torso. He was bulkier than Fenrin, with curved taut muscles and that dark, unblemished skin. He had a tattoo—a long, supple lizard running down his stomach, the head disappearing into his waistband. There was something a little bit Gypsy about him, and it made me wonder what kind of witch he'd be, if he were one. He lay down in the sunshine and I sat beside him, running grass blades through my fingers.

"Do you think I got Summer into trouble?" I asked him in a low voice.

"Perhaps." He had his eyes shut and his ankles crossed. "She can handle it." One eye opened a crack. "She likes you. Don't worry."

I shifted, pleased and anxious. "I shouldn't have been there. It's not my business."

"You are their friend. You are concerned. Sometimes they forget that other people are in their lives. Sometimes deliberately, I think."

I gazed at him, trying to work out what he was thinking. "What was all that about, in there?"

"Thalia."

"And Marcus."

He was silent for a moment, maybe weighing up how much to tell me. "What do your school rumors say of it, then?"

"I heard . . ." I hesitated. "He's obsessed with her. Dangerously?"

He shrugged.

"You've known the Graces most of your life, right?"

"All," he said firmly. "All my life."

"So you must know Marcus."

"I do."

"Is he dangerous?"

"Are people in love dangerous? Yes, then."

"But would he . . ." I tailed off.

"I believe he's changed recently," he said. "That's what you mean to ask, right? He was always sweet, if a little anxious. Now he's . . . angry. Desperate."

"What do you think they'll do?"

"Nothing." Wolf propped himself up on an elbow. His stomach muscles twisted. I tried not to look. "They will act as if nothing happened."

"Why?"

"Because that's the Grace way. Image is everything."

"Can't they . . ." I hesitated. "Can't they do something? To make him go away?"

Wolf was silent.

"You know what I mean," I said. "Right?"

"No. Explain." But he did know. He was testing me. You didn't hang out with the Graces all your life without knowing that, of all things, about them.

I shrugged. "Can't they do some magic?"

"You believe in that, do you?"

"Yes," I said, without hesitation. Another test. "Don't you?"

He lay back down, closed his eyes.

After a moment, his voice came again.

"So which one are you in love with?"

"Excuse me?"

"Which one?" he repeated. "You must be in love with one of them. You hang around like a dog hoping for scraps."

"Wow," I said, trying to sound amused.

"I don't mean to offend you. It's the same for me. I have no reason to keep coming back to this house." He paused. "No reason except one."

We stared out across the garden together. I felt closer to him again.

"Which one are *you* in love with?" I asked.

Wolf's mouth curled into a vague smile.

"We love just one, but we love them all as well," he said. "The Graces. We want to be them, and love them, and for them to love us. It's a curse. Don't you see? The Grace curse."

He fell silent. The air was still. I didn't want to leave, but neither did I know what to do, so I copied Wolf, lying down on the grass and letting the sun push me gently into the ground, hazing up my senses.

"Wolf," I said, after a while.

He grunted.

"What if we broke the curse?"

A buzzing bee wound its way through the quiet.

"How?" he said.

I didn't reply.

"With magic?" he continued tonelessly, and I still couldn't tell what he thought about it at all.

"No, with scissors. Yes, with magic."

"Have you done magic before?"

"I . . ." I hesitated. "I've done some with Summer, recently. And I've been reading up on it."

He regarded me. "So you know how to break a curse?"

"Well . . . not exactly. Do you?"

He was silent.

I nodded toward the house. "But we could find out."

Wolf sighed and lay down again. "You are crazy."

"Let's at least try," I urged, my mind racing, alive, shouting *yes, yes.* This was what we were supposed to do, surely. This was the way I would prove myself to them.

"You think generations of Graces haven't tried before? There is no point in even trying to try."

"Oh come on," I scoffed. "You think the human race would advance if people just decided not to try where others had failed before? Just because it's not been done doesn't mean it can't be. What if . . ."

His eyes were on me.

"What if it needs outsiders?" I finished. "Maybe it's always been Graces who tried, but the curse can't be broken by a Grace alone. You know what they're like—they don't talk about that kind of thing outside the family. I bet they've never even thought of asking a non-Grace for help. What if that was all it took?"

He was wavering. I could see it in every line of his body.

I gave him one last push. "They'd be free to be with whoever they wanted. All of them. Wouldn't that be worth it?"

I think I actually saw the moment he made the decision. Maybe he was thinking about the one he secretly loved. I wondered which it was—Thalia or Summer. I couldn't decide. He was very good. He gave nothing away around either of them.

"What do you propose?" he said.

* * * * *

We made our way back into the house. Warm to cool, bleached to dim.

Wolf peered into the kitchen.

"Esther and Gwydion are not there," he reported, and I felt my shoulders go down. "I think they must be in their wing of the house."

I peered around. "Well, let's avoid that area. I don't want to make them any angrier."

"Thalia has books in her bedroom. We could start there."

I must have looked doubtful because he shook his head at my face.

"She's not here. She's staying at the house of a family friend tonight. Even so, it's no problem. I'm in there all the time."

Still, I hesitated. It was one thing to contemplate exploring alone, but now that Wolf would be there, it felt like another test of loyalty. He went to the bottom of the stairs, looking back at me expectantly, his body cocked forward like an eager puppy.

I couldn't help it—I laughed.

"Oh ho," he said. "Now she laughs at me. She with the plan. Are you scared?"

I thought of Fenrin. His trembling anger. Each Grace alone with their private pain, unable to break out of the secrets they had all locked themselves into. I knew something of that, and I wouldn't wish it on anyone.

"Nope," I said. "Let's go."

We made it to the second floor, treading as softly as we could. Summer's bedroom door was firmly closed, and I couldn't hear anything from the outside.

Wolf pushed on the door to Thalia's room, and it opened without a squeak. He went straight to her bookcase, running his fingers along the spines, but I stood in the doorway, uncertain.

"Haven't you been in her room before?" he said, glancing up.

I shrugged. I'd been in Summer's and Fenrin's, but Thalia had never invited me into hers.

"Come in and shut the door." He went back to the spines, his lips moving as he read off the titles to himself. I did as he asked, allowing my eyes the luxury of wandering over Thalia's things unchecked. It was a beautiful, poised girl's bedroom, filled with carefully chosen, well-placed objects. On the fireplace, stones sat in an earthenware bowl, and beside that a thick glass jar filled, on closer inspection, with salt. A delicate-looking knife with pearlescent strips set into the handle had been pushed all the way to the hilt inside, nestling among the grains.

I'd have given anything to have a study desk like hers. Or at all. The wood had been painted the palest of greens. The top was covered in clay pots filled with various plants, interspersed with fat candlesticks and wooden tea light holders. I could imagine sitting at it and feeling like I had access to the secrets of nature. Like I was a witch through pure atmospheric osmosis.

Was Thalia the most powerful Grace? She went to great lengths to be unknowable. She would forever dance out of your reach to maintain the glamour. I admired it, but I couldn't like it. Summer was different. She had her set of masks and fronts she used to survive, like all of us, but there was something truer about her. Something more beautiful, despite Thalia's obvious loveliness.

With a room like this, I wouldn't have minded the feeling that I was born into the wrong family. I felt like I'd come from a cuckoo egg, and my parents had never noticed that they were raising the wrong child.

Or maybe they had noticed, but they couldn't bring themselves to face it.

Wolf's voice cut into my thoughts. "This was your idea. Help me out."

I joined him at the bookcase and pulled out a book at random. The four I'd amassed in the box under my bed were embarrassingly meager in comparison to Thalia's collection.

"We could be here forever," I muttered. "Know anything about breaking curses?"

"No."

I read out loud the title of the book I'd chosen. *"Plants and Their Medicinal Uses Through the Ages.* Wow."

"She studies," he agreed, flipping through another. "Oh yes, I remember this one. *Druidic Circle Rituals*." He showed me a drawing.

"Would make a great tattoo," I commented.

"You should get one."

"Sure."

"Why not?" Wolf was smiling. He had a mischievous smile that was hard not to respond to.

"I don't have wonderfully bohemian parents like you," I said drily. " My mother would lose her mind."

She might not even notice, to be fair, but he didn't need to know that. I often liked to present my mother as grossly over-sensitive and controlling to make up for the fact that she was never around.

"My mother also," said Wolf.

"But you already have a tattoo."

"That one is different."

"How come?"

He paused, as if trying to find the right words. "That one was chosen by them for me."

I stared at him, uncomprehending.

"It's a tradition in my family," he said, under the weight of my gaze.

"Really? You're all tattooed?"

He shrugged a yes.

"But . . . what for?"

"Tradition," he repeated, stubbornly.

"What does your lizard mean?"

"Salamander," he corrected. "It represents fire." He snapped shut the book he was holding and turned away, searching for another one, and it seemed I would get nothing more.

It didn't matter, though—I thought I had my answer. It sounded like Wolf was a fire witch. I tried to remember what they were supposed to be like. Strong, wasn't it? I'd have to go back and reread Marcus's website the first chance I got.

"What are you doing?" said Summer, from the doorway.

I flinched, froze, everything that made me look guilty. But Wolf didn't even pause.

"Looking through your sister's books for something," he said, as if it were the most normal thing in the world.

"For what?"

"To help River with her plan."

I shot him a look.

Summer came farther in and glanced at me. "What plan?"

* * * * *

Summer led us up to the third floor, where Fenrin's and Wolf's bedrooms were. The cock-and-balls floor, she called it. When she pushed open Fenrin's door, I hung back—surely he didn't want to see us—but Wolf took the lead and I wasn't going to be left behind.

Fenrin was sitting on his bed, his feet up, reading.

"Fen," Summer said. I wondered if everyone could hear the tiny strain in her voice when she was acting brave in a way she didn't feel, or if it was just me.

"I'm sorry, Fenrin isn't here right now," he drawled without looking up. "But you can leave a message with his rather gorgeous secretary, and he'll get back to you when he feels like it."

Summer picked up a towel folded neatly over his study chair and flung it at him.

"Tell him he's a horrible prick," she said, above his muffled laugh.

He pulled the towel off. "He knows," he replied regretfully, and just like that, it was fine between them again.

She slid onto the end of his bed. "River's got something to say."

*She does?* My heart triple bounced.

Fenrin looked up at me, and then his eyes strayed to Wolf, lurking against the wall.

"Is it something about what a hideous family we are and that she's moving to the moon to get as far away from us as possible?"

*Oh Fenrin, you have no idea the lengths you'd have to go to get me to hate you. I'm not going anywhere.*

I glanced at Wolf for support, but he just shrugged, as if to hand me the spotlight.

"I think we could find a way to break the curse," I said.

I swore the air in the room grew colder.

He folded his arms. "What are you talking about?"

"I know you said you don't believe in it—"

"I don't," he replied flatly.

"But just suppose it's real."

"Let's not."

"We could find a way to stop it. Research it. Somehow. We could . . ." I cast around helplessly. When I'd thought about it, it was perfect. It would bring us together as a proper coven, working on solving a problem and protecting one another. It seemed so lame now that I was saying it out loud. "Look through books, and things. You guys must have family history and stuff. Maybe there are patterns or clues—"

The look on his face stopped me.

"Well, god," I said. "I'm just trying to help. I want to help."

"Fen," said Summer. "She came up with a good idea. She's not a Grace, so she's not under the curse, and neither is Wolf. I think involving them might do something different—"

Fenrin made a snorting sound. "It's a bullshit family myth created to keep us from straying, Summer."

"I don't believe that."

"I don't care."

Summer raised her hands in a helpless gesture. "Well, what do you want to do? Sit around and wait for things to get worse, like everyone else?"

"Maybe if you just talked to Marcus—" I offered.

"Jesus," Fenrin snapped. "Don't you think we tried that? This was a problem long before you came on the scene."

"Hey," said Summer sharply. "Don't be an asshole."

Fenrin sighed and tipped his head back. "I'm sorry. I will start again. I tried. He won't hear it. It's my fault. I bitched about my family once too often to him. Now he thinks we're all toxic and evil and that we hate his guts. He's really lost it. Nothing we say makes any difference."

"So we have only River's option left," said Wolf, softly. "If you don't believe in the curse, what harm could trying to break it do? And if it works, and the curse is broken, you could be free to be with whoever you wanted."

I watched Fenrin's gaze fall on Wolf, his expression dark, and then travel to the rest of us.

"Thalia won't let us do it," he said, finally.

Summer spread her hands. "So we don't involve her. There are four of us, right here. One for each element, four to complete the circle. It's perfect."

"You want to do this behind her back."

"Fen, she will freak out if we tell her, and she'll probably even tell Esther. She's all high on guilt and fear, like this is her fault. You know she thinks messing with the curse might make it worse, even though there's no evidence of that. She can't think straight about this."

He sighed shortly. "Fine. I must be desperate. Let's try it."

A tense quiet settled over the room.

Summer raised an eyebrow. "Shall we set a date?"

# SEVENTEEN

IT WAS DECIDED.

We would try to break the curse on midsummer's eve, in just over a week's time.

Midsummer was all about driving away bad energy—it would be perfect. But most of all, Thalia wouldn't be around. Midsummer was next Friday—she was staying at a family friend's house until that Sunday night. We'd have to go to the woods straight after school, all four of us, and Fenrin had a few days to come up with an excuse as to why Thalia wouldn't see any of us that evening.

They were a family of secret keepers, but Summer once told me that the three siblings had always sworn to never keep secrets from one another, at least. Fenrin brooded, and everyone around him at school caught his mood and talked over his head, making uneasy jokes, waiting for the moment he would shake it off with a laugh and be himself again.

Wolf was back in the city the rest of the week, as always, but he would meet us outside school on Friday. In the meantime, we had to get on with our lives as if this plan, *my* plan, didn't weigh around our necks, shade our eyes like scuffed sunglasses, making everything else hard to focus on.

We hung out together over the next few days, mostly with other people. When it was just us we didn't talk about the plan, as if we'd jinx it by saying it out loud. Even in a crowd of others it felt like we were bound together by invisible threads. I couldn't get the woods out of my mind, and I didn't think the others could, either. I didn't even care when Niral spent one lunchtime talking to Summer with her back deli¹ rately to me, shielding me from view, so I spent a good half an hour sitting in silence. It didn't matter anymore. Niral was on the outside now.

I was officially in.

* * * * *

I spent one furtive lunchtime of that week in the computer lab, combing Marcus's website for anything relevant, anything I might have missed.

I looked again at the witch types:

*Fire* — Protectors. Confident. Powerful.

*Water* — Charmers. Restless. Persuasive.

*Air* — Seers. Truth tellers. Sensitive.

*Earth* — Leaders. Grounded. Calm.

Wolf had hinted that he was fire. From what I knew of him, it seemed to fit. Summer—I was now sure she was air. Fenrin was water, the charmer, through and through. That meant, for this to work, I had to become earth.

I was no leader. I was not grounded. I knew no herb lore, and I couldn't make anything practical to save my life. But I could learn, if that was what it took. I had determination. That had to count for a lot.

I came across the story of the Four Bells again, tucked away in the resources section of Marcus's site. In my previous searching, I'd found the tale described as an anonymous local myth, but here it said that the story was attributed directly to the Grace family, way back in the dark ages of the local history. One commenter remarked that it was as if the land around here had spit them up when it was still forming.

The widely accepted version of the story was this:

One day a handsome stranger came to town, and the local girls fell in love with him, but only one caught his particular attention. The man was really the devil in disguise, and people could give him devil stones in return for wishes that he willingly granted. But his wishes always ended badly, with the moral of the "nice, official version of the story" (as the site said with what seemed like a sneer) being a literal take on *be careful what you wish for*. The virtuous girl the devil fell in love with was the only one who resisted him. He tried to tempt her, but she wanted for nothing, and having come up against a pure soul he could not break, he flew into a rage. While he was incapacitated by his anger, she and her three sisters, who had positioned themselves in the bell towers of the four town churches, began ringing the bells at the same time. The pure sound was too much for the devil, who fled the town howling.

The site went on to say that local folklore offered an older, less hideously insipid version of the story. In the older version, a wish demon disguised as a beautiful and mysterious boy ran riot over the town, granting everyone's most horrible desires. Half the population were dead by the time he took the girl he wanted for himself—and that would have been that, except that she was part of a coven of witches who were understandably upset at the loss of their sister, so they banded together and defeated him with their combined strengths. The coven was made up of four witches, each with a different power—the air witch, the girl he fell in love with, could see what the demon really was; the water witch persuaded him not to hurt them; the earth witch made a potion that boosted their powers; and the fire witch fought him and won.

It was a great story.

It was a neat story. The reality was probably messier—surely magic was tricky, more elusive than that. It could punish you for daring to use it. Maybe one of them had died as a consequence of what they'd tried to do. Maybe they hadn't won, not really.

Magic didn't seem to make things easier.

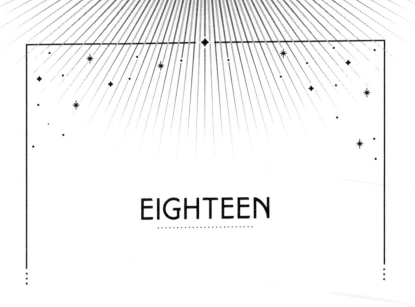

# EIGHTEEN

FRIDAY ARRIVED, AND WITH IT MY GUTS WERE CHURNED to sour butter, my insides greasy and strange.

A note in my locker that morning on parchment paper in Summer's sprawling scribble outlined the plan. We would meet at the Malan tor, a huge standing stone that rode the top of a hill outside of town inland from the sea. It was unmistakable, clenched like a fist on the horizon, the note said, and it detailed which bus to take and where to get off. We were to leave separately after school and meet there to avoid suspicion.

Fenrin had told Thalia he would be with a girl for the evening, which was apparently enough to make her eyes roll and question him no further. Thalia once said that she never took the trouble to learn whichever one he was dallying with at any given time as they changed so often. I remembered this because she used the word "dallying," whose pretty prissiness had stuck in my head. Esther and Gwydion were joining Thalia at their friend's house for the evening, and Summer had weaseled out of going as well by complaining loudly that she had end-of-year coursework to hand in on Monday that she had barely started, something she did so often with homework that she was notorious for it. They weren't even aware that Wolf was in town and not in the city, but he came down so often no one would bat an eyelid to find him in the house on Saturday morning.

They used truths to tell lies, and they were very good at it.

On my way out of school, I passed Summer in the hallway laughing with a couple of friends. For one awful, treacherous moment I imagined that the whole thing was a setup, that I'd get to the tor and no one would be there. But when I glanced up at her, she dropped me a wink. My fears fell away. I walked on.

The bus was filled with people from school, laughing and nudging and swapping phones, chatty and rowdy. I felt a couple of curious gazes light on me. I even thought I heard a whisper or two. I was best friends with the Graces, the gazes and the whispers said. What was special about me?

I wouldn't have been able to explain it to them even if they'd had the courage to ask.

By the time I got to the bus stop nearest to the Malan tor, the bus was almost empty. I stood, looking up at the hill we were to meet on, marveling how it jutted into the sky like it wanted to break it. It was hot and bright out, and my battered black-and-purple backpack already weighed heavy on my back, sweat running a trickling stream down the dip of my spine. I had butterflies, an army of ants, a bucket of feathers tickling my insides.

I crested the hill. It was bare. They weren't here yet.

The Malan felt dark and enormous this close up. I shrugged off my backpack and let it slump to the ground as I stood and stared upward, wondering what this rock had seen. Maybe they used to sacrifice animals against it. Maybe even people, when things were going badly enough. Crops failing. Enemies attacking. If I let myself drift, I could see it all. Arms held back, muscles straining. Mouths open in silent screams. Blood running down the stone, a little of it soaking in every time. This rock might have ancient blood on its hands.

I stretched out a hand, and my fingers traced the stone's dark veins that twisted through its surface. Then I dropped my hand hastily when I heard movement from behind. Their voices scouted ahead of them before they came into view, tramping across the dry ground, brown grass blades flickering under their heels. Summer, Wolf, and Fenrin.

Four of us, for the four elements. Earth, air, fire, and water.

"Let's go. Come on," said Fenrin, as soon as he saw me. "I don't know why you wanted us to meet here."

"It's on the way," said Summer mildly. "Besides, River doesn't know where our spot is. She had to meet us somewhere obvious."

He walked past us. His bad mood hung off him in ribbons.

"Ignore him," said Summer to me.

"What happened?"

She shrugged. "This stuff always puts him on edge."

We walked on, down the other side of the hill and toward the woods that hugged this part of the land. It took only a few minutes to be enveloped by the cool calm of the trees.

"I love woods," said Summer. "When you're in them, you feel like the world has disappeared on you. Like you could step into a different reality if you could just find the right path."

"It's not Narnia," I joked, but she turned serious eyes on me.

"You don't have any places that do that to you?"

*Your house*, I thought.

"I guess," I said vaguely, and let it drop.

Fenrin was walking behind us alongside Wolf. At one point they'd been talking to each other in voices too low for me to hear. It made me happy to see that they could get on. Something had obviously happened between them in the past to make them act so cagey around each other. I wondered if either of them would ever tell me, or if one day soon I would dare to ask. Wolf might tell me. We might sit in the garden together again, just the two of us, and talk secrets in the sunlight.

"So where are we going?" I said.

"We're going precisely here." Summer had stopped in a clearing. "This is our place. We've been coming here forever. It has a feel to it." She lifted her arms over her head, as if about to dance. Then she stretched, her eyes half-closed and a sliver of her flat belly showing.

"How do you even know this is it?" I said, dropping my backpack to the ground. "It looks like any old clearing."

"Look up."

I did.

It took a moment, but then I saw them. Dangling from the branches were thin twine ropes with different objects swaying gently on their ends. There were shells: purple-blue mussel shells, curled winkles and whelks, pink tellins, corrugated cockles, razor clams, otters and sand gapers. There were feathers, long and glossy black, or stubby white fluff, or thick white and gray and shaped like knives. Glossy chestnuts. Pinecones. A big piece of bark shaped like a hand.

"We tie a few more every time we come," said Summer.

"Where do you get the shells from?"

"The cove. Always the cove. We bring them with us. It makes it feel like it's our place."

I peered upward. Some of those ropes were tied really high. "How the hell did you get them all up there?"

"Summer is a freakish climber." Fenrin was crouched, sorting through the bags they'd brought.

Summer took a bow. Then she tilted her head back, opened her mouth, and howled like a dog. To my astonishment, Wolf did the same. And then Fenrin joined in.

I stood, listening to them howl, voices wavering up and down, shrinking into myself. It went on just a little too long. I didn't know where to look. Should I watch them? Ignore them? Join in?

Before I could do anything, it was over.

"Sorry," said Summer. "It's just something we do. It's very freeing. Want to try?"

"Maybe later," I said with a laugh. Was it a good laugh, an easy laugh? I felt too embarrassed to tell.

We hadn't bothered to bring tents. Summer had said we needed to be close to the stars, not shielded from them. It wasn't supposed to rain, but I didn't think I'd mind if it did. Rain might feel significant, like a dark adventure. Rain made me think of Summer, laughing through the wet strings of her hair. Asking me to come to her house.

We built up a pile of wood to make a fire. I had no idea what I was doing, so I took directions and watched, fascinated, as the pile grew as tall as our waists. Snatching glances at Fenrin, I saw him relax and laugh, wrestling with Summer. Wolf had abandoned his usual careful reserve for a teasing, playful kind of mood that made me want to hug him. Despite the trees, it got hot as we worked, and both boys took their shirts off to our claps and whoops.

We broke for food, chattering. Summer bumped shoulders with me. I looked around the clearing, suddenly alive with our noise and our life. This was what people meant when they talked about their friends with shining eyes. This was what they meant when they talked about things I'd always thought were impossible clichés from movies, those hazy summer scenes where beautiful people laughed and shoved each other and spent hours together just being who they were. The appeal of it filled me up to the brim. This was my life. This was a perfect life, and I was finally getting to live it.

We waited until the light started to turn. As the woods darkened, Fenrin lit the fire. He fiddled, his arms in the teepee of branches up to the elbow. Then he crouched back and stood up beside me as flames rolled up the wood.

I watched it catch and grow, and I felt its rushing warmth. It spat, and Fenrin put his hand on my arm. "Careful," he said. "It's probably moss, but we should stand back."

He pressed with his fingers, moving me. When he let go, I scrabbled for something to make the moment stretch out.

"Are you all right?" I said. "You seem kind of tense about this whole thing."

He shrugged. "Thalia is the one who takes all this more seriously. She can be a bit Queen of Nature about it. It winds me up, that's all."

My heart sank. I watched him. "You don't believe in it at all, do you."

He sighed. "All it's ever brought my family is misery. Why would I want to believe in something like that?"

"You've never . . ." I hesitated. "You've never seen it do good?"

"I've never seen it *do* anything. I mean, I've never seen evidence. Like, x equals y—do *this* spell and you get *this* effect. So I stopped doing them."

"Maybe it doesn't work like that. Maybe it's not as easy as that."

"Oh yes," he replied with a grim smile, "now you sound just like a Grace."

It wasn't a compliment.

"Thanks?" I said with a frown.

"Look, I'm just pissed off at Thalia. I keep telling her to stop believing in the curse. It's only when you believe in a thing that you give it power over you. But she won't see it. Sometimes I think she *wants* to be miserable." His voice dropped. "Like she thinks she deserves it. And sometimes I want to punish her for being so stupid. Let it get so bad it teaches her a lesson. Let there be consequences."

"Wow."

He paused. "I didn't mean any of that. Ignore me."

I folded my arms, trying not to sound irritated. "If you don't think it will do anything, why are you even here?"

He tried to grin, tried to shake it off. "Ah, it makes Summer feel like she's helping. She goes crazy when she can't fix things. And it's better than doing nothing, isn't it?"

He walked over to the others, leaving me with an ever growing sense of doubt.

Was he going to wreck this because he didn't believe?

We sat around the fire, quieting our hearts in the dusk.

I watched Summer take out a taped-up bundle and unwrap it to reveal a square glass jar with a stopper shaped like a lightbulb. Dark, thick red liquid sloshed inside it.

She unstoppered the jar, lifted the base with one hand, and upended some into her mouth.

"What's that?" I asked.

"Liquid courage," said Fenrin, taking the jar from her and doing the same. I was the last to receive it. I took the jar from Summer. It was a heavy crystal, the base weighting my palm down. I sniffed the liquid.

"It's homemade wine," said Summer. "Herbs from the garden, fruit from the grove."

I lifted the jar up and took a swig.

It tasted like the dark; sweet and thick.

"More," said Summer.

I took another swig.

"More."

I took one more swig. My throat started to burn. She took the jar off me and drank. We passed it round until it was empty. The wine spread through me, warming and fuzzing as it went.

We talked, laughed. I felt my head swim slow, lazy strokes as the light fled us.

We began.

Fenrin had a glass jar of water in front of him. He sat with the shell necklace he always wore clutched in one fist, the leather thong trailing out beyond his fingers.

Summer had her amber bird. I didn't understand what she'd do for the air element until I saw her chest rise and fall and realized—it was all around her.

Wolf's hand was pressed against his stomach. The salamander tattoo. His object. And fire was right in front of him—all he had to do was let himself feel it.

I had a small cup I dug into the ground in front of me, filling it with dry earth and crumbling leaves. I was sitting on my coat, and from the pocket I wrested out the black doughnut stone from the bowl in my temporary Grace bedroom. It was my witch object. My connection to them and their power. I curled my hand tight around it.

The fire cracked. We sat with darkness at our backs.

Summer said, "What is our intent?"

"To break the curse," I offered. My voice came out clear and precise. It was the opposite of how I felt.

*Focus*, I told myself. *They need you. They need your will.*

"To break Marcus"—Fenrin began and caught Summer's eye—"'s obsession."

"To break the curse, Fen," Summer told him, and she was calm, very calm. I'd come to think of it as her witch voice. That calm, that surety that what we were about to do was right and correct and would absolutely work, and there was no other way.

"To break the curse," he said, and for a moment I could almost think he believed his own words.

"To break the curse," echoed Wolf, staring into the fire.

"Marcus and Thalia will part as friends," said Summer. "He won't visit anymore. He won't talk to her anymore. She'll be nothing to him. And there'll be no more curse."

I pictured Marcus and Thalia passing each other in a shadowy corridor. Vague smiles on their faces. A polite "hi" on their lips. Friends, that was all. Marcus could get his life back. Thalia could stop being afraid. Fenrin could stop being angry. Summer could stop fighting with him.

And maybe. Just maybe. I could be a Grace.

This was the real test. All I had to do was will it to be so.

I saw Marcus leaning over Thalia in her bedroom, pleading with her. Trying to grab her hand. Pushing her down. Forcing his mouth on hers.

Fenrin's voice was in my head: *Sometimes I want to punish her for being so stupid. Let it get so bad it teaches her a lesson.*

I forced it hastily away.

We worked together, Summer had said earlier. We combined our collective power—the power of four instead of one, the power of a circle. I watched Fenrin take up the jar of water in front of him and pour it, a steady stream, into the edge of the fire. It crackled and spat and hissed. I took my cup of earth and did the same, careful to throw my handful onto the branch nearest me. Summer opened up her palm and blew on it into the fire. Wolf lit a match, and I watched as the flame danced near his pinched fingers. He threw it into the heart of the blaze.

And we closed our eyes.

This wasn't like the thicket with Summer that day. That had felt like kids' tricks in comparison to this. As I sat there, I heard the fire and the soft breeze above us winding through the tops of the trees. The longer I closed my eyes, the farther away the world seemed. Even the stone in my hands felt like someone else was clutching it. Someone else's thumb rubbed over its smooth surface, though I knew it was mine.

No one talked. No one coughed. I started to believe, implicitly, that I was all alone, and that everyone had left me. I just knew if I opened my eyes, they'd all be gone. But I didn't. I would not wreck this. I would not give in.

I could no longer feel my body. If I wiggled a toe or shifted, this, whatever it was, would break and I'd come crashing back to earth. I was a star, looking down on this world from up high. It all seemed so unimportant. So very unreal. I was lost somewhere inside, and I felt nothing. It was a joy.

It might have been hours later, or maybe only minutes, when I felt warmth on my ear, and a whisper. "River, wake up."

I blinked.

Summer was crouched in front of me, her head cocked. Her eyes were wide and wet in the dark, bare arms slick. The fire was low, wisping, and the night air sharp against my skin.

"It's done?" I said, somehow surprised my lips still worked properly.

"It's done." She handed me a plastic goblet filled with wine. "Now we party. Keep the energy raised, as long as we can. For hours, if we can do it. Can you do it?"

In response, I brought the goblet to my lips and downed half the wine, feeling it spill out and dribble down my chin. I didn't care. I swallowed.

Summer smiled.

# NINETEEN

SCHOOL WAS OVER. IT WAS THE SUMMER HOLIDAYS, AND endless rippling time stretched out before me.

I usually dreaded it. You could only be enough company for yourself for so long, and I got sick of watching bad daytime TV and fusing into the sofa through boredom. Now I was worried it would go too fast. In my mind the immediate future was filled with sparkling light, like the sun on a river, a compact mirror shining into my face, painting everything peach gold.

It had been over three weeks since the night in the woods. During that time, Marcus hadn't even shown his face in the cafeteria, and I'd barely seen him around school. Thalia had come back home without incident. Fenrin had an easy grin permanently on his face, Wolf had become ensconced at the Grace house, and Summer and I had spent every minute we could together. More often than not we'd been outside, sometimes collecting leaves or stones she liked, talking and planning for the holidays. We had spent one lunch hour at school making daisy chains. She had worn hers like a crown the rest of the afternoon, the salt white petals contrasting gorgeously with her raven hair—and none of the teachers had blinked. We were all too close to freedom.

Fenrin and Thalia had survived their exams unscathed. I often wondered what they would do after school ended for them next year, because they never talked about it, not even among themselves, or at least not when I was there. Summer often spoke to me about vague grand plans—study music, play in a band, be a rock star—but with an air of fantasy, like it was a silly child's dream that she knew she should let go of but couldn't quite. It wasn't in their nature to volunteer their secrets when pushed, and so far my tactic of listening and just being there when they felt a sudden and fleeting urge to open up had served me well. I would not ruin that now by pushing them to examine futures they seemed unwilling to think about.

Anyway, it was the holidays, and all of that was far off, a distant hazy horizon. We were here, and we were now, and if there was one thing the Graces enjoyed, it was being full and present and alive in each moment—a philosophy I found, in the quiet privacy of my own head, incredibly sexy.

* * * * *

August 1, the twins' birthday, dawned heavy with clouds, and the promise of on-again, off-again rain. Undaunted, they'd simply moved their plans indoors and prepped the house for their impending guests. One or two were apparently already in town. My mother had remarked on it with a fascinated kind of sniff, saying she'd seen a lanky man with fluffy white blond hair like a dandelion "head to toe in Gucci or something" standing in a supermarket line, as out of place as a butterfly among toads.

Once he'd bought his groceries, he had left with a rounded older woman who looked, according to my mother, like she was in costume as a Victorian pirate. She'd thought they were part of some kind of parade until a friend at work had told her they were "Grace people" and that they flooded the town every year around this date.

She'd spent a good twenty minutes on the topic while I squirmed silently, concentrating on the TV as she talked. I hadn't exactly gotten around to telling her who I was spending all my time with. All she knew was that I had some friends, which was good enough for her. We'd been here less than a year, but she'd integrated just fine. She was always off at her work friends' houses, which made life easier—we didn't mix easily when we were together. She liked feeling normal. I didn't. She didn't want to talk about my father. I did.

Though recently I'd found myself not even thinking about him, or his disappearance, for whole days at a time. It was hard to concentrate on the past with so much present to look forward to, filled with sunlight and Graces and magic. It was better that I'd begun to let him go. Didn't that mean I was finally moving on?

\* \* \* \* \*

Learning my lesson from the last birthday party, I arrived at the Grace house over an hour after Summer had told me to be there, though it was still a couple of hours before the party was due to start. When I stepped into the hallway from the back door, Summer barked at me from the second-floor landing.

"You're late. Why are you late?"

Resigning myself to the fact that I would never get it right, I took my shoes off at the bottom of the stairs and ran up to her room, feeling my steps get lighter and lighter as I went toward her.

"How's it going?" I greeted her at her bedroom door, but she whirled away from me.

"No time for that. Brush your hair out."

I watched her curiously, letting my bag slip to rest on the floor by her bed.

"What are you jabbering about?"

She fixed me with a dark, mischievous gaze. "I have plans for you."

\* \* \* \* \*

"Summer, I don't know about this."

I stared at the sludgy brown mess in the bowl.

Her hands were covered in stained gloves so she settled for wiping her forehead on her arm.

"Too late," she said. "I've worked my ass off making the mix. Anyway, what makes you think you have a choice?"

"The party's in two hours. What if it's a total disaster?"

"You'll wear a hat. Come on. Since when have you been afraid?"

*Since my whole life,* I thought.

Summer already had her fingers in my hair, sectioning it off with clips. I clutched the towel tighter around my shoulders. She'd greased up my hairline and neck with coconut oil—stuff that looked like lard to me—and made me face the long mirror hanging on her wall while she worked.

She scooped the gritty mud onto my head, and I felt it ooze over my scalp.

"This really doesn't look right," I tried.

"Henna always looks like cowpats but it'll come out amazing. Especially on your hair. Esther makes the stuff. She imports the henna, and it's pretty much the purest quality you can get. And she makes it up with these different oils and butters. You'll look like a goddess. Just trust me."

She gently massaged my head.

"So who's coming tonight?" I said, trying to ignore the way the sensuous feeling of her fingers on me ruffled up my spine.

"Aunts and uncles and cousins. Wolf's parents. Friends of the family."

The entire house would be filled with Graces. Summer laughed behind me.

"Don't worry," she said. "We get to disappear back upstairs a bit later. We usually hang out in Fen's room. Maybe he'll even dance to *Footloose* again this year."

"He dances to *Footloose*?"

"Only on special occasions."

"Is he any good?"

"He's amazing. A regular Kevin Bacon. Don't ask him about it, though, or he won't do it. He thinks he's too cool. Oh, but I should introduce you to a couple of people first. One of my great-aunts does tarot cards. She always brings a deck with her and does readings for people who ask. She's brilliant at it. We should get yours done."

She could see my face in the mirror, and I shrugged, smiling. "Yeah, sure."

She finished off, and then tightly covered my whole head in plastic wrap.

"Seriously?" I drawled.

"Ha, you look stupid." She peeled the gloves off and dropped them into the bowl. "Now we wait. Don't get it on my carpet or Esther will raise an eyebrow at me."

"Sounds bad."

"Trust me, it's enough."

I swiveled carefully on the chair and watched her clean up.

"Summer," I said.

"Yeah."

I opened my mouth. I didn't know what I wanted to tell her. Something profound. Something intimate.

"How come you started hanging out with me?" I laughed, awkwardly. "I mean, you had friends already. And I'm just some girl."

I waited.

Summer shrugged. "You just seem different from everyone else. More honest. Most people don't have the guts to be, but you do. That's important. Why do you hang out with me?"

She said the last suddenly, as if the words that had just come out of her mouth hadn't set my world on fire. As if she couldn't see me burning up with guilt.

Why did I hang out with her?

Not for the same reasons as everyone else did. Not because she was popular. More because I had the very real, heart-pounding hope that the Graces could tell me who I was.

And lately, for the plain, simple reason that I liked her. I liked them all. I couldn't seem to help it.

"Because you're amazing," I said, deciding to try for the honesty she thought she saw in me. "Thanks."

She looked up at me. "For what?"

*Letting me in.*

I shrugged. "Being you."

I thought she'd laugh at me and mouth some perfect quip, but instead she looked wrong-footed, like I'd caught her stealing. "Yeah, sure."

She left the room to dump the bowl and gloves.

When she came back, she put on an album I actually liked, which I laughed at her for until she protested that she'd taken it from Fenrin's room. The henna was surprisingly heavy on my head—I had to move carefully, like my neck was cased in cement, and it kept cracking her up, and I kept telling her to be quiet, until the buzzer on her alarm clock sounded.

Summer sat up, her eyes shining, and marched me to the bathroom. We rinsed and rinsed and rinsed, until my neck ached and my thighs pinged from kneeling over the bath for so long. When we got back to her room, she made me keep my eyes closed while she blow-dried my hair.

I sat, my ears filled with noise, hair fluffing around my face.

"Don't you dare open your eyes until I tell you," she said for the fifth time.

"Seriously, I'm not going to!"

"Just sit really still."

"What are you doing?" I said, out into the quiet around me.

Something cold and thin touched my forehead, and I flinched.

"Er, do not move."

"Summer . . ."

"I'm just going to trim your bangs a tiny, tiny bit. Don't freak out. I'm nearly finished."

I waited. Friendship meant trust, didn't it?

"Okay, I'm done. Open your eyes."

I stared at the girl in the mirror.

The girl in the mirror stared back, transformed.

* * * * *

Esther was flitting around the kitchen when we finally went downstairs. She glanced up at us.

"Ten minutes," she said distractedly. "Then the first people will be here."

"Anything we can do to help?" Summer asked.

"Choose some music for the living room." She eyed Summer. "From my music collection, not yours." Her gaze fell on me. "I thought I told you to only bring River tonight, dear."

Summer rolled her eyes. I stood confused.

Esther gasped theatrically. "Oh, my word! It *is* River! What have you done to your hair?"

"Summer did it," I blurted. I touched my new bangs self-consciously.

"Oh, it looks *gorgeous*." She came up to me and reached a hand out. "Oh yes, and the green eye shadow really frames your eyes. You look like a totally different person. Just lovely."

I squirmed, delighted and cringing. "Thanks."

"And the hair! Fiery auburn, like autumn personified."

"Summer and Autumn? Just no," I said. "Summer and River is hippy enough."

Summer scoffed, but Esther frowned. "I don't understand."

"It's a joke," said Summer. "Never mind. Come on, we'll sort the music out."

We wandered out into the hallway.

"Is that what you're wearing tonight?" Esther called after us.

Summer had gone for a look that was best described as "goth sorceress"—a black dress with delicate lacing that spidered across her collarbone, a long, full skirt, and pointed lace-up boots. She looked dark and sexy as hell. I wished I could do that.

"Erm, yes," Summer called back.

Silence.

"Quick, before she says anything else." She pulled me into the living room and pushed the door shut.

* * * * *

Thalia and Fenrin made their joint entrance about twenty minutes into the party.

I learned later that this was a traditional English ritual called Lammas—the Graces observed it every year. The music cut off. A bell tinkled sweetly in the hallway, and the guests gathered at the foot of the stairs, their heads tilted expectantly up to the second-floor landing.

After a moment, Fenrin appeared to whistles and claps. He was so lovely to look at, it made my throat close up. He wore a white muslin shirt, with his shell dangling through the shirt's open V. His hair was loose and tousled, and his grin was extra lazy. He looked fresh as the wind and cool as the sea.

He waited on the second-floor landing, and then Thalia appeared, to more noise. Fenrin offered her his arm and she took it with a coy smile. She looked incredible in a white drippy gown covered in crystal bead patterns that caught the light, and her hair was done in a loose knot at the base of her skull, as if she'd just carelessly swept it back—a chignon, she called it. I could just see her horse-hair braid twined into the style, its coarse ridges nestled against the soft lines of her hair. A pure white feather dangled from the tie down her bare back.

Two members of the audience, a different two each year, approached the foot of the stairs, each with a half loaf of bread. They proffered up the bread halves to Thalia and Fenrin with bowed heads and raised hands. Solemnly, the Graces took them. Fenrin winked at Thalia as he took a bite out of his, and she raised a brow back as she did the same with hers. Then they gave back the rest to the two bread bearers, who melted into the front of the crowd.

Together Fenrin and Thalia walked slowly down the stairs, and the waiting audience of Graces clapped in time with one another, a deliberate, strong beat that pumped your blood for you. I wanted to join in, but I couldn't quite shake the embarrassment. Summer led us back into the living room before the clapping died down.

"They'll split the bread again," she said to me when we were alone. "And then the four pieces will be put at the four corners of the house, for three days. It's a good luck thing."

"Thanks for letting me watch it." I had the impression that it was something outsiders weren't supposed to see.

She smiled reassuringly. "It's okay. I vouched for you."

"Is that why Fen and Thalia don't get to invite anyone from school to their birthday? They don't like people seeing that kind of thing, do they?"

"Well, there's that, and then there's this thing, this accident that happened at a party when they were, like, eight."

Matthew Feldspar.

"I may have heard about that," I admitted.

Summer sighed. "Yeah, I figured. They only let me have other people at my birthday because I promised we'd always stick to the cove, but ever since the thing at that party, we don't have friends come to the house anymore. It just added fuel to my mother's paranoid fire that letting anyone who isn't part of the family near us always results in total tragedy."

"I'm near you," I said, trying to joke.

"I've had to fight for that."

This, more than anything else that had gone before, affected me so much I suddenly felt in real danger of crying. I blinked and turned my head from her.

"Don't be upset," she said, anxiously. "They're fine with you being here. I mean, they can obviously see how awesome you are. God, Summer, shut up. I shouldn't have said anything."

"Honestly, it's fine," I said carefully. "It's just . . . that's the nicest thing anyone's ever done for me."

Silence.

"Here, have an exotic canapé," Summer said, trying to break the tension. A plate appeared under my nose, and I took one gratefully. At that moment, the door to the living room opened, and in poured the guests.

I must have looked panicked. Summer murmured in my ear. "You okay?"

I nodded. "Yeah. Just not used to so many people, I guess."

So many people I needed to impress.

"It doesn't matter," said Summer, as if she could read my thoughts. "Most of them aren't even worth talking to. None of this means anything, you know."

But how could I tell her that it did? The fact that so many people wanted to be in the same house at the same time. The ritual of it. The easy pattern of intimacy. The effort in making it happen, energy so unthinkingly spent. It was so normal that it had become boring for her.

"Don't worry," Summer was saying. "You'll have fun. I promise."

She was right. The next couple of hours were a blur of color and riot. Summer kept me close by her and kept introducing me to faces I could only vaguely latch on to before they were replaced. They all liked my hair, once Summer told them what she'd done. Even Thalia cooed over it when she saw it.

"Oh my god, henna," she said approvingly. "It looks great." I felt helplessly pleased. Summer basked in every bit of praise, loudly exclaiming how fabulously beautiful I was to whoever was in earshot. After the first couple of times, I managed to stop turning puce with embarrassment. Summer's glee was infectious. She kept us topped up with the sloe gin cocktail from the brimming set of giant crystal bowls in the kitchen, and I swiped us the best of the food whenever I saw a chance.

So far I'd only caught sight of Fenrin from across the room, in deep conversation with different people. Thalia was with her mother most of the time, and together they laughed glittering laughs and made lovely teasing smiles. I would never be one of those who drew everyone to them like magnets and pins. I could try; I could study. But some people had it, and some people did not.

I wondered if Thalia enjoyed it as much as she seemed to.

Summer played a game with me. She'd point at someone in

the room, and I'd try to guess what they did for a living. Most of the time I got it utterly wrong, much to her amusement. Her eyes fell on a man like a stringy cat with a restless energy to him. He had on violent blue eye shadow that popped against his dark skin.

"Him," she said.

"Oh god, I don't know," I groaned. "He's probably in the circus."

"Ha! That's the closest you've come so far. His name's Glorien, and he used to be a ballet dancer. One of the best."

I leaned into her, mock despairing. "That's not even a bit close."

"You are pretty bad at this," she agreed with obvious delight. "What about her?"

I glanced over at the woman she was pointing to. She was short, with strong features and a simple black patch over one eye, which gave her a sharp kind of edge.

"Um. Pirate?" I said hopefully.

"Now you're not even trying."

"Dog-training school?"

"Dear lord, stop. Her name is Miranda Etherington, and she runs a 'consultancy firm.'" Summer crooked her fingers in air quotes. "Which is really just code for saying that she reads people's futures for them. One of her company's clients is a guy who works high up in the government."

I stared at the woman. "No way. Does she do it with, like, a crystal ball or something?"

"God, no, she thinks that stuff is trashy. She says she sees their futures in her dreams." Summer's face changed. "Oh, no.

My slobbery uncle Renard is coming this way. Help me. Hide me."

"Hi," said someone in my ear.

I turned and found myself inches from Fenrin's mouth. I'd moved too quickly, and he was still drawing back from me.

"Hi," I said. "Happy birthday."

"Thank you."

Beside me, Summer was kissing a rotund man on each cheek as he exclaimed at her fondly. She'd give me hell later for not rescuing her, but Fenrin was there, so close I could smell him, and right now it was hard to think.

His eyes fixed on my hair. My makeup.

"What happened here?" he said.

"Summer wanted to play around. I don't know."

He seemed surprised. "And you let her?"

I half shrugged, feeling weird, and then annoyed that I felt weird. He thought I looked bad. He liked natural girls, didn't he—those surfer types with their perfect skin.

"No offense," he said. "But it's just not . . . you."

"Have you noticed how when people say 'no offense,' you know you're immediately going to be offended?"

"It's just . . . as if you're her doll. You know? Like she's tried to make you look like her."

*Like I'm trying to be one of you.*

I hated myself for being so painfully obvious. I wanted to rub the eye shadow off. I looked across the room. First chance I got, I'd go to the bathroom, take my makeup off, and try and make it look like I hadn't. I didn't want to upset Summer by spoiling her creation.

"I'm sorry," he said, and I was startled back to him. "That was mean. Just don't let them . . . consume you." I was still looking at him. He laughed. "I'm not making much sense. I'm in a weird mood. Ignore me."

"What's wrong?" I said.

"Oh nothing. I have nothing to complain about." He smiled. "I really don't."

Maybe this would be another movie night. I shouldn't push. I waited, letting him find his way to me. This was what made me different in his eyes. He could tell me the truth. He didn't have to pretend. Wasn't that what had made him like me in the first place?

He wasn't looking at me. His eyes roved over the room, and he stared, but I couldn't make out who had his attention. I followed his gaze and saw a couple talking to Esther. The woman had thin features and dyed white blond hair that made a sharp contrast against her pale olive skin. The man was tall and imposing, with a salt-and-pepper beard.

"Are those Wolf's parents?" I said.

His eyes immediately dropped away from them.

"Where?" His voice was casual.

"Talking to your mom."

"Oh yeah. The Grigorovs." He rolled the 'r' dramatically.

"What are they like?"

"Solemn. Reserved."

"Like father, like son, I guess."

Fenrin shrugged and didn't smile. "They're okay. I've known them since I was born."

The joke felt stupid now, like I was bitching. I tried to make up for it. "You all grew up together, right? How come?"

Fenrin swirled his drink, looking into its depths. "Our parents have been best friends since they were teenagers. They're more like extended family than anything else. Since they moved to the city Wolf is over here all the damn time. It's only about an hour's drive, I suppose. But still, you think he'd have his own friends."

"Doesn't he?"

"Oh, well. He talks about a couple of people every so often that he seems to hang out with, doing city things like going to art galleries and concept nightclubs." His voice turned a little savage. "One guy in particular called David who sounds like an asshole. But then, Wolf has always had a penchant for those." Fenrin grinned into his drink.

I wondered what that meant. Was Wolf the type to hang around with the kind of people who gave parents heart attacks? Maybe he'd been in trouble a lot when he was younger. He seemed sweet to me, underneath his careful blank exterior, but he could be sweet and he could be trouble. People were complicated.

"What was he like as a kid?"

His face shifted. "Horrible little shit."

We both laughed.

"He used to have tantrums about the stupidest things. And he swore in Bulgarian because he knew he could get away with it. We had no idea what he was saying, but you didn't have to. It was all there in his scrunched-up, cross little face."

"And now?"

Fenrin shrugged. "Oh, now he's all silent, like he thinks he's better than the rest of us. No idea where he is right now, actually—probably lurking upstairs like an antisocial mute."

Thalia appeared at her brother's side and whispered in his ear.

He turned to me with a smile. "Gotta go. I'm being summoned."

"Oh?" I said lightly. "Sounds serious. By who?"

He waved a hand. "The party gods. See you later."

He tucked a strand of my hair behind my ear and left, weaving his way to the hall.

I stood there and tried to understand all the signals he'd given. He'd come and found me to talk. He'd insulted my hair, but then apologized for it. He'd then left without even a pause, like I meant nothing, but he'd touched my hair and my ear like I meant something. People didn't make affectionate gestures like that to people they didn't like. I knew that. I had to hold on to that.

Was it progress? If it was, it was just too damn slow.

*You should kiss him.*

What if he laughed at me? Or pulled back? Or turned away so that I missed his mouth and kissed his cheek instead, like an awkward five-year-old?

What if it all went wrong and he told the rest of them?

"Drink?" said Thalia, breaking into my thoughts. She gestured dreamily at my empty glass.

"Yeah." I raised my voice over the music. "Is there any of that cocktail left?"

She made a grab for my glass but missed, and her fingers brushed my hand.

She smirked and said, "Ooooops."

*No more for you, though,* I thought.

I hoped her parents hadn't caught sight of her like this. Or maybe they were bohemian enough not to mind, but from what I'd seen of the care they took over appearances, I somehow doubted it. Either way, she was practically rolling on her feet. Why hadn't Fenrin noticed and said something before running off to wherever?

"Hey," I said. "I'll get it."

"No, no, no. Mmm hosting."

"It's your birthday," I tried. "I should serve you, not the other way around."

She stood, uncertain and glazed.

"Stay here," I said. "I'll get us both a drink. Okay?"

I scanned the bodies in the room for Summer, but she wasn't there, then Thalia started off to the kitchen.

I grabbed her arm. "Hey, where are you going?"

I couldn't even pick out words among the slurring sounds that came back. I couldn't leave her like this.

"Come on," I said. "Come with me."

I tugged gently on her arm. I could practically see her thoughts running to catch up while her body responded automatically. We weaved through the crowd and she dragged on my arm like a reluctant child. Steering was too superhuman a feat for me—she bumped into about five people, and I went faster and faster, trying to get us out as quickly as I could. Fresh air would help.

We cleared the hallway and I managed to push through to the back door. It had stopped raining, and the air had a sweet, sharp tinge to it. The garden lights were on, giving a soft glow to the night. There were a few people outside, smoking and talking.

*The grove,* I thought. *It'll be quieter.*

"Stars!" called Thalia too loudly, as I dragged her along, her hand in mine. I saw heads swivel to watch us as we passed. "So gorgeous. Don't you think?"

"Stunning," I muttered. Even under stress, I had time to appreciate the feel of her hand, so thin and fine-boned, so rare and alien a touch to my fingers. I felt like I could snap her beautiful wrist with one squeeze.

We stumble-walked our way through the garden, down the stone path that led to the pond and the apple tree at the start of the grove, its huge craggy branches black against the sky. The sounds of the party grew quieter, and I started to breathe more easily. Thalia was tugging back on my hand, her movements more and more urgent. I stopped, thinking she probably wanted to throw up.

But then I saw a shadow moving just before the apple tree.

"Thalia," it said.

Thalia turned away, hanging off my hand. "Oh god."

"Thalia," it said again, and stepped into the faint light from the house.

It was Marcus.

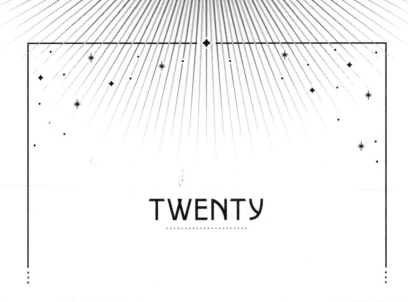

# TWENTY

HE STEPPED FORWARD.

"You should not be here," I warned him. "Marcus, they're going to freak out if they catch you here."

"I just wanted to see you," he said, his eyes on Thalia. "I thought . . . it's the party tonight, there'll be a hundred people around, you could slip away for a minute."

His tone was pushy and oddly uneven, as if he'd forgotten how to speak and was trying to remember each step of the process. He looked disheveled, like he hadn't slept properly in days.

Thalia's eyes were shut, as if she could make it all go away as long as she couldn't see it.

"Please don't," she whimpered. "Please. I said I was sorry. It's over. I told you. We're done, we're done."

Marcus held up a hand.

"Don't," he said. "Because every time you open your mouth, what you say is so very much the opposite of what you really think that it kills me. What you're doing is killing me." Frustration leaked out of him. His voice rose. "I just . . . want to talk to you. That's all it's ever been about these last few months. But you just shut me down. Do you know what that *feels* like?"

He was trembling. I could see his shoulders shake.

"I've known you all your life," Marcus said. "Don't you think I can tell when you're lying?"

Thalia's mouth was open and her eyes were wet. "Marcus."

Incredibly, he laughed. "No, look, it's okay. It's okay. See, I've got it all worked out—a way to solve this."

He held up the hand that had been dangling loosely by his side.

In it was a knife.

The silence was absolute.

*Oh no, Marcus,* I thought. *Oh no, no.*

"That's my . . . ," Thalia said, faintly. "That's my athame."

It wasn't some kitchen knife, but a pretty, polished blade. I saw a pearlescent glimmer between his fingers, and I remembered where I'd seen it before—pushed into a jar of salt in Thalia's bedroom.

Thalia took a step back. "You've been in my room. When?"

"I just slipped upstairs. No one was even . . . it was just for a minute. It doesn't matter. Listen to me." His voice was fast and urgent. "It's got to be a blood pact, Thalia. Remember how we used to talk about it, but we never actually did it? If we're bound together by blood, then nothing can keep us apart. Not your parents, not the curse. Everything falls away before a blood pact. It's the strongest magic there is."

Thalia's eyes were locked on the athame. "No, it's too dangerous. It's really, really dangerous."

"Not if you do it properly," he insisted. "You just need to judge the amount of blood loss right."

I tried to swallow my panic. "Marcus," I said. "Look at me. You're under the curse."

He frowned, distracted. "What?"

"This is not you. This is the Grace curse."

"You don't know what you're talking about. God, you're just like the rest of them."

"Look at yourself. You're acting . . ." I bit off the word *crazy*. "Irrational. You look weird right now. Like you can't even see straight."

"I'm drunk," he said matter-of-factly. "That's why."

"Then just think for a second about what you're doing."

The alarm in my voice made him frown again. "It's a blood pact, not a human sacrifice. Thalia? What do you say?" He stepped forward.

"Stop," said Thalia faintly. "Marcus, please don't. I don't want you to get into trouble. It's true, okay? It's all because of the curse, what you're feeling. It's not real."

He stared at her, his head weaving a slow no, over and over. "Don't you get it?" he said finally, his voice reasonable. "There's no curse. I've been in love with you since we were kids. Forever. I've felt like this forever."

He stepped forward again. "All your life you've let your family decide your fate," he said. "What do *you* want?"

My arm came out to push Thalia behind me. He was inches away.

He held out the knife toward her, point first.

He was ruining everything. Esther would know. It would all

go wrong for them. I didn't want it to go wrong. This was supposed to be a perfect summer. We were supposed to have *fixed* this. Instead, here was the curse in full force, showing me up, mocking me and my pathetic attempts to stamp it out. How would I ever become a proper witch if I couldn't even fix *this*?

I remembered what they'd said about that day he'd been caught in her room, forcing her down, and I felt a roaring anger claw its way up and out of me.

"Just stop," I said, furiously. "She doesn't love you back. You're being a creep. Can't you see that? You're scaring her!"

"Get out of the way," he said, but then I saw his gaze falter. There was a sudden cracking, popping sound behind us, like jars smashing to the ground, over and over.

I watched his eyes widen as he looked past me, and I turned without thinking.

Together we stared at the mess in the light of the garden path lamps. Normally, the path was lined with delicate little clay pots of sage and asters, but now several of them lay scattered and broken on the tiles, as if their sides had burst.

A rustling pulled me back to Marcus. I turned, suddenly terrified that he was lunging toward us, but then I saw the glint of the athame nestled in the grass where he'd dropped it. His dark shape hugged the edge of the garden, and I heard the side gate bang shut. He had gone.

Only then did I let go of my fear, feeling it drain away and my shoulders come down. I caught Thalia's eye.

"That's . . . weird," I said cautiously, my eyes on the pots. "Did you do that?"

"I was nowhere near them," Thalia managed. "It wasn't me. It wasn't me. Oh, shit. Esther's going to have a meltdown."

"Maybe something knocked them over. Do you have a cat?" It seemed impossible that a cat could have done all that, but there was no explanation I could think of that fit.

She shook her head.

"A fox, maybe?"

Thalia glanced at me in sudden horror, as if I'd inadvertently hit close to home.

"What?" I said, curious.

She ducked her head down. "I think I'm going to throw up."

"Oh god. Look, he's gone. Let's get back to the house. At least to the toilet. Can you make it back inside?"

She gave me a half nod. Good enough.

Her hand stretched out and pointed to the athame. I bent down and grabbed hold of it. I didn't know quite what I expected. Would it feel strange, heavy, unnaturally hot or cold? But all I could feel was a knife, the handle gently warm from Marcus's hand.

I slipped my arm around Thalia's waist. She palmed the athame from me and slid it handle first into her armpit, gripping it to her side with her arm to conceal it. We walked slowly back to the house.

"Thalia?" said one of the partygoers, peering at me with mistrust as we approached. "Something going on?"

I opened my mouth to snap back—I was their friend, I had every right to be there—my mind whirring with an explanation. But I didn't need to.

Thalia raised her head and gave a little laugh. "Oh god," she said, embarrassed, with barely a trace of alcoholic waver in her voice. "These idiots from school were trying to gate-crash. You know how it is. They get jealous. They smashed up a couple of Esther's pots, though. They looked pretty drunk."

"Don't worry about it," said the guest. She was smooth and oiled, slicked-back hair, all in black. "We'll get her some more tomorrow. Go enjoy your birthday."

She smiled. "Thanks."

I felt her shift beside me, and I walked her on, concentrating on the back door. It was incredible, really, watching her put on a show like that. As soon as we were out of sight of them all, her face dropped and her eyes half-closed.

We reached the hallway toilet without incident. I pulled Thalia in and locked the door behind us. She went straight to the toilet and sank to the tiles, placing the athame next to her. I took the hand towel off its wall peg and laid it over her lap—I couldn't bear seeing that beautiful dress get ruined. It looked like the kind of delicate thing that wouldn't withstand a drink spill, never mind a good vomiting. She kept her hair back from dangling around her mouth with one hand and leaned over the bowl. Small neat movements, as if it was a routine she'd grown used to.

*After all, you do it a lot,* I thought. *Isn't that what Fenrin had said that night? Did he mean drinking, or something else?*

The only light was over the sink, and it cast a soft, dark glow over the small room. The tiles echoed with the sounds of retching, and I tried very hard not to listen. I rubbed her back with one hand and held a long strand of her hair away from her mouth with the other. That was what people did, so I did it. I distracted myself with thoughts of Fenrin. Where was he right now and what was he doing? Probably not, let's face it, helping someone puke.

It took me a while to break the silence. I looked down at her head. It was shaking very slight, fast shakes. Then I heard the sound people make when they're crying really hard but don't want anyone to hear it.

I cautiously took my hands away from her and sat back against the wall. I always did this kind of thing in private. I guess she did, too, but the drink had punched through her defenses. I could never have imagined Thalia crying in front of me before this.

"Can I get someone?" I said at last. "I can go find Summer."

She shook her head.

"Do you want to talk about it?"

"Don't want your fucking sympathy," she snapped, her voice blotted and wavering.

"Fine." I got up to leave.

"Don't."

I stopped. Sat back down again. Listened to her shudder.

Her tears turned to coughs, and then she retched again, and I turned my face away to give her privacy. Eventually, the sound of movement drew me back to her. I watched her bend to the sink and run the tap, washing her mouth out and spitting. The weak set of her body was gone, flushed down the toilet with everything else, but I thought I could see her fragility now, running like spider web cracks underneath the glossy finish.

"What are you going to do?" I said, quietly.

"Nothing."

"Nothing? What kind of a solution is that?"

"The only kind." Finally, she sat on the floor and rested her back against the wall, her legs drawn up. She was greasy and pale. Earlier, her hair had looked sleek and glorious. Now it clung to her scalp in strings. "River, just drop it. It's got nothing to do with you."

"Wow. That attitude must really solve all your problems, mustn't it? For your information, it's got everything to do with me."

"Why?" she shot back.

*Because I'm trying to break your stupid curse.*

*Because if I can do that, I can be a Grace. I can fix me.*

"Because I care about you guys, okay?" I said. My chest was tight with growing, blooming tears. Not here. Never in front of them.

Thalia laughed. It was a bitter, withered sound. "Maybe you shouldn't. Maybe you'd have an easier life if you just left us alone."

"I can't," I said. It was all I could say, and it was the stark, simple truth.

I loved them. Maybe I was like Marcus now, too. Maybe I was under their curse.

*Too many curses going around,* I thought grimly, and stood up.

"Come on," I told Thalia. "Let's get you to bed."

She shook her head. "I can't. I have to go back out there. It will look bad."

"God, fuck appearances, for once in your life," I said sharply.

She glanced up, startled. I thought she'd fight me, but she was too tired. She just nodded.

I helped her up.

# TWENTY-ONE

"HELLO?" I CALLED INTO THE HALLWAY.

The Grace house was quiet. It was almost a week after the party, but the last of the extended family had only gone the day before, leaving a cavernous silence in their wake. Gwydion had taken the opportunity to travel to the city with a cousin who lived there and wouldn't be back for another couple of days. Esther was holding court at Nature's Way and would be holed up in her workshop there until very late, Summer had assured me. I found it easier to be here when they weren't. Easier to breathe.

I dropped my bag at the foot of the stairs and wandered into the kitchen. The fridge purred gently, underlining the quiet. Outside the sun sparkled over the patio stones, but in here it was calm and cool. A huge bowl of strawberries sat in the middle of the table, gleaming red. Fruit in this house always looked like it would burst open on your tongue and fill your throat with clear, fresh juice.

"Eve and the apple," said a voice behind me.

I flinched, turned. Fenrin was in the doorway, watching me. Sometimes it still hurt to look at him and have him look right back. I should have been used to it by now.

"Huh?" I said. Evocative. Eloquent. As always.

He pointed to the strawberries. "You looked like you were undergoing some kind of struggle with temptation. Forbidden fruit." He misinterpreted my expression as alarm at being caught and laughed. "Relax. You know you can eat them. You can have anything you like."

*Can I?*

Was I making this conversation seem loaded, or was it him, talking temptation with that flirtatious slant to his mouth?

"I haven't seen you since my birthday," he said, coming in closer and picking up a strawberry from the bowl. "Did you have a good time?"

A good time? Yes, up until the moment it all started going wrong.

*See, Fen,* I wanted to say, *the plan had been for us all to sneak out of there together, go upstairs and hole ourselves up with alcohol and music. The plan had been for me to watch you dance to* Footloose *and cheer and clap and hug you and feel your hand lightly skating my back in a way that didn't say "friends," and then later, when everyone had finally fallen asleep, the plan, Fenrin, had been to just lean forward and kiss you with no warning, and feel your hands around the back of my head, pushing your mouth into mine as if you couldn't get enough of me and had been twisted up inside waiting for this for so long.*

The plan had not been for Fenrin to completely disappear for the rest of the evening without any kind of sorry or why.

The plan had not been for me to spend my time getting Thalia upstairs to her room without any adult partygoers seeing us and helping her into bed. She'd asked me not to tell anyone about Marcus's visit, and I hadn't, but I couldn't keep it secret for long. How far would he go next time? Would it be my fault if something happened? I had to tell Summer, at least. The closer I got to her, the harder it got to lie to her. I liked the way she trusted me. I wanted to be the kind of friend who earned that trust. Now that she was no longer preoccupied with her visitors, I could get her on her own and we'd work out what to do.

"Yeah, it was fun," I said. "Thank you for inviting me. Did you have a good time?"

"I did, actually." There was a secretive kind of a smile in his voice. "Summer said something about swimming down at the cove today. You up for it?"

"I have a towel with me and everything."

He raised his eyebrows. "You are aware that you could just borrow one from us."

"I'm aware," I said, mock haughtily. "But my towel is better than yours."

He smirked. I watched him take the strawberry into his mouth whole and bite down.

There was a short, sharp, loud shriek that echoed through the hallway.

Fenrin cocked his head. "What the hell?"

"Was that . . . a cat, or something?" I said.

"We don't have pets."

"Bird?"

"Maybe. It came from outside."

He disappeared out of the kitchen, and I followed him to the back door. He was standing, his back to me.

He was absolutely still.

I gave it a moment, but the moment stretched and grew strange.

"Fe—"

I bit his name off as he moved fast, jerking into action, racing across the patio and down the stone path. Startled, I ran, too.

"Fenrin, what—"

But he didn't turn around and he didn't talk. He reached Summer, who was standing in the middle of the garden, holding a mound of mud in her hands. She was looking down at it.

Fenrin took hold of her arm.

"Summer, what's wrong? *Summer.*"

I reached them, trying not to pant.

"Can you see it?" Summer said to him. Her voice was normal. Very, very normal and extremely calm.

"See what?"

"Look at it."

She was staring down at the mud ball in her hands.

Fenrin looked at it. "It's just mud. What is it, like a chunk of stone?"

"It was just lying there," Summer went on. "There's that clear patch of soil right at the back, near the oak tree. We don't plant around that tree, you know? We don't plant anywhere near it. But the soil was all scattered, and this was lying there next to the hole, as if it had just been dug up."

"*What's* been dug up?" said Fenrin, growing impatient.

I stared at the mud ball.

It was kind of elongated, like a mini football. A dirty red brown.

"You don't see it?" said Summer, her voice whispery, paper thin.

"There's a tube coming out of it," I said, getting curious.

"It's a heart."

Fenrin went still.

I looked at it. The more I looked, the more I could see it.

"No."

"Yes," said Summer.

"It's too small," I said cautiously, my body humming with anxious dread.

Fenrin extended a finger, thought better of it. "Animal."

"Fox," said Summer.

"How the hell would you know that?" Fenrin shot back.

"There was a bit of fur. It was orange and white."

"Could be cat."

"It's fox."

"How do you know for sure?" I said.

Summer pursed her lips. "Because I know what you need a fox heart for."

We watched each other.

"Well, for christ's sake, stop touching it," Fenrin said suddenly, and Summer dropped it to the ground like it scorched her. "And you should wash your hands because god knows."

I stared at the dirty heart on the ground. "What do you need a fox heart for?"

"It's bad," said Summer. "Old magic. We don't do that sort of thing. This is really bad." Her eyes widened with a new urgency. "If there was old magic working against us . . ."

"What are you talking about?"

"That night in the woods. We tried to get Marcus to go away, right?" She turned to me. "Well, what if someone had already tried? But they used old magic to do it. And then we did ours on top. That could really mess things up, two spells working against each other—"

Fenrin scoffed. "I've never even heard of that. How do you know what would happen?"

"Seriously," I said. "What does a fox heart do?"

"It's about cunning and manipulation. The trickster. You see?" Summer looked down at her dirt-streaked hands. Dirt plus something else? My insides gave a gentle roll. "Thalia cast a spell on Marcus to manipulate him."

"You make me sound like a calculating bitch."

Summer full-body flinched.

Thalia was standing, framed by the house, as we stared back at her. She looked calm, but it was a lie, and if I could see it, then everyone could. Her mouth was drawn and her eyes were too wide.

"Thalia," said Summer. "What did you do?"

"What did *you* do?" she snapped. "You did a spell in the woods? Without me? *On* me? How could you?"

"Thalia," Fenrin joined in, gently. "Come on. What the hell is this?" He pointed to the heart on the ground.

Maybe it was the sight of her twin, the skeptic, the hater of magic, asking her. But she broke.

"I just wanted to not end up like all the rest," she said.

"What do you mean?"

"Like our aunts and cousins. Like our grandparents, and like Esther."

"You tried to break the curse," Summer breathed.

Thalia wrapped her arms around herself. "No, no. No one can break the curse. I just wanted to make it so he didn't like me anymore."

There in the sunshine, it sounded so thin and unreal.

"When?" said Fenrin. "When did you cast it?" His face was cold. I knew what he was thinking. *You kept this from me.*

"A while ago. After the thing at Christmas." She swallowed. "I didn't want him to end up like all the rest of them from our amazing family history. Dead or mad. It's him or me, isn't it? That's how the curse works. I liked him too much, okay? He didn't deserve that. I wanted to save him. But it didn't work." Her voice had a quiet wail to it. "He's gone crazy anyway, hasn't he? So I'm screwed. It'll play out like it always does."

"But . . . it's better," said Summer cautiously. "I thought he was better. It's working. Isn't it?"

Thalia's eyes met mine.

*Tell them.*

She sighed. "No, it's not. He was here at the party. He was . . . he was not okay."

Fenrin threw up his arms to the sky, turning his back on her. He rubbed his hands over his face, there in the bright sunshine, and it looked odd because we'd all been brought up to believe that sunshine and darkness couldn't exist in the same place, but they did, they did.

"That crazy—what did he do?"

The athame, gripped in his hand.

*A blood pact.*

"It doesn't matter," said Thalia. "All that matters is that the curse exists, Fen, you have to see it does, because nothing we do works. It's stronger than all of us."

"Come on. That's twice he's tried to attack you," I said. Her heavy, tragic fatalism was starting to grate on me. "Are we just going to sit back and see if third time's the charm?"

"Twice?" Fenrin echoed, baffled. "What the hell are you talking about?"

"Well, the first time was in Thalia's bedroom." Fenrin was blank. Thalia's eyes were on the ground. "The thing that started all this? Your parents throwing him out?"

"They threw him out because Esther walked in on them having sex," Fenrin said coldly. "They actually threw him bodily out of the house and told him he was never allowed to even speak to Thalia again. And she went along with it—she's utterly ignored him ever since. Our crazy, ex–best friend. Why, I hear you ask? Oh, because she was risking the curse by being with a nonwitch, wasn't she, the good old nonexistent curse, and let's not forget that Marcus isn't the one they've chosen for her. Is he?"

They were staring at one another. I felt the undercurrent of something unsaid all around us, pulling and tugging, but I didn't know what waters we swam in now.

"So," I said, in my most reasonable voice. "You, what. Told everyone at school that he attacked you? Why? To save face?"

"I never said that," Thalia tried to snap, but her voice wavered with unshed tears.

"But you didn't deny it, either, did you, when the rumors started?"

She looked away, her mouth trembling.

"What rumors?" Fenrin demanded.

I rounded on him. "How the hell can you not know? It's all anyone at school ever talks about when he walks into a room. They've made up all these lies about him because none of you ever told them what really happened. He's practically a rapist in their eyes. That's really unfair. At the least, he's some kind of creepy stalker—"

"Well, that part's true," Summer said, and then she held her hands up when my eyes landed on her. "Look, he is. You can't deny how he's been recently. And I didn't know about the rumors, not really. I mean . . ." She paused, uncomfortable. "Maybe I overheard something one time. But no one talks about anything to do with us around us, River. They all get this look on their faces, like we'd take their heads off if they so much as breathed a word of it."

"And whose fault is that?" I said.

"No one's." She shook her head. "We didn't ask them to be like that. It's just the way it is."

*No. You never ask, do you? People just part for you, and bend around you, and flock to you, and it's not like you encourage it. It just is.*

*But you don't discourage it, either.*

Why would they, though? Who would discourage power? It was all anybody ever wanted. Power got you through the day when everything seemed gray and bleak. I knew this.

My anger drained away, leaving me tired.

Summer was staring at her hands. "What are we going to do about this?" she said.

I nodded at the brown, withered heart on the ground. "We're going to take off this fox spell. Have you even thought about the fact that Marcus's recent behavior is because of it?"

"It was supposed to do the opposite," Thalia said, her voice wispy and small.

"River's right." Summer glared around. "I'm going to wash this horrible shit off my hands. And then we're going to fix it."

# TWENTY-TWO

WHEN THE DAY STRETCHED INTO EARLY EVENING, WE gathered in the garden.

Wolf had turned up late in the afternoon, back from a day trip he'd taken into the city with his father. He was enigmatic at the best of times, but tonight it felt like he was trying to disappear into himself, barely raising his voice over a grunt. Someone had evidently filled him in on the day's events, and he didn't seem happy about it—it looked like he and Fenrin had fallen out. They kept circling each other like angry cats and now sat on opposite sides of our ragged, five-pointed circle.

I'd spent the afternoon at the cove with Summer, but no one else had wanted to come, and it hadn't been carefree and fun the way I'd imagined it. She'd scrubbed them clean, but every time I looked at her, I flashed back to her dirt-streaked hands and the heart they had held.

We gathered, and at first no one talked. Thalia was draped in a wicker chair next to Summer, silent. Summer was staring off into the distance, her fingers tapping out a rhythm on the grass only she could hear. Wolf was fiddling with the cork in a bottle of wine. Fenrin seemed lost in thought.

I had a role to fulfill. I was the disruptor. The outsider. The one forcing them out of the comfortable rut of secrets and silence they were accustomed to, and into action.

*Be brave.*

"So what magic needs a fox heart?" I said. "I mean, what does it do, exactly?"

"It's an old way of doing things," Wolf said, unexpectedly. "You offer an exchange, a sacrifice, instead of using your will. You offer up something else instead of using yourself."

"Bad magic," Summer said, gloomily.

Thalia was very still and small.

Bad magic?

I didn't think magic could be bad. It depended on the person doing it, not the thing itself. It was like a knife. Inert until someone forced their will on it, driving it into action. It could be used to cut someone free or kill them. It was all things, and no things, given purpose by an outside force.

Magic was only bad if you were, too.

"Well, come on," said Fenrin to me. "The spell in the woods was your idea. What do you think we should do to fix it?"

Wolf raised his head to look at me. And then they all did.

I felt myself start to melt under their collective staring. I searched, stumbling around half-formed thoughts. "What do you want me to say?"

Fenrin folded his arms. "You must have a plan of action. You said we had to take off the spell on Marcus, so let's hear it."

"I don't have a plan," I said, uncomfortable. "I'm not an expert on magic. I was just . . ." I faltered.

But his stare was hard. He was challenging me.

*Be the disruptor. Be brave.*

So I said, "I was just thinking about bad magic. I don't think that's the problem here. I think it's to do with intention."

Summer was frowning.

"I think when we did the spell in the woods, our intentions weren't pure," I carried on. I wouldn't look at Fenrin for his reaction, not until I'd finished.

Maybe he didn't even remember what he'd said to me, anyway.

"We all wanted to break the curse," Summer said. "That was the intention. Why would anyone want something different?"

"Maybe someone wanted to punish her."

"Who? Thalia?" Summer was mystified. "Why?"

I opened my mouth, but I couldn't say it.

It didn't matter, though, because Fenrin said it for me. "Because maybe I thought she deserved it for being a coward."

There was a shocked silence.

His eyes fell on mine.

"Thank you," he said, clearly. "Very sweet of you to let everyone know."

He stood up and walked off down the path toward the grove.

Out of the corner of my eye, I saw Wolf twitch as if to go after him, but he stayed still.

"What is he talking about?" Summer said.

I didn't dare look at Thalia.

"River, just tell us." Summer's voice was urgent. "We can't do a spell without knowing everything. We could screw it up again."

It felt like a betrayal. He'd confessed it to me—you didn't tell other people's confessions. But god, there were all these knotted, tangled secrets, strangling us. We were choking to death. I wanted to save us.

"He told me something," I said. "That night in the woods. He said he wanted to punish Thalia, not help her."

Thalia laughed, only it sounded more like a gasp.

"Look, I'm sorry."

"You're sorry," she echoed, her voice flat, and laughed again.

"So you're saying it's Fenrin's fault." It was Wolf.

I eyed him. "I'm not saying anything like that. People can't help what they really feel inside."

Wolf shifted, folded his arms. "No, but it *is* his fault, then—whether he wants it to be or not."

Fenrin felt guilty. He remembered what he'd told me and thought the same as I did—that this was all going wrong because of him.

"I'll go and talk to him." Summer shifted.

"No, I'll go." I got up and walked down the stone path to the grove. I could see him in the half-dusk, just beyond the apple tree. As I contemplated his outline, alone and stark against the tree trunks, I made a decision. In the spirit of the evening, I would finally tell him the truth about the way I felt.

He was leaning back with his arms folded, facing away. He heard me approach and sighed.

"I'm sorry," I offered.

He said nothing. I waited a moment, but a nervous energy was sparking in me, and I walked around to stand right in front of him.

"I'm sorry," I repeated.

He looked at me. "Are you the type to bring out people's secrets when it suits you, like a good card hand?"

"What? No. I didn't tell them to hurt you. I just . . . we shouldn't let everyone think it's all going wrong because of bad magic, when it might not be. We should all know everything between us. Shouldn't we?" I hated how my voice sounded, like I was pleading with him. Pleading didn't sound like I was right. I tried to change my face, my stance.

"Was it really up to you to tell them?"

"Well, were *you* going to tell them?"

He was silent.

"Why not?" I said.

"Why not?" he exploded. "It's bullshit. We didn't do anything that night in the woods. Nothing."

"Will you just stop lying to yourself? You believe, Fen. Why else would you be acting so weird about this?"

He laughed, raising his hands helplessly. "Jesus, another zealot. You're really starting to fit in well, aren't you?"

I wanted to hit him.

"Why do you use that as a put-down with me, as if it's just so pathetic to like you?" I stopped. "All of you," I amended. I bit the inside of my cheek hard, to replace the emotion with pain. To regain my control.

He was turning away from me. *Don't turn away from me.*

"It's not because I met you guys and then suddenly decided magic was real, okay? I've always believed, before you came along. Maybe *not* in magic, but in something."

Fenrin stopped. "What do you mean?"

I'd gone too far without even realizing. "Nothing."

"No," he said, renewed. "You're so damn mysterious. You never talk about yourself, you just let us go on and on about our own unimportant crap. You sit there like a mirror, and all you do is magnify all of us. You have to tell us your secrets, too, River."

"There's nothing to tell!"

"Come on. There's always something."

"No! I'm the most boring person in the world! Okay? Is that what you want to hear? That I hang around with you because I want to be interesting, to be *loved*." I spat the word out. "Loved and adored, like you are. That's what I want. You happy now? I'm just as pathetic as you think I am."

I stopped, shocked at myself. How had this happened? How had I let so much out when I'd worked so hard to keep it all in?

"You're not," he said, shaking his head. "I've never thought that, River. Not once."

My heart moved, stirred. It was the confirmation I'd been looking for from him all this time. I felt tears trying to leak out of me, and I just panicked. I did it badly as well, kind of gulping in a breath like I was about to take a dive, and moving up to him, trying to concentrate on his mouth.

I leaned in. This was it. The moment I had been thinking about for months.

But I didn't even get close enough to touch. His hands were on my shoulders, stopping me.

"What are you doing?" he said. He sounded alarmed.

I could see a sickly realization creeping across his face. He wasn't happy.

He wasn't happy at all.

"River, I—"

I tried to laugh. Bad, bad mistake. It came out stuttering. "It was just a joke. You should see your face."

He dragged in a deep breath, fighting for words. "This is. I didn't even realize."

It was a compliment, of sorts. A testament to how good I was at hiding my true self.

I was looking at the trunk past his face, tracing the bark cracks with my eyes. "We should get back, okay?"

He said nothing. So I walked away.

As I walked I heard rustling, and he came up beside me. "Don't just walk off," he said. "I'm sorry."

"What for?" I replied, offhand.

He breathed a short, sharp sigh. "I like you, I do. But—"

But. There was a but.

"I get it, okay?" I interrupted. "Just fucking drop it." I turned my face from him as if I didn't care at all.

"Fine," he said sharply, and walked on ahead.

I stopped. I had to. My chest was shrinking, pushing inward and squeezing all my air out. I leaned against the nearest tree and took in a deep breath, counting to ten. Let it go, counting to ten.

I would not cry here.

I would go back to them, and I would be perfectly easy. I would be the River they knew. I would be their equal. The only way to be what you wanted to be was to pretend that you already were. One day you would stop feeling like you were acting. One day there would be no need, and finally, oh finally, you would be able to relax.

*What if Fenrin tells them?*

I ignored the voice.

*He will.*

He wouldn't.

I reached the garden. Fenrin was laughing, and for an awful screeching moment, I thought it was at me, but it was at something Summer had said. She lashed out, kicking his ankle, and he staggered dramatically.

I walked up, and no one said anything, and nothing more was said about spells and magic at all that night. But it hung over us, stretching and straining our time together.

He hadn't told them. But what about tomorrow? Summer would be so disappointed in me. I was half-convinced the reason she had liked me in the first place was because I had seemed so disinterested in her brother. Because it meant I wasn't going to try and use her to get to him.

I hadn't. I hadn't done that. But it would look like I had.

Thalia was silent in her chair, sunken into the bright, brittle chatter around her. I felt Wolf's eyes on me more than once, but I acted as if I didn't. Fenrin laughed like his usual self. Summer suggested music, and a stereo was dragged out on the end of an extension cord. Twilight rose all around us, and we switched the garden lights on—fairy twinkles strung through the trees, solar lamps around the edges of the lawn, fat candles lining the patio stones. I watched the light fall across their faces, as it must have fallen across mine. Did that make us seem the same, somehow?

Fenrin was right, about everything. I did sit like a mirror. I told him there was nothing to see inside me that was worth seeing. Sometimes I thought that was true. Sometimes I thought it was better if all I did was reflect.

After the fourth bottle of wine, they started playing games—hopscotch, dares. The promise of more magic lay forgotten between us as the moon came out. I stayed where I was, chasing that nothingness I had felt during the spell in the woods. Chasing the life of a star.

At some point, I was passed a different bottle, something homemade. It tasted like spiced honey. Summer pulled me to my feet with a wild grin. The others were chanting nursery rhymes, over and over. It should have felt stupid, but it didn't.

*Oranges and lemons, say the bells of St. Clements.*

Summer was spinning me. We weaved and swayed. I fell over twice. It was loud. The garden was black outside our circle of light. The endless night stretched all around us, so we told each other that we had to be close together, together in the dark.

I remember only images, snapshots burned into me, bleeding into each other until I no longer knew the order they had happened. The flash of my bare arms as I stripped off my sweater. Thalia standing up and shrugging off her long skirt, peeling it down until it pooled at her feet. Cool grass tickling my back when I lay down and looked at the stars, Summer's hand in mine. Thalia's long hair wrapped around my fist as I played with the strands. Thalia's or Summer's, all the same color in the dark.

That night I think we were trying to fight against death, against boredom and banality, against everything that made us cry and stare at our futures full in the face with dread. We drank and played games to be in the now, to be in each moment as hard as we could, because the moment was all that mattered, at the end of it all. I remember I felt intoxicated on life and darkness.

I felt powerful. It was the most natural thing in the world. This was why we were alive—to be powerful and free.

It was only in mornings that spells were broken. In mornings, reality always came back in a sick, rolling wave, and the glittering black night before had become something gray and wrong in the daylight.

The next thing I remembered was a sound like a rusting jackhammer. Then another overlapping it. And another. Magpies calling to one another in the dawn light.

I opened my eyes and was immediately sliced with pain.

Grayish light. My skin was cold.

I managed to roll over. My head was surging.

The fruit trees whirled and rustled, whispering. I knew what they were saying.

*We saw what happened.*

I was in the grove, and I was alone.

Then I heard voices, calling my name.

Then: "Fen!"

"Where are you?"

They were coming closer. I tucked my bare arms around myself, huddling in a thin, sleeveless T-shirt that wasn't mine. Maybe it was Summer's. God, it was cold. Dry leaves pricked my skin, scraping against my jeans.

"Fen! River! Where the hell did everyone go?"

*Find me,* I thought. It was all I could think, and I thought it with everything I had.

They found me. Thalia and Summer came through the trees. I heard their voices, but I could only stare at the ground.

"River! What are you doing?" Relief, then nerves creeping their spidery legs into that voice. Summer's voice.

"Are you okay?"

"I'm cold," I said.

Summer crouched down next to me, her eyes full of concern.

"I thought we all fell asleep on the garden chaise lounges. When I woke up, it was just Thalia and me, and you weren't in the house. How come you came out to the grove by yourself?"

"I don't know."

"Have you seen Wolf and Fen?"

I shook my head.

Thalia sounded strange. "Sum, I think something's happened."

"Don't freak out," snapped Summer's voice. An arm came around my shoulders. "We should go back."

"Maybe they went down to the cove."

"Yeah, maybe."

"It's like five minutes away. Shall we just check?"

"Okay—but let's do it quickly. If they come back to the house and find us gone, they'll do the same thing we're doing and we'll be here all day."

They were using matter-of-fact tones. I knew what those tones meant. They were pretending that everything was fine.

It wasn't.

Summer helped me to my feet and we walked. The end of the grove came to an abrupt halt. Beyond was a worn dirt track that led into the dunes, sandy hills covered in long windswept heather, rolling away from us and curving down to the sea. It was going to be sunny again. The sky was pink and gold. Summer was murmuring in my ear, but I couldn't really concentrate on anything she said. She wanted answers I couldn't give to questions like, "What happened?" and "Are you okay?"

The closer we got to the cove, the more wrong everything felt, as if while we'd slept, we'd slipped into another version of this world, almost the same as ours but made of black glass, distorted and dark. They must have felt it, too, because when we got down to the cove and saw something slumped on the sand near the shoreline, none of us broke into a run, as if we weren't even surprised.

It was Fenrin.

He didn't move when they called, but when they rolled him over he woke, his eyes slitting against the light. He looked at us like he had no idea who we were, and for a moment everything dislocated because I was *convinced*, right then, that we had slipped into an alternate reality. But then he blinked.

"What?" he said, his voice rasping. He coughed, and his brow furrowed as if he couldn't remember why his voice would do that.

"Where's Wolf?" said Thalia.

He looked around, bemused. Then shook his head.

"Ah. My throat hurts."

"What are you even doing down here?"

Fenrin sat up. He had his jeans on, at least, but the top button and zipper were undone.

"I don't know."

"What d'you mean, you don't know?"

His face screwed up. "Stop," he said, irritated. "I just woke up. I don't remember last night very well."

Thalia glanced at Summer.

I knew what that glance meant. They didn't remember last night very well, either.

My body rolled with sickness. I crouched on the sand and threw up.

"Oh god," said Summer, behind me. "We have to get her back."

"We need to find Wolf." Thalia's voice was tight around the edges.

"Well, maybe he went back to the house already."

"He wasn't there when we left. And we would have passed him on the way here."

"We should go back and tell Esther."

"She's not awake, and there's no point in saying anything yet. He's probably around somewhere."

"But—"

Their voices rose and rose. I tried to block everything out, but that was worse. There was nothing in my head I wanted to see or hear or feel.

Summer stayed with me while Thalia and Fenrin went back to the house, gathering up my sweater, shoes, and bag and bringing it all to the cove. They used my cell phone to call a taxi. When it arrived, we would clamber over the rocks and then up to the Gull, the pub that sat on the main beach. And I would go home.

Fenrin looped the cove over and over while we waited.

He didn't find Wolf.

No one did.

PART
TWO

# TWENTY-THREE

I'M RUNNING THROUGH THE WOODS IN THE PATCHY purple gray of morning so early it's almost the night before. I'm running barefoot and I can feel the sting of crisp leaves scoring the pads of my feet.

I don't know why I'm running. Only that if I stop, I will be caught.

Then I hear a whoop through the trees, and the noise gets me skimming across the ground, barely touching it, skating desperately. For a moment it feels free, victorious. But then I see shapes close in through the rods of tree trunks. They're matching me.

More whoops. Howls, one, then two and three and four, joining to make a rising and falling cadence that makes me want to be sick. The pack is hunting.

I don't know how long I run, but I'm going nowhere. The trees don't break, there's no flat plains beyond, there's no end to it. I know they've spelled me so I never get to the edge of the woods, but knowing a thing does nothing to stop it. I can't fight this. I can't think.

They're right behind me now. The howls have stopped, and I feel their steady breath coming hot and fast on my shoulder. I'm slower, and slower. My legs wind down like a toy with dead batteries. Something touches my shoulder lightly, but it's like being slammed into a wall. The next thing I know is that I'm on the ground, and they're prowling around me.

I try to speak.

I try to say "please."

But nothing comes out. My jaw is wired shut.

Summer is closest. The others hang back now. She grins at me, all fangs.

Please don't. God, don't do this. But my voice won't form words. My throat feels like it's bleeding with the noise I'm trying to force through it.

Summer has a long, curved blade in her right hand.

I can't move. My arms and legs are heavy as mountains and as impossible to move. All I can do is lie there and watch her crawl up to me like a spider.

I feel myself crying, long tear strings rolling into my ears.

"Shh," Summer says, as she raises the knife. "It'll all be over soon."

She stabs it into my chest. I feel the dull smack of it vibrating through my whole body.

\* \* \* \* \*

I woke up.

I woke up with the heel of my hand pressed into my breast-bone, as if to stop the blood I knew was spurting out from it, leaking my life away. I woke with a shout caught in my mouth, stopped before it could get out so it was more like a strangled gasp. I woke and I could still feel those cold, crunching leaves pressing into my back, the weight of Summer on me.

It took what felt like a long, miserable, heart-stopping time before my brain finally realized that what I had just experienced wasn't real.

The tears were real, though—my hairline was wet with them.

# TWENTY-FOUR

THESE ARE THE ONLY THINGS I REMEMBER ABOUT THE time immediately after the disappearance of Wolf:

The funny expression on Summer's face that day in the cove, while they were still looking for him and I was throwing up on the sand, when I said I didn't want to go back with them, that I wanted to go home instead. I think it was the first time I'd ever chosen my own home over hers.

How I spent the rest of the day curled up in bed, cove sand still clinging to my skin, a blank, black hole for a head. The look on my mother's face when I came in the front door, the surprise and then the panic, quickly swallowed.

The way the police interviews went. I remembered that they checked over and over what we drank and what we ate. We were truthful. I think that helped sway them over to the conclusion they eventually drew. I know we had a lot that night. I know that alcohol wasn't all we had. I remember us all taking half our clothes off and dancing around wildly. At the time, it had felt like freedom. Afterward it was just excruciating, especially when you had to explain it to a police officer and watch the expression on her face.

How my mother, not long after my first interview with the police, caught me by the arm and shook me. Her hand gripped hard as she asked me what the hell was going on. It shocked me to tears. In between hard, dry sobs, I told her that I had absolutely no idea.

How I don't remember living as much as existing. How I barely left the house and mostly only came out of my room at night, going to sit in the kitchen in the darkness, a blanket wrapped around me, watching the moon out of the window.

It had all gone so bad so fast. It only took a moment for your life to stop, and a gray, sickly version of it to slip quietly in and take its place. Every day when I woke up, it felt like a punishment.

When nearly three weeks had passed, the police search continued only halfheartedly.

They thought they knew exactly what had happened. We'd partied too hard and all passed out in drunken stupors. Wolf and Fenrin had woken up in the early hours of the morning, still drunk, and wanted to go swimming. They'd gone down to the cove together, and Wolf had been caught in a vicious tide. He'd been washed out and broken on the rocks, probably while Fenrin was passed out on the beach. They were confident in finding his body any day.

In between all of this, Summer had called me fifteen times.

Sometimes I picked up the phone, sometimes I didn't. Our conversations tailed off into uneasy nothings, and there was only one thing to talk about, which meant we always ended up asking each other exactly the same questions.

"Have you got any news?"

"No. You?"

"No."

"Do you remember anything more about that night?"

"No. You?"

"No."

"Have the police interviewed you again? What did you tell them?"

That last was a favorite of hers. After a while, it started to grate on me. What did she think I'd told them? I knew the Graces would close ranks when questioned, and I did the same. What else was I going to do?

"Just like before," I always said. "That we got drunk. Really drunk. That I don't remember anything after being in the garden that night."

A pause.

"Okay. Because the way we found you in the grove . . . it looked like maybe you tried to go after them, or something."

"I don't know, Summer."

"Okay."

And then the silence, and then the "I'd better go" from her, and the click on the line as she put the phone down, and then just me, alone, wondering if she could hear the lie in my voice.

Because I did know. I knew exactly what had happened to Wolf. I was there. I saw it.

And I was the only one who seemed to remember it.

# TWENTY-FIVE

SUMMER HAD TOLD ME IT WAS BEST NOT TO COME round for a while.

Just a little while, she had said on the phone when we were a few days into this nightmare, until they could all stop feeling like they were under a microscope. Her parents weren't happy about the police's involvement. Because, what—they could have handled it better on their own?

No. Because they could have handled it quietly. Secretly. The Grace way.

Fenrin was the one who had called the police. He'd taken charge, ringing Wolf's parents, calling his friends in the city, checking, alerting, growing louder and more desperate with every phone call. Wolf's parents had come to stay at the Grace house while the police search continued, and they were still there. Another reason for me not to go over there and be caught in the midst of their grief. I was relieved to stay away, more than anything else. The lie I'd told Summer about not remembering anything lay gasping and flopping like a dying fish between us, and I couldn't believe she couldn't see it, smell the stench of it.

I should tell her.

No. I'd wait.

Did Fenrin remember? If so, why wasn't he saying anything?

No. I'd wait until Fenrin said something. If he never remembered, there was absolutely no point in ever bringing it up. They assumed Wolf was lost to the sea at this point, anyway. I'd just cause them all more pain. I didn't want that. I'd never, ever wanted that. I wanted to keep them from pain because I loved them. That was what you did with loved ones, wasn't it?

I shut my eyes. Summer was on the phone again, and I had picked up this time, unable to stop missing the sound of her voice. I let the words in my ear wash over me, knowing I was a coward, feeling the coward's sickness rising up from my belly, bulging in my throat. We were back in school tomorrow, and I was utterly, completely dreading it.

When I opened my eyes again, my mother was standing in my doorway.

"Summer," I said into the phone. "I have to go. Yeah. See you at school. By the lockers? Okay. Yeah. Bye."

I put my phone down.

"So that was Summer Grace," she said, her arms folded.

I waited, wary.

She launched straight in. "You know, all those times you were on the phone, or texting me to say you were at a friend's house, or out in town with some people, and I never gave it a thought.

Because you never told me it was the Graces you were friends with. And I suppose I still wouldn't have known if not for this poor Wolf boy disappearing."

I felt my hackles rise, defending me from attack. "You never asked me. You never ask me anything."

"I don't keep tabs on you. I'm not that kind of mother. I let you have your freedom, as long as you don't do anything silly with it—"

"Like have friends?"

"Like have *those* friends."

"What's wrong with them?"

She sank into the doorway. The frame dug into her soft, round shoulder. She always looked tired.

"There's a lot said about that family around town, love, and not much of it's good."

"You're judging them based on gossip?"

Mom shot me a sharp look. "I just want what's best for you."

I hated this line. It meant nothing at all. It was a line you could use to justify anything you liked, and she often did.

"It's a big school," she offered, after a moment. "Lots of kids you could hang out with."

"Mom, there's no one else for me."

"Don't be silly. You're a bright girl. Funny. Well read." She tried to grin at her longstanding bookworm joke, the one I used to feel proud about whenever she made it. "Anyone would love to be your friend."

My laugh came out watery and childlike. "No, they wouldn't."

"Yes, they would! You just have to give them a chance. You

never give it a *chance*. How do you know it won't suit you if you don't try it?"

*It* meant *normal*. It always meant normal.

"Mom," I said. I was pleading. I could never make her *see*. Why couldn't I speak her language? Why couldn't she speak mine?

She shuffled. "If you want . . . help," she said carefully. "We can—"

I buried my face in my hands. "Please, please, not this again."

"Your father—he meant well."

"He wanted to lock me up!" I said, my voice rising. "He thought I was crazy!"

"He just . . ." She cast around wildly. "He just *suggested* it—"

"He'd already signed the forms! He didn't want to deal with me! He just wanted to get rid of me!"

I sank downward into myself. I was drowning again. Just like last time with my father. Just like every time. Drowning, clawing desperately up.

"What's wrong with me?" I whispered.

"Nothing," she said, so forcefully that I looked up. "There is *nothing* wrong with you. You are normal and you are fine. So you listen to me. You'll stop seeing those Graces. They are no good for you. No good, do you hear me? Look at what's happened. Drunken parties, a boy dead." She rubbed her face. "Life isn't all fun and playacting because, sooner or later, the fun stops, and all that's left is misery. I'm sorry, but there it is. You just have to get on with things, sweetheart. You have to learn to be happy with who you are and what you've got."

It felt like I had a pillow over my face, suffocating me.

She shifted, obviously pleased that the conversation had gone the way she'd wanted it to. "Now come downstairs, and I'll make us some tea. And you should get ready for school tomorrow. It's a new year. A new start."

When she left my room, I noticed how she'd never put a foot in it the whole time. She never came near me anymore.

I heard her heavy tread down the stairs.

There was nothing I could ever say that she would ever understand, and it had always been this way, and it would always be this way. She and I lived in parallel universes, similar enough from the outside, but look closer and you'd see subtle differences, here and there. Tiny little changes that kept us worlds apart.

I was alone in this.

No, not alone. I still had Summer.

# TWENTY-SIX

ON THE FIRST DAY OF SCHOOL, I TURNED IN TO A COR-
ridor and caught sight of Summer leaning against my locker.

She was surrounded by people, crowding close, trying to share
in her tragedy. Her long black hair was in a plait down her back.
Black jeans. Buckled biker boots. Oversized checked shirt that
rested against the tops of her thighs, the sleeves turned up into
thick cuffs that hung against her forearms.

She didn't see me as I bolted back the way I'd come. That
moment, the moment I was running away from, was supposed
to be our big reunion after days and weeks of "no, it's kind of
weird right now." We were supposed to be the only two people
in the corridor who would understand what the other was going
through. Everyone else would make a shell around us and we
wouldn't even notice them.

It was supposed to be like that.

But now that I was confronted with Summer for real, I felt
like my body was turning inside out. What would happen to me

when I saw Fenrin, or Thalia? How would my body betray me then?

Maybe I'd hoped I could slip back into school and everything would be the way it was before the holidays. I knew how stupid that idea was the moment I stepped through the gates. Never before had I gotten the distinct feeling that everyone I passed knew exactly who I was and had already heard a hundred different rumors about me. Their eyes assessed me like they were deciding which one they were going to believe.

First period was homeroom, orienting us to the new school year. I couldn't get into the classroom fast enough. I was the first one there, leaving behind the crowds milling the hallways as they squealed at each other and caught up on holiday gossip. A shocked whispering frenzy about what had happened to the Graces had already begun, rolling through the student body faster than a wave, though it seemed like everyone already knew everything there was to know about it.

Of course they did. This whole town was tuned to Radio Grace.

New year meant new rules and new seats, so I chose a desk right at the back in the corner. I kept my head down as people came in, which meant I wasn't sure if they were staring at me or not.

We were officially waiting for our new homeroom teacher to show, but the buzzing in the room had nothing to do with his absence and everything to do with the fact that Summer hadn't walked in yet. I tensed every time the door opened, but it was never her. I wondered if she'd try to sit next to me or go for her old friends again.

Like Lou, who was leaking tears noisily at her desk a couple of rows ahead of me. "What an amazing guy he was," she sniffled. "It's just so tragic."

"Oh my god, did you know that guy who died?" said someone else sympathetically. Several other people around Lou turned to look with curious faces.

"Wolf?" She said his name with a casual slant to her voice. "Oh yeah, I met him loads of times. We hung out together at parties. He was so great. Such a nice guy."

My heart contracted painfully.

"Where's Summer?"

Lou sniffed. "She's got a meeting with the headmaster and the counselor, so she's skipping homeroom."

Disappointment flooded me. Relief crept up in its wake.

"Wow. This must be so awful for her. He was their best friend, right?"

"I think he grew up with them. He was practically a cousin or something," Lou said. "More like family than friends."

Gemma was lining her eyes in a compact mirror. "I don't know why she's even back in school."

At that moment our new homeroom teacher swept in, launching immediately into an eye-watering speech about how important this year was going to be for us all. He even mentioned Summer with a sorrowful, grave air, and told us all to be sympathetic to her needs at this difficult time.

I was close to choking myself just to be out of this sycophantic vomit show.

It went on like this until lunch. Stares and whispers. I caught words and phrases like "police" and "that girl there, no *there*, walking past us," as I struggled my way through the morning. This was a nightmare. This was a horror film.

Weren't you supposed to act like everything was normal when people were grieving, give them the comfort of a familiar routine? I wouldn't have been able to stand it, people like packs of dogs around me, licking my heels. Teachers giving me sympathetic looks, those awful pity eyes. *You don't have to do any work. Just take it easy, okay? You can leave class if you need to.* The "are you all right" hand on the shoulder. Protective clumps of people surrounding them, closing in, shielding them from the outside world. Some people cried, making sure to do it in public where everyone could see them. These people, I was absolutely sure, had barely ever met Wolf.

Tension always drew eyes, like we were designed to see it clutching at someone's shoulders, the worst of us pointing it out, finding a way to exploit it. My whole body was rigid with it, and it only made me more noticeable at a time when all I wanted to do was disappear.

As the bell for lunch rang, I leapt up so fast out of my chair that it almost toppled over. I caught it just in time, and I skittered out of the classroom with my face heating, knowing everyone was watching me, and went straight to the library. It wasn't hiding, I told myself. If Summer wanted to find me, she could, just like the first time. In the meantime, I could be alone.

Except I'd forgotten about the one person you could find in the library more regularly than me.

* * * * *

Marcus was by himself, while the rest of the school was stuffed into the cafeteria, the better to gossip freely, churning the same rumor mill that had cast him as some sort of sadly obsessive pervert. He was no such thing. He was someone who had snared Thalia.

*That's what someone spelled by a Grace looks like,* I thought.

I wondered if I was looking into a mirror.

I remembered what he'd said the night of the party. His shameful, desperate abandon. The knife in his hand.

In the library, Marcus looked up, and his eyes landed on me, and I felt a shiver going down my spine. His mouth opened as if to speak, but suddenly I just couldn't face it.

He'd ask about Wolf, wouldn't he? And what would I say?

I ducked my head, walked back out, and spent lunch in my empty homeroom instead.

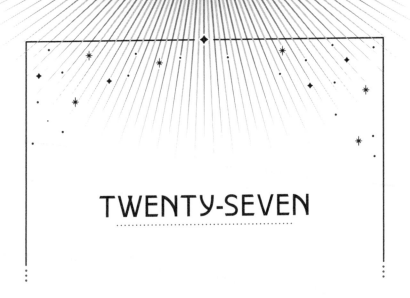

# TWENTY-SEVEN

*IS SOMETHING WRONG? WHY ARE YOU AVOIDING ME?*

I cupped my hand around the note.

I was afraid and glad at exactly the same time, the strangest sensation. She still wanted to be my friend. I still had her. I wasn't alone.

I wrote on the back and folded up the note, sliding it onto the desk next to me. I could see it, just for a second, the barest hesitation as the girl there contemplated trying to read it.

Then she passed it to Summer, still folded.

*Parental unit told me I couldn't see you anymore. Can't be obvious.*

I watched her read it, then scribble something back in tiny letters at the bottom.

*Meet at the end of my lane, midnight tonight?*

\* \* \* \* \*

I waited until my mother's bedroom door was closed, and the tiny television in her room was pouring out a comfortable burr of canned laughter.

I crept down the stairs, every muscle creaking with effort, and slipped out the back door and through the communal garden we shared with the rest of the building. It had been raining a lot the past few days, and the garden's concrete ground was dark with patches of wet, but tonight the air was clear and fresh. I breathed in deeply as I walked, feeling the tight band around my middle ease up. Air was good. Air cleaned. I felt like I was surfacing. Just the thought of the house, Summer, spells, and secrets got me twitching and itching, nervous and afraid and excited all at once.

When I reached the top of their lane, I had to switch on a flashlight. It was pitch black around here—no street lamps. I kept it pointed downward just in front of me, hoping no one was around to catch me looking dodgy as hell. I checked my watch. Ten to midnight. I found a spot underneath the hedge, sat down and curled up, waiting, the flashlight dangling loosely from my hand, listening for noises.

It was so still and soft down this way, so sheltered and alone. This place was like a bowl they couldn't climb out of. Too much honey at the bottom to suck on to bother thinking about what might lie over the lip of that bowl.

As my eyes adjusted, the house made a black, brooding shape against the sky. It was clear, the stars full out. Sitting in the dark, listening to the cool rustle of the grass in the night wind, alone and still, I felt a kind of peace, the first in weeks. It felt natural. We were supposed to sit in the dark, *with* it, not ward it off with electric lights and buildings like cold, square cocoons. After a while I thought I could hear the sea, a rolling, perpetual murmur underneath life. A rolling that would go on after I was dead.

A rolling that had claimed Wolf.

My heart shriveled. My peace was gone. I felt cold and shitty and small and scared and awful. The black pressed in on me. Where the hell was Summer?

I checked my watch under the flashlight. Half past twelve.

Should I go? Had it all been a lame kind of joke?

No. She wouldn't do that to me. Not Summer.

I stood up, legs stiff and jerking, and made my way slowly down to the house. My feet made so much noise over the sandy gravel I was convinced the whole place would be flooded with light, everyone awake and calling the police to report burglars. But when I reached the front garden it was dark and still. I went through the wooden gate that took me down the side of the house. I remembered the last time I'd done this in full daylight, sun streaking over my shoulders, lying with Wolf in the garden, his stomach muscles twisting as he talked to me in a low voice about secrets but not the one secret he should have, and I had to stop for a moment as my insides rippled; in a panic I thought I might be sick there and then. But it passed. I'd learned that every feeling passed, eventually; except love, and except hate.

I knew which window was Summer's, but I was still terrified of getting it wrong. Picking up the smallest pebble my grasping hand found, I stood for the longest time, too nervous to throw. Twice my arm went up, and twice it came back down.

But I'd come all this way.

And then Wolf flashed in my head, and the pain took over, and my arm came up by itself and loosed. The pebble clacked against the bottom of Summer's window.

The lights would come on. I'd be caught like a rabbit, crouching and cringing.

But nothing happened.

I waited.

Nothing.

I took another pebble and threw, quickly this time. It rattled against the pane and then fell on the window ledge and stayed there.

*Please, Summer. Wake up.*

I waited. I couldn't do it again. I waited under the moon as it bathed the back of the house in silvery light, and I closed my eyes and felt every bit of life drain out of me. They'd find me in the morning, curled up in the garden, comatose.

"Hey."

A sharp whisper.

I looked up, nerves dancing and jumping. She was at the back door.

She turned as soon as I was near, disappearing silently back into the darkness of the house. I followed, easing the door shut, taking my shoes off and carrying them for fear of making noise. We walked through the house, and I felt like it was breathing around me.

When we got to her room, Summer closed the door behind us. She switched a lamp on. The place was spotless. Another sign of the alternate reality we seemed to live in these days.

"Sorry," she said in a low voice. She was fully dressed, her boots and coat on. "The parents are asleep and Fen's not in, but I had to wait until Thalia went to bed. She's usually out like a light by eleven, but she hasn't been sleeping that well recently."

I slid onto the end of her bed.

She seemed so normal. So Summer. Wasn't she supposed to

look different? Like a shadow of herself? Shouldn't some kind of pain be etched all over her in thick, sharp lines?

She perched on the bed next to me and started unzipping her boots. I felt an urgent itch between my shoulder blades, a feeling that made my stomach turn over uneasily. I shouldn't be here.

We both waited.

"How are you" was so ridiculous it hurt.

"This is so awful" was redundant.

There was nothing, nothing to say.

"I'm sorry," said Summer.

Except that.

I turned to look at her. It was the first close-up look I'd had in so long. She wasn't quite the same. She seemed kind of hollow, like all her insides had been scooped out and replaced with something thin and collapsible.

"I haven't been around," she sighed, rubbed her neck. "I'm really sorry. I didn't mean to avoid you like that after what happened, but it was all just too much. And his parents, they've been basically living here the last few weeks. Everything is just so strange right now. I mean, he can't be dead. He just can't."

I wanted to say how sorry I was, too. It had come out easily from her, but the word seemed so ridiculous in my mouth that it stuck in my throat and choked me.

"How . . ." I plunged ahead before I could stop myself. "How's Fenrin?"

Summer's face twisted. "Not good," she said quietly.

My tone was careful. "Yeah. I can imagine. I mean, I can't. Not really. But it must be the worst for him."

I felt her gaze on me like a heat lamp.

But she still didn't say anything. She still didn't trust me enough to tell me, and that hurt—so I told her instead. It was bravery, but it was also, *Look what you didn't know I knew. And see, I kept this secret for you, from everyone, even though I've been carrying it around for weeks. See how loyal I am.*

"Summer . . . I lied to the police," I said. "I remember something about that night."

"What?"

Not a "what do you remember?" A "what" of utter disbelief.

I ploughed on. My stomach was trying to climb up my throat.

"I know why I wasn't with you guys in the morning. You and Thalia. I woke up in the middle of the night and I saw Fenrin leaving. I didn't realize Wolf was with him, he must have been ahead. Anyway, I saw him go and I wanted to know what he was doing. So I followed his flashlight down to the cove."

I had still been drunk, and it had seemed to take forever, watching that bobbing circle of light and trying not to let it get away. It wasn't until we hit the dunes that I understood where we were going. There was only one flashlight, so I thought it was only him. Fenrin. Like the police, I supposed he'd gone down there to swim. And this was my chance.

No joking around this time. I'd ask him how he really felt about me. Maybe he'd just been awkward in the grove earlier because I'd taken him by surprise. He'd told me he liked me. Maybe he just needed time to work out what I was to him. Maybe we'd even sit on the beach together under the moonlight, and he'd pull me to his chest like he'd done on movie night, and we'd talk about everything. He'd tell me secret things, and I'd tell him secret things, and he would lean in, his grin softened by desire, and he'd kiss me. Maybe more.

I knew it might not go the way I'd had it in my head for so long, but it would still be electric, even awkward electric. We'd have plenty of time to get better at it, and we wouldn't be able to get enough of each other. We'd be that couple that everyone is loudly sick of and quietly jealous of who are always touching in public, who have to be near each other at all times.

I was drunk. It had made sense in my head at the time. It had seemed like the only thing to do.

It must have taken me longer than I'd thought to get down there. I know I stumbled once or twice. And it was lighter than I'd expected—the moon was full, low over the sea, and the sky was clear, which meant everything was gray and silver. It also meant there was enough light to see them by.

At first I thought they were fighting. I got closer and closer, and I was standing full up, out in the open, but they didn't even see me.

They *were* fighting.

But they weren't.

I saw Wolf's curly black hair and Fenrin's smooth arms. They were making the strangest noises, and I thought, it can't be what I think it is because who the hell makes noises like that? But they were, and then I saw Wolf pin Fenrin to the sand, and Fenrin gave a kind of a snarl, and then Wolf dipped his head down and they were kissing like dogs ate, and it was kind of disgusting.

But I couldn't stop watching.

Their jeans were dragged down almost past their hips and I saw the crouched Wolf press his thighs down and I heard

Fenrin groan. Their arms tangled and Fenrin's feet dug into the sand.

I saw them, and they didn't see me.

To Summer, I said, "Fenrin and Wolf, they . . . I think they were seeing each other."

She didn't reply.

"I saw them," I tried. "Um, they were kissing."

"That's what you remember? That you saw them kissing?"

"Yeah," I said.

"And then what?"

I swallowed. "I left. I ran back."

*You miserable coward*, said the coal-black and coal-bright voice inside me that I hated and loved.

But there was a point where I *had* run. I had run until I'd reached the grove, and then I must have collapsed because the next thing I remembered was waking up, morning light in my eyes. I was telling Summer the truth.

*Telling part of the truth is not the same as telling the whole truth.*

Summer leaned back. "Man," she said, shaking her head.

I watched her.

She laughed, relieved. "Oh, god, you really scared me for a second there. I mean, River—I already knew about Fen and Wolf. We all did."

"Why didn't . . ." I tried not to sound as deeply wounded as I felt. "Why didn't you guys tell me?"

"I don't know, really. I guess we thought you already knew. I mean, it was so obvious."

Obvious.

It was so *obvious*.

Then why hadn't I seen it?

*Because you didn't want to.*

"It's been that way for years," said Summer. "Thalia knew from the beginning. They didn't tell me until later. And then they only admitted it because I threatened to scream the house down unless they did. Protect the baby sister." She gave me a bitter smile. "It's our natural instinct, you see, to lie. It's hard to fight against."

"But . . . he's always had all those girlfriends."

"He likes girls, too, I think. Just never anyone the way he likes Wolf. He's been in love with him since they were kids."

No wonder my spell hadn't worked. He was already in love with someone else. Could magic not fight against that? Couldn't you change people's minds? Otherwise, what was the point of it?

Why hadn't it fucking *worked*?

If it had, none of this would have happened. If they'd just *told* me, none of this would have happened. Wolf would still be alive. We'd be the Graces, we'd be together, we'd be giggling and getting wasted, and everything would be beautiful and passionate and perfect.

I was so angry. I sat there and I was so angry I could have burst and killed everything in the universe right there and then.

She saw something in my face because she said, "What's wrong?"

I could feel my arms trembling with the effort of holding in all my hate at the unfairness of the world, the exact set of circumstances, things that had to be timed in just such a way to make Wolf dead. There were so many ways it could have been prevented. We'd never even have known it as a possibility. We'd have just gone on with our lives, and death would have had to slink off by itself, utterly beaten.

"What's the point?" I said. "What's the point of magic and spells when it never turns out like it should?"

Summer drew back, ever so slightly.

"Why do I get the feeling sometimes," she said all slow, as if testing the words out, "that you only like me because you think I'm a witch?"

I gaped at her. "I *think* you're a witch? What does that mean?"

"It means that I wonder if you even see me. Or if all you see is a Grace. I think it would straight up kill you if you realized how ordinary we are." Her eyes were curved in half moons of bitter amusement. "Wow, how disappointed in us you'd be."

"No. No. This is another test of yours. Magic exists. I know it does. *It has to.*"

Summer was shaking her head like I'd lost my mind.

"Look, say it does, right? Say it's all true and we really are witches. Take a look at us, then. Do you think magic has made us better? We're not better than you. We're so screwed up it's not even funny. Don't you think we could have . . ." She stopped. She stopped for so long I lifted my eyes a little, just long enough to catch her odd expression, like she was trying to make a funny face.

Then I got it. She was trying not to cry.

"Don't you think Wolf could have just, like, *not died*, if we were these amazing magical beings you're so desperate to believe we are? Don't you think he could have protected himself somehow against something as stupid as drowning?"

A part of me had wondered about that. But he couldn't, and

he hadn't, and all I had now was the awful truth about magic that I'd suspected from the start—that it didn't just fix things, that it wasn't as simple as that. Because this was real life, and nothing was ever simple.

Summer sighed, a riffling shaky sound. She leaned back, drawing her slim legs up against herself. "It's like . . . that's why I like you. You're so *you.* You act like nothing could ever be more certain in your life than being *you.*"

*Because I'm the best actress you've ever met,* I wanted to scream in her oblivious face. *Because I'm pretending to be a Grace.*

"You really don't get it at all, do you?" I said. "No one wants to be who they really are. No one except people like you."

"People like me?"

"People who get all the luck in the world and don't even know it. All the money you'd ever need, all the friends and the chances. The beautiful house and the beautiful *things* and everything is just so easy for you, isn't it?"

She blinked rapidly.

"Look," she said, her voice sharper. "I get it, okay? You have your divorced mother and your father who just up and left you and your government housing and your beans on toast for lunch. You need magic because you think that'll give you control over your life."

"Oh my *god.*"

"But no one has control," she insisted. "You've got to let it go."

"Stop the therapy talk. Please, I can take anything from you but that. The 'poor you' pity party when you look at me. Is that why you became friends with me? Charity case?"

Summer looked horrified. "No!"

But I could sense the panicked "maybe" lying just underneath her skin. I remembered all the lunchtimes where she'd given me her food, saying she wasn't hungry, or she'd already eaten two breakfasts. What did they see when they looked at me? What did they *really* see? A poor little powerless ugly duckling they could make over with secrets and magic? The desperate new girl, hanging on their every word, willing to do anything to bask in their sunlight?

Is that what they'd thought of me all this time?

My fury was coming, and with it the fear that was always swept along in its wake, drowning in its tidal wave.

I had to go. Now. Before I let myself think one more thought or say another word. I got up and left Summer's room, running down the stairs. I heard her call, but I wasn't going to stop. I couldn't stop. I walked out the front door this time, posting the key back through the mail slot after closing the door. It was Thalia's—it had that amethyst drop dangling from the plaited keychain.

Why did I always cry with my fury? Why couldn't I be steely, powerful magnificence? What the hell kind of reaction was it to *cry* when you were angry? My chest felt like a screw was being drilled into it, tightening everything around it, because she just didn't see it and so I couldn't explain.

I couldn't explain because there was no telling what would happen if I tried.

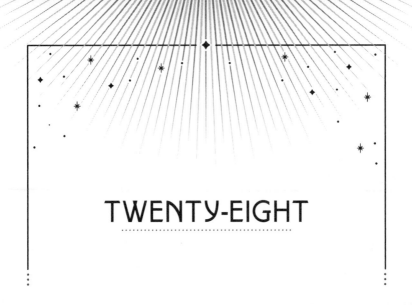

# TWENTY-EIGHT

IN THE MORNING, SUMMER WAS WAITING FOR ME OUT-side the school gates.

She stood there, in the way of everyone, the crowd parting around her like a wave around a rock. People talked to her, and she gave them absent smiles. They tried to stop, but two bodies caused a blockage and the complaints behind them began, so they had no choice but to be swept along, away from her. She didn't even turn her head to watch them go.

She saw me before I saw her. There was no escape.

The crowd had thinned to a trickle by the time I reached the door, but it didn't stop the stares as I walked up to her, my grip tightening on my bag straps.

"I'm sorry," I said, immediately. "I'm sorry, okay?"

It was the most awkward apology in the history of humanity. I heard the brittle anger and shame in my voice and cringed.

Her face softened. "Don't be an idiot. It's fine."

And then she swept me into a hug.

My nose was buried into her hair. It smelled of licorice. She was so alive underneath her shirt. I could feel the smooth planes of her back under my hands, the alive, beating warmth of her. Her arms had gone all the way around me, crushing me to her. I wondered what she smelled on me. I wondered if desperation had a smell.

I pulled away.

"I just got so angry," I said haltingly. "I didn't want you to see me like that. I had to leave. I'm not good when I'm angry."

"*You wouldn't like me when I'm angry*," she said in a droll voice. "You're like She-Hulk."

I tried to laugh.

Summer sighed. "God, I've had screaming matches with every member of my family recently. I get it."

She took my hand and pulled me into the building. Stares followed us like spotlights.

"I said some shitty things to you last night," she said, not looking at me. "You know we don't see you as a charity case, right?"

"Yeah, I know," I said, with conviction I didn't feel.

"Okay, good. I don't want to be one of those horrible people who don't even know their own privilege, you know?"

"Sure," I tried.

I tugged her hand to get her to stop beside my locker, and I popped the door open.

"So let's forget it?" she said, hopefully, and I melted.

"It's forgotten," I said. "Like it never was."

"Good," she sang, hanging off my locker door.

If only everything in life were that easy.

As I rummaged through my textbooks, I felt her come close to my ear, her voice low. "Listen, we could use your help with something."

Despite everything, my skin tingled in that old familiar anticipation.

"What is it?" I murmured.

"We've been trying to get Fen's memory back."

*Oh, Jesus.*

"We've tried every charm we know, and nothing is working," she said. "I said I thought it was because his brain has blanked it out on purpose, and he just . . . *lost* it with me. He just needs some kind of closure, you know? I keep telling him, look, you don't really want to remember seeing your . . . you know, *drown*. How completely heart-stoppingly awful would that be? He's so angry and devastated. He's so . . . ."

She stopped. In complete, panicking alarm, I could see her eyes filling with tears.

It wasn't just Wolf they'd lost that day. Now they were losing Fenrin, too. Thalia was halfway to basket case. Summer was desperately trying to hold them all together, but they were tearing themselves apart. She needed me.

She needed me, and I needed to step up, and screw the consequences. I would take whatever was waiting for me at the end of this. That was what it was to be brave.

"You were there," she said. I looked up at her, sick with sudden adrenaline. "I know you left and you don't remember what happened afterward, but you saw them together in the cove. I think you're the missing piece. If we include you in the spell—maybe we could get *your* memory back, at least? Would that . . . would that be okay?"

Her eyes flashed past my shoulder, and I heard a voice behind me.

"Yes, River, *would* that be okay?"

I'd know that drawl anywhere.

Fenrin moved around me, coming to rest beside Summer.

It was the first time I'd really seen him up close for weeks, and he looked, truth be told, kind of awful. It was easy to romanticize tragedy, like you suddenly transformed into some sort of Byronic hero, sitting in darkened rooms with crystal glasses of whiskey, hair tousled and artfully lank from all those sleepless nights staring at the walls and cursing the gods.

Fenrin looked a lot like he'd been doing exactly that. His eyes were bloodshot, rimmed with red. His hair had dulled to a dirty blond, and his skin was almost gray in places.

I stared at him, too shocked to speak.

"Yeah," he said with a smile. "I look like shit, don't I?"

I opened my mouth, but nothing came out.

"So." He folded his arms. "I hear you saw us that morning in the cove."

My eyes flickered to Summer. Her whole frame was tense.

"Um," she said. "Well, I had to tell him, River. We tell each other stuff."

"We tell each other everything," Fenrin corrected.

"You mean, apart from the time we did a spell on Thalia without telling her?" I said. "Apart from the fox heart spell she did against Marcus without telling *you*? Apart from probably a hundred other things you guys hold back in your hearts like future ammunition?"

I hadn't meant that to come out. I had meant to think it, not say it.

"Well, well. You're so eloquent when you choose to be, aren't you?" said Fenrin, sounding amused rather than angry. "Don't stop now, let's just get it all out in the open. So you saw us. Wolf and me."

He wasn't even bothering to keep his voice down. Curious looks were tossed our way.

What was I supposed to say?

"Go on," he goaded. "What did you see?"

His feet digging in the sand. Wolf's hands on him, holding him down. The way their jeans were dragged down past their hips.

"What do you mean?" I said, my cheeks heating.

"Did you see him die?"

"Fen," Summer warned, his name a humming sound in the back of her throat.

"Did you?"

"Of course she didn't. Leave her alone."

"Summer, I love you, but kindly fuck off," Fenrin said calmly, and her mouth snapped shut, her eyes hurt. "So you don't remember anything about what happened?"

There was a crowd gathering, listening in. I could feel it around the edges of me.

"Why are you doing this?" I stammered out.

Where was the Fenrin who used to pull me to his chest and whisper secrets in my ear, who did a spell with me in the woods to save his sister, to save his family? Who laughed and flirted with me as easily as breathing? There was no trace of him in this glass-eyed boy. This boy who looked one step away from an awful precipice.

"You've been avoiding us," he said. "It's been weeks since you've come to the house. Summer said you could barely talk to her on the phone, but at least you talk to her. When you pass *me* in the corridors, god, never mind talking, you won't even look at me. Why?"

My gaze slid to Summer. She was stricken. Stricken but mute. However reluctant she was about how this was playing out, she was not going to stop it.

I guess I understood that. I would always come in second to them.

"I just . . . feel bad," I said.

"Why?"

"Do I need to spell it out? Because of Wolf. I liked him," I whispered, and the awful truth of it hit me. I *had* liked him. Sullen, intriguing, unexpectedly kind Wolf.

"So did I," Fenrin said, nodding. A horrific understatement. How could my pain compare to his? "Which is why I'm like this, River, I think you can get that. And I think you know why I'm pushing you. Because I think I know why you've been avoiding us. You *do* remember, don't you?"

I was a maddened, fluttering moth, trying to escape, attracted back to the burning light, trying to escape, back to the light, away, back.

I hadn't prepared for this. It should have felt momentous. My full confession. Here they were, waiting for me to speak the truth at last, and all I could feel was the burn at the back of my throat that told me I wanted to be sick.

"Yes," I said, and out of the corner of my eye I saw Summer recoil.

"What did you see?" said Fenrin, his voice flat and calm.

"I saw you there, both of you, in the cove. And you were so close to the shoreline, but he was closer. You'd left him behind and you were coming up to me, to talk, maybe to explain. I don't know. And this wave . . ." I swallowed. "This wave, it came out of nowhere. It came and it knocked him off his feet. Then he comes back up, and for a second I think it's fine. But it's not. Because before he can get out of the water, another wave comes, bigger than the first. And it rolls over him. And when it pulls away, he's gone. He's just gone."

"Oh my god," said Summer, and her voice was tearful. It tore at me.

Fenrin put his arm around her and hugged her to his side. His voice, when it came out, was low and vicious.

"Did you know that his parents don't believe the police? They think he ran away. They think he's still alive." Fenrin's eyes were half-closed, as if he was in pain. "I thought he was still alive, too. Even though I knew, the more time went by, that it was impossible. Every day I've been waiting for him to come back. You could have saved us that."

"Why didn't you say anything?" Summer choked out. "Why would you keep that from us?"

"I don't know. I don't know." Panicking, I ran through explanations in my head—but there was no reason I could give them that would save this. "Everything was so messed up. And with the police—none of you remembered anything except me, so I figured it was best if I didn't, either. It would have looked weird if it was only me that remembered, and I was there when it happened. I was scared. The whole thing was so . . . it all happened so fast."

I was losing them. I could see it. I was powerless to stop it.

"I'm sorry," I whispered. "I'm so sorry."

Fenrin shook his head. "It's too late for that."

I watched him walk away, Summer pressed against his side.

I watched them walk away from me, and did nothing.

# TWENTY-NINE

I FOUND THE FIRST ONE HANGING FROM THE HANDLE of my locker.

It was a tiny doll made of sticks of wood, no bigger than my thumb, a shapeless piece of orange cotton wrapped around it like a dress. Little black daubs for eyes. A piece of string around its neck, the other end tied to the locker handle like a noose.

At first I thought it might be a bizarre gift from Summer. A secret message of some kind.

It was a message, but not a good one.

Then I came into homeroom one day and found the chair I always sat on wrapped tightly in reams of black ribbon.

I knew exactly what that one meant.

Every morning, in those few nothing seconds before I woke up properly, my life was a blank slate, and I was just a girl with everything before me. Then I remembered the way things really were and I started to feel sick.

My mother's way of noticing was to ask me if I needed to go

back on the meds I'd been taking just after Dad disappeared. I didn't have the strength to get angry with her—I knew it was only her way of trying to help me. I told her no. I didn't want to shut everything out like I had back then. Maybe it was dangerous, but I wanted to feel this, every minute of it.

She didn't press. She never pressed. I couldn't stop going to school, though—she worked nights now, which meant she was in the house during the day, and there was nowhere in this tiny, claustrophobic town to go without running the risk of being spotted cutting classes.

Every morning I walked up to the school gates, as late as I could make it without getting into trouble, so no one would be there to start whispering when I went past. I went to my locker, scanning for a telltale flash of color or a shape that meant something had been stuck to it or hung from it. More often than not nothing was there. That was the worst thing about it. They were so irregular I could never know when I'd find something, so every minute of every day was spent drenched in expectant dread.

I tried to pass Summer notes in the classes we took together, like before. The first one I watched her read, then screw up and drop on the floor where anyone could pick it up, like there was nothing I could say that deserved to be private. The next couple I left in her locker. I never got anything back from her.

Twice after school I made the trip to the Grace house. If I just turned up there, she'd have no choice but to see me. And maybe the sight of me would click together comfortably in her head, reminding her of all that had gone before, all the things we had done in that place together, how *well* I fit in there—all that was too good to throw away.

The first time I got to the top of their lane and then turned back, nervous. The second time I got as far as the front door before suddenly realizing I was drenched in sweat, my heart trying to punch its way out of my chest. Rather than keel over on their doorstep, I retreated, pulling my phone out, fumbling. My thumb hovered over the 9 button. But as soon as I reached the top of their lane, I was all right.

I felt like eyes watched me walk away. I clutched my phone tightly all the way home on the bus, but the feeling had gone, and I was too afraid of my own treacherous body to try again.

At lunch, Summer was either completely surrounded at a crowded table, or she wasn't even in the cafeteria, outside on the courts, or anywhere else. On those days she was obviously in the thicket, and I always noticed the people missing along with her—Gemma, Lou, Niral—though Niral seemed to be ill a lot at the moment, off school here and there.

For a second, I let myself feel shamefully triumphant about that—maybe my spell was finally working. But a binding didn't make people ill; it just stopped them from doing what you wanted them to stop doing. Niral was likely spearheading this entire campaign against me—the goddamn mastermind of it. She often stared at me in the corridors, nudging her friends as I walked past. Once I saw her near my locker. She caught sight of me, stepped back, and disappeared around a corner fast. When I got there, the dial of my padlock was covered in some kind of oil. I was too afraid to touch it, and had to make do without my textbooks for the rest of the day. Her illness was total coincidence, the universe mocking me. My spell on her had failed. My spell on Fenrin had failed. Our attempts to break the curse had failed.

I would never be a witch.

A crow feather placed carefully under my chair in history class.

Clove rubbed into my coat so it stank of it for days.

Broken eggshell pieces poured into the open slot of my bag when I was turned the other way.

A twisting symbol scrawled onto my locker with a Sharpie.

Every single thing was a form of warding, binding, protection.

Protection against me, not for me.

I waited for a tingling sensation, or something like mild suffocation, something that would tell me their charms were working. But nothing like that ever came. I had bad dreams, but I'd always had bad dreams, and I couldn't honestly say if that was them or me.

I started incessantly calling the Grace house. I couldn't stop myself. If they'd just let me explain.

But no one ever answered.

* * * * *

The noise woke me from one bad dream into another.

That wasn't my mother's voice. It was all smooth, with sweet notes.

And there—a man's low burr, words indistinct.

I cracked an eye open and peered at my alarm clock. Mom had work friends round sometimes, but it was early Saturday morning, which seemed like a strange time for a visit.

Or maybe it was the police again. Maybe the Graces had told them that I'd lied about what I remembered.

Adrenaline got me upright and dressed in a matter of seconds.

I crept down the stairs.

The kitchen door was shut, and the voices were muffled. I hugged the wall, straining to hear. No good. I didn't have to wait long, though. Before I could rabbit back up the stairs, the door opened, and Mom poked her head out. She caught sight of me, and her mouth shut. She'd been about to yell for me, it looked like.

"Oh, you're up, are you? You'd best come down here, then."

She disappeared back into the kitchen. I left the bottom step and stood just outside the door, heart kicking and kicking. It was quiet. Very quiet. What was I walking into? Scenarios buzzed anxiously through my head. Not one of them prepared me for who it was.

Esther and Gwydion Grace were sitting at our rickety kitchen table.

I stood in the doorway, cycling fast through surprise, fear, wariness.

"Hello," said Esther pleasantly. "Late night?"

I regarded her. She shone, luminous, in the dull light of her surroundings. Her hair was loosely wrapped in a thick trail down her back. She seemed the same. But how were you supposed to be when someone close to your family had died? Crumpled, maybe? Something? Gwydion looked like he'd walked straight out of an ancient forest fairy tale and had been persuaded into normal clothes to blend in. There was a plate of biscuits on the table, and they both had mugs of dishwater-colored tea in front of them, big thick mismatched mugs that didn't fit with their supple, fine-boned hands.

I glanced at my mother. The Graces seemed perfectly content to sit and say nothing, but that wasn't her way. Perhaps they'd figured that. She fidgeted, clacking her pink nails on the tabletop.

"Well," she said brightly. "We've been talking quite a bit while you were sleeping, haven't we?"

"We have," said Esther.

I would give them nothing until I knew what their game was because it couldn't be anything good.

"We've been talking about you and Esther and Gwydion's family." Their names sounded so thick and jerky coming out of my mother's small mouth. "About everything that's happened. And we think maybe it's a good idea, right now, to be giving them a bit of space."

"What does that mean?" I said.

Esther's cat eyes were cold. "It means that we are grieving over Wolf right now. Our hearts are broken. Summer and Thalia and Fenrin, they need some time away from everything."

"I'm not stopping them from that."

"Oh, honestly," Mom snapped, growing red. "Put a lid on the backchat for once, please. You're not doing well. You're bad for one another. After what's happened . . . I've had letters from the school, too."

I went still. Most of me didn't care, but there was still a hushed, secretive bit of my soul that wanted to be the normal, popular girl who got great grades, the one people liked. That one who was going to do well in life and make her parents think she was such a lovely girl. They'd smile when they talked about her. You could long for something you'd never been, even if you could never know the real shape of it.

"I know you've enjoyed spending time with Summer," said Esther, her voice soft. "And I'm sure that what happened to Wolf has been hard on you, too, so I'm sure you understand. There'll be no more wild parties. Everyone in my house has spent too long being given free reign to do what they like, and I don't want them to end up like Wolf. You need to stop calling the house every day, and you need to stop coming round."

"You've been calling their house every day?" Mom's face was creased with a dismayed frown. I was silent. Sides had already been chosen before I walked in. I didn't have a chance.

Maybe that was why I said what I said next, the last sting of the bee before dying.

"Is this about the curse?"

The hit I'd scored flickered across Esther's face.

"Excuse me?" she said.

"The curse. The one about how if a Grace witch loves a non-witch, one of them dies or goes mad. I mean, that's part of why you're so obsessive over their private lives, isn't it? You don't let them go out. You don't like them having friends that aren't one of you. You never let people stay over at the house. You interrogated Summer about me because she dared to invite me over to watch movies. I mean, it was just movies. What did you think we were doing?"

I felt a hand grab my arm. "Stop that," Mom said, shocked. "You can't talk like that to them. Apologize right now."

I wouldn't. Not to her.

"Apologize, young lady!"

It was demeaning, seeing my mother flap in their presence like this. Beauty. Glamour. Money. They all weighed heavy on the room, sucking the air out of it until you felt like you had to breathe double time just to stay upright.

Esther held a hand up. "It's quite all right," she said mildly. "She obviously needs to talk. Please, go on." She directed the last at me with a little smile, as if there was nothing else I could say now that would affect her.

So I damn well tried my hardest.

I folded my arms, holding myself together. "You threw Marcus out of your house, and you terrified Thalia into cutting him out completely, making her miserable and driving him crazy because he's in love with her. That's not a curse. That's just cruel. Your cruelty is her cruelty now. She's learning from the best."

"I don't know what you've been told—"

I ploughed on over her. If I stopped now, I wouldn't start again. "They don't have to tell me, I've *seen* it. I've seen how Fenrin could never even show anyone that he loved Wolf. They had to sneak around behind everyone's backs because they were afraid—"

"Because he *knew* it was wrong!" she hissed, suddenly. "He knew it was—"

She stopped. But it was too late because I could already see the word half-formed on her mouth: disgusting.

She thought it was disgusting.

She sighed. "And I suppose it was Summer who told you all of this? What else did she tell you?"

"Why does it matter?" I shot back.

"Because you're not a Grace, so how could you possibly understand us?" Her voice was tinged with a sickly kindness. "You're not like us. You'll never be like us. You want to feel special, don't you? Well, here's the ugly truth—some people are ordinary. The best of them at least have the intelligence to know it. Be a little more mature. You already have a place in the world, and it's here, with your mother. You don't belong with us."

Esther sat back and folded her arms. Her jewelry tinkled.

"I wasn't sure we needed to do this," she said. "But I'm worried for you, River, and for Marcus. You're both very sensitive individuals. We've been discussing it, and we think the best course of action would be to take Summer and Thalia and Fenrin out of school."

"What? You're going to homeschool them?"

"No. They'll be going to boarding school, away from here. Of course, Thalia and Fenrin only have to finish out the year and pass their exams. If they do well, they'll be taking a year out to go traveling together abroad. Summer will stay at her cousins' in the city on the weekends and board at her new school during the week." She gave me a sympathetic head tilt. "You won't be seeing them anymore."

For a moment, I was struck dumb.

"You can't . . ." I swallowed away the crack in my voice. "You can't do that."

"Of course we can." Gwydion's voice was matter-of-fact. "We do what's best for our children. Your mother will understand. So will you, one day, when you have children of your own."

"I'm sure you can make some new friends," Esther remarked, taking a biscuit from the plate in front of her. "You seem like a nice girl. Maybe even a boyfriend? I hope you like surfers—we tend to have those in abundance around here."

She dropped me a wink as if we shared a secret and took a bite out of the biscuit. I felt a panicking fury like vomit in my mouth. I wanted to run. I wanted to hit back. Anything not to feel this yawning black hopelessness that told me I offered nothing, that I was nothing, and always would be until I was dead.

*Some people are ordinary.*

*You don't belong with us.*

"Esther," said Gwydion, leaning toward her.

Her beautiful face had gone bright red. Her throat shuddered.

"Esther."

Her chest tried to heave. She gripped at her throat.

"Oh god, she's choking," Mom breathed. "Water, let me get you water!"

Esther struggled. I was sinking in horror.

This was not happening.

It wasn't.

I could not watch someone else die in front of me, and yet I just stood there, frozen. I heard Mom turn the tap on, splashing and sploshing frantically, but the sound seemed to come from very far away, like a television in another room. I watched Gwydion pull his wife to him and bring his fist down on her back. She was making the tiniest flat sound of no air going in. He took hold of her from behind the chair and pulled his clasped fists back into her stomach. I watched, mesmerized at the violence of it.

Esther was hacking, dragging air in as mashed biscuit leaked out of her mouth.

"Can we have a tissue please," said Gwydion, calm as anything.

Mom brought a box over, her hands shaking. Esther pushed a big handful of tissue to her mouth, cleaning up. Her head hung down as if she were ashamed.

We sat in silence.

"Those bloody biscuits, they're so dry," Mom ventured, in her most tentative voice. "I'm so sorry. I hope you're feeling better, Mrs. Grace."

Esther was staring at her mug. "Perfectly fine, thank you," she replied, eventually. I half expected her voice to come out all squashed, but she sounded the same as before.

"I think we should be going," Gwydion said. He had one arm still protectively around Esther's back.

"Of course. I think we can all agree that it's best if everybody just keeps to themselves for a while. Let people come to terms with things." Mom shot me a look. She had her bright, blank face on. "Thanks for coming to have a chat. I think we've got it all quite clear."

She pulled on my arm, moving me out of the kitchen doorway.

I didn't protest.

I didn't even know what to do now.

Esther and Gwydion stood, maneuvering carefully around the table. He hugged her close and wouldn't let her go. I found myself wondering why he loved her, and how they'd met, and what they had been like when they were my age. Had time hardened her into this frightened, controlling thing, or had she been fixed from early on? What did she believe in? What made her happy?

We watched them go from the front doorstep, and with them I felt the last of me drain away, my light, my life. My coal-black and coal-bright voice was silent. Maybe I'd never hear it again.

"Well," said my mother. "She was a bit snobby, wasn't she?" She put her arm tentatively around my shoulders.

I burst into great, shuddering tears.

Away walked the last chance of fixing me.

Away walked the last chance of ever getting my father back.

He was gone. That was it.

"It's for the best" came my mother's voice above my head, soft and final, as she hugged me to her. "I know you want to believe that everyone can get along, and we're all the same, but people like them stay in their corners, and we stay in ours, and that's how the world works. It's for the best," she repeated.

I wondered, at last, if she was right.

# THIRTY

I WAS LOCKING UP THE CAFÉ WHEN I FIRST FELT IT.

It was Friday night. Only a couple of weeks to Christmas, and two months since Esther and Gwydion's visit.

Things were different now.

I preferred to work these days. I'd been spending all my time alone again, so it made sense to put all those hours of nothing outside of school to good use and get some more money coming in. I'd been lucky enough to stop off at this place just as they'd put up a handwritten sign recruiting for a new waitress. It was better to be busy because busy kept me from thinking. Busy helped me ignore the reaching, yearning feeling in my guts.

I'd given away my witchcraft books to a charity shop. The lady running the place had shot me the filthiest look when she realized what they were—maybe she burned them instead of selling them. I found I didn't really care, one way or the other. That part of my life was over.

It had been a long shift. There was a family who wouldn't

leave, with one of those beautiful golden-haired kids who alternately screamed the house down and charmed the pants off you. They came in regularly, so they must have lived around there. They liked the café because, as the mother told me once, "It's artisanal." I didn't know what to say to that, so I just nodded.

It was a nice place, anyway. Kind of dingy, but Delia, the manager, had done pretty good with the furnishings. She called the style natural vintage, but all I could think of was that sometimes, when I let it, it reminded me of the Grace house, and my heart tipped over.

They did great cakes at the café. People raved about them. There was some small magic in food, I was learning. I wondered sometimes if the baker who made them might be an earth witch—her cupcakes looked and tasted like feelings. Maybe I wished I could be her. I wondered if she was happy. I wondered if she spent all day in chunky earth knits and heavy jewelry, whirling around a warm-tiled kitchen with her fingers covered in flour.

Delia had only just started trusting me to lock up the place by myself on the evening shift. It was a stupid thing to feel pleased about, but there was something so quietly enormous about another human being placing so much trust in you with their things. I didn't want to screw this up. I wanted to be River 2.0, the one everybody liked. Kind of quiet, okay, but reliable and worth having around. This was my second transformation. I liked this one best so far. This one made me feel capable, and normal, and in control. I worked as many weeknights as I could get, and weekends, too. Mom liked that I had a job and my own income again. She said I could be independent. That it would keep me out of trouble.

But as soon as the key turned and the door gave that sliding click, I felt it on my neck, like someone was watching me. When I turned, I was alone on the street.

I had the house to myself that night, at least—Mom was on a night-shift rotation, and I wouldn't see her until late afternoon tomorrow, when she got out of bed. Delia slipped me leftover cake occasionally, as a bonus tip. I was grateful—they made life just a tiny bit more bearable. I had a tub of her homemade peanut butter ice cream in the freezer and a favorite book on standby—my preferred method of temporary forgetting.

Which was smashed to pieces when I got home because Summer was sitting on my doorstep, hunched against the cold.

She was huddled there like a lost puppy, and it was a lie, a big fat lie, because she was no puppy and she had never been lost. She'd cut her hair since disappearing off to boarding school. It was still dyed licorice black, but now it followed the angles of her head, cropped to her skull at the back, flopping forward at the front. She looked like a supermodel.

She broke the bubble first.

"River," she said.

Just her voice, saying my name, was enough to make my insides flare.

"What are you doing here?" I said, astonished. "You can't be here. We don't do this anymore."

We didn't talk. We didn't call. We didn't do anything. I hadn't even seen them around town—Esther had been true to her word. Two months ago they had vanished, and I'd learned to live with the hole they'd left behind.

Summer sniffed, annoyed. "Stop looking at me like I'm breaking the law or something. I just wanted to see you. It's been so long. I just . . ."

She tailed off and hugged her arms close to herself. It was really cold. I had no idea how long she'd been sitting there.

"I just wanted to know how you are," she finished.

"Does anyone else know you're here?"

She hesitated. "No. I'm supposed to be staying at school this weekend, like a good little girl." The dry way she said that last melted me a little. Just a little.

"Look," I said. "It's just better if we stay away from each other. If we stay away, like we've been doing, no one else is going to get hurt, okay?"

"I never agreed to that."

I stared at her. "Are you kidding me? You ignored the hell out of me for weeks, and then you all left! You just left me behind!"

"You lied about Wolf. I didn't take it well, okay? I hate it when people lie to me! It makes me so f—" She stopped. Dragged in a deep breath. "I was angry with you. I couldn't believe you didn't trust me enough with the truth."

I snorted, and she rolled her eyes. "Look, I get why *now*," she said. "Now I've had time to think about it. I guess we're all really good at keeping secrets. And look where that got us."

She shivered. "Please, can we just talk? Preferably inside where my balls aren't going to freeze up and drop off?"

"You don't have any balls."

"Ouch. Well, maybe I've grown a pair since I've been away."

I hesitated.

But it was too late. The moment I'd seen her it was all too

late. I was buzzing again, like I'd spent the last two months without power and she was my own personal battery.

It was just a conversation.

* * * * *

I hunted in the cupboards for hot chocolate while Summer perched at the kitchen table.

"Esther let you come round, then," I goaded as I switched on the kettle.

"She has no idea I'm here. This is the first time since we left that she's not at the house. She and Gwydion are out of the country, frolicking somewhere warm for the weekend, so I took the chance to pay the old hometown a little visit."

I sat down and pushed a mug of hot chocolate toward her, warming my hands on my own. I took a sip to give myself something to do. It was still hot and burned my tongue.

"Can I ask you a question?" she said suddenly.

I waited, wary.

"Do you believe in the curse?"

She gazed at me intently. I opened my mouth and then shut it, caught by surprise.

River 2.0 did not. River 2.0 was normal, and sensible, and recognized that those kinds of things were beguiling but childish fantasy. It was easy to let yourself get all hysterical, to get swept up in the drama of it—but in the end it caused only trouble and hurt.

"I've been thinking a lot about coincidence recently," I said at last. "I mean. Marcus, he's unstable. Maybe he just couldn't handle being shut out."

Summer tilted her head. "The spells we did," she said. "The things that happened. You think it was all just coincidence?"

"Well, none of it worked, did it? I mean, we never saw any real evidence of it."

"Wolf," she said quietly. "He drowned?"

"Of course, he drowned," I said irritably. "I was there. He was drunk and he was standing too close to the water and he drowned." Was she here to pick a fight with me about that again? I'd managed to not think about Wolf for a while now, and I couldn't bear reopening that wound.

For the longest time, she said nothing.

"Are you telling me now that you don't believe?" I prodded. "Because you certainly always acted like you did."

She was staring into her mug.

"I don't know. I don't have any answers," she said. "I never have. It depends who you ask. Ask Fen . . . you know what he'd say." Her mouth pulled into a wry twist. "Ask Thalia . . . you know *she* believes. It's part of why she's so bloody tragic about everything."

"And you're, what? Piggy in the middle?"

"Haven't really made up my mind about it all," she said, leaning back, her gaze resting on my face. "Not yet."

I felt scrutinized.

"What are you here for, Summer?"

She shrugged, evasive. "We were best friends. Not that long ago, you might recall."

The word "best" made my insides lurch.

"Not anymore," I said evenly.

"Come on, you didn't give me a chance. We were still all screwed up over Wolf. Fen was falling apart. Thalia had been falling apart for a while. We just needed time."

"Your mother came in here, into this kitchen, and categorically told me to stay away from you. Like I'm some horrible influence or something. Like I walked in and screwed up *your* life instead of it happening the other way around."

"You did," she said.

I gaped at her. "Me? *I* did? You have no idea the effect you all have on people, do you?"

"What do you want me to say? If I say yes, you can call me arrogant. You can accuse me of playing it up. If I say no, you'll call me blind and stupid. Maybe even a liar. Either way I don't win!"

"Well, this has been fun," I said, pushing my chair back. "But I have a life I have to get back to, and I'm sure you do, too. So thanks for dropping by."

"What?" She looked genuinely panicked, enough to stop me. "I'm not going yet. I can't. We need to talk."

"There's nothing to say."

"Yes, there is!"

"So say it!"

Summer stared at me, wide-eyed. Then she collapsed back in her chair. Her boot slammed against the table leg, slopping hot chocolate over the mug rims.

"God!" she exclaimed. "You never made it easy, did you?"

I was mystified. "Made *what* easy?"

"Telling you I missed you. Telling you that you were my best friend. I don't have best friends. *They're* my best friends. But then you came along, and I realized how much I needed that. You changed us. You changed everything."

She paused, staring at the hot chocolate puddle seeping around the bottom of her mug.

"I seriously have not had a chance to come back home again until now. It's been miserable. I've been all alone, okay? And you didn't try to see me. I'd fantasize in class about how maybe you'd find out the school's address and you'd sneak into the grounds one night and find my window and throw stones at it like you did before. I honestly thought you would. But you never did."

She was inscrutable, rocking back on her chair. Then suddenly it slammed down again, changeable as the wind. The Summer I remembered. Her coyness fell off and she looked me directly in the eye.

"So. Are we going to be best friends again?" She flung her arms wide dramatically. "Despite the world trying to keep us apart?"

The grin threatened to crack my face in half unless I let it surface, so I did. I had all sorts of good reasons for not doing this. For moving on with my life and leaving them in the murky past, a past I would take out only occasionally, like an old photo album buried in a box somewhere in the back of the attic.

There were reasons. Just right now, I couldn't remember what they were.

"Would you tell your parents we were hanging out again?" I said to her.

She tilted her head. "You're going to have to give me more time on that one."

I snorted.

"Would you tell your mother?" she said, soft and knowing.

I took a deep breath. "You're going to have to give me more time on that one."

She grinned. She seemed so relieved, like I'd suddenly made everything right again. We stared at each other, both feeling exactly the same thing, connected, and glad for it. It was a very simple, powerful feeling, to be wanted.

Summer raised her hands. Her silver rings winked in the light. "We need to do it better this time, though. No more secrets. We tell each other everything, otherwise it won't work. It's what you said we should do, isn't it? You got all high and mighty about it. Well, you were right."

I was taken aback that she remembered. "Okay."

"Deal?"

"Deal," I said.

*Deal? Really? You're going to tell her? Everything?*

"I'd better go," she said. "Sorry about the mess." She indicated the spilled chocolate.

"Don't worry about it," I said, sinking into disappointment and trying not to let it show.

She stood, shrugging on her jacket. "Do you want to know what you're doing tomorrow?"

"What?"

"Having breakfast with me."

"I am? Maybe I'm busy. Maybe I'm working."

"You're not."

"How would you know?"

"I know things." She glanced at me slyly. "So? I mean, if you can get past your mom."

A golden warmth spread through me. "She's on a late shift—if you come by at nine, she won't even be back yet. I'll leave her a note."

"Cool. I'll be here just before nine, then."

"Really? I figured you'd tell me it was an inhuman hour or something. Since when do you even know what nine looks like on a Saturday?"

She grimaced. "Oh, boarding school has totally screwed me up. I'll tell you all about it in the morning over eggs, if you like. And I'll tell you a secret. And you tell me one. And that's how we'll start it. We'll just do it, like ripping off a Band-Aid. Secrets and eggs."

"Secrets and eggs," I echoed.

She winked at me, punching her hand lightly into my shoulder as she brushed past.

I heard the front door slam closed.

Tomorrow. Secrets and eggs.

It took a few minutes for the nerves to start kicking in.

This wasn't going to work. How could it? From now until forever, there would always be Wolf between us, his ghost curled around our necks like a cat, weighing us down.

What was I doing?

What was I *doing*?

# THIRTY-ONE

SHE WAS TRUE TO HER WORD—THE DOORBELL BUZZED just before nine.

"Are you even allowed to drive?" I said as I slid into the passenger seat of her borrowed car.

"Nope," Summer replied cheerfully. She had her long black coat on with the oversized buttons and lined knee boots. A red knitted hat capped her raven hair.

"Are you taking lessons?"

"Sally's been teaching me the last few weeks."

I guessed this was the friend at school whose car we now sat in. "Seriously?"

"Esther was never into the idea of us all learning to drive. She always said we didn't need to go anywhere by ourselves that wasn't in this town, until we were actually leaving home for good."

"Wow."

"Yeah."

She pulled out slowly and we headed into town, toward the seafront. She looked like she'd been driving for years. I didn't think she ever bothered with anything she wasn't immediately good at.

"So," she said casually. "What did you tell your mom about where you are right now?"

I glanced at her. She'd never been so worried about my mother before. Was she as nervous as me?

"It's okay," I tried to reassure her. "I left her a note saying I picked up an extra shift at the café. She won't expect to see me until this evening, when she wakes up."

Summer seemed satisfied. It was a short ride, and neither of us talked much. We parked and went to Blue Juice, a cute little place right on the front. It was probably too early to run into anyone from school in here, but I was still jumping in my skin. I wanted them to see us and I didn't want them to see us. Summer seemed to be in the latter zone, as she chose a booth at the back, hidden from the whole place except the table right next to us, and it was pretty empty right now.

I didn't know the waitress, but she might have been a couple of years older than Thalia. She stared at Summer like she had grown two heads. She didn't write down my order, even though I said it twice. Summer was blank on the outside, but inside I could tell she was shrinking, squirming.

"Hello?" I said to the waitress. "Maybe stop staring at her and do your job?"

The waitress gave me a dirty look. "Excuse me?"

"I want scrambled eggs on toast and black ginger-nut coffee.

She wants poached eggs over spinach and green tea with honey. Maybe you should write it down?"

"I can remember it fine," she said. "Everyone round here has a great memory, actually."

She threw Summer a hard stare and then walked off.

"Wow," I tried to joke. "What was all that about?"

She shrugged, sullen.

"Come on."

"The tide is turning," she said, mysteriously. "It does, every so often."

I frowned. "I don't get it."

"It means that some of the more gullible people in this stupid town think we killed Wolf." She laughed, sharp.

"What?" I said, astonished. I wasn't exactly in with the crowd at school anymore, but I hadn't heard anything like that. I wondered if my mother had. I wondered if she just hadn't been telling me. "That's ridiculous."

Summer looked away, fiddling with the corner of the menu.

I watched her. "Do you want to go?"

"No, it's fine. It'll be the same everywhere. They'll get over it eventually."

I cleared my throat, trying to think of things to say.

"Hey," she said suddenly. "I just realized, I've never ever asked you what your favorite color is."

I searched, caught off guard. "That midnight blue, purple velvet kind of color. Yours?"

"Burgundy. Like wine. Like old blood." She grinned. It was a very Summer color.

We went on like that for a while, trading favorite things, and it started to feel better, but everything was still drenched in expectation. Jokes were funnier and words more carefully chosen. Too much had happened, and it crouched between us, an ugly, patient toad waiting for a mistake.

The waitress came back with our food, and despite her venom-tinged silence, our breakfasts looked and smelled amazing. I picked up my fork and opened my mouth to say something stupid about eggs and balls, but Summer was looking away from me, smiling, and I glanced round right into Fenrin's chest.

The world froze.

"Hey," she was saying. "You're disgustingly late. As always."

"Oh, stop your moaning. You had a good substitute." He winked at me.

For a long, long moment, I had absolutely no idea what to do.

Fenrin slid into the booth next to Summer and nudged her. "She doesn't look happy to see me."

"It's been a while," she said.

"It really has." He flashed me a beautiful smile, and I felt my whole body quail.

He looked lovely again, like nothing had ever happened to him. He wore a thick fisherman's sweater over a loose shirt, and his blond hair was tousled by the wind. I could see the top of his turret shell necklace poking just above the V of his collar.

I had not let myself think about him because all that was over, over, filled with pain and shame. And yet now here he was, as if no time had passed at all.

"What . . . are you doing here?" I managed.

"Sorry, I invited him—"

"Sorry, it's my fault—"

Summer and Fenrin both talked at once, looked at each other, and laughed awkwardly.

"It's my fault," Fenrin said again. "I said not to tell you I was coming. I thought maybe you wouldn't show if you knew I was here."

I tried to relax my grip on the fork. "Why on earth would you think that?"

"The last time we saw each other," he said. "I didn't handle things very well. I'm sorry. It was not a good time for me." He spoke carefully, and I wondered if it was to conceal the pain underneath, like speaking carefully, as if he'd rehearsed it, was the only way it would come out.

"Don't worry about it," I said. "I messed up, anyway. I mean . . . I'm sorry, too. I should have . . . I should have told you everything."

He was silent. I stared into my eggs as hard as I could.

"Well, now we're all very sorry for being complete asses to one another," said Summer brightly. "Let's eat before our food gets cold."

I tried to laugh, and stabbed at a yolk.

Fenrin grabbed the menu tucked behind the salt shaker. "What's good here?" he said. His voice was nearly as cheerily forced as Summer's.

And so, in a slow, halting way, it went. Fenrin ordered waffles drenched in wildflower honey, and I kept my eyes down when he ate. I'd never been able to watch him eat without craving him. He and Summer laughed and flicked each other and joked, but there was something to it, an edge I'd never noticed before, and I thought maybe it was new. But then, I couldn't expect everything to be exactly the same between us after all that had happened.

"So what are you guys up to this weekend?" I asked them, after we'd all finished eating.

"Taking advantage of the fact that our parents are away and running riot over the house," said Fenrin, pouring himself some coffee from the pot we were sharing. "You should come round."

"You should come and visit us," Summer said, at exactly the same time.

I laughed. "Guys, you have to stop doing that. It's weird."

"God, stop copying me," Fenrin said, shooting Summer an evil look. She stuck her tongue out at him, but he missed it as he turned back to me. "So?"

"So?" I said.

"So are you coming round? We could watch movies or something, like we used to."

My chest tightened like a vise.

"Probably not," I said slowly. "I have loads of schoolwork to do this weekend."

"Schoolwork?" Summer rolled her eyes. "There are more important things in life. Like this horror film I found about dead serial killers resurrected as ghost clowns." She waggled her eyebrows excitedly.

"Christ alive, Summer," Fenrin said, "we want her to come round and hang with us, not promise to give her nightmares."

I smiled weakly. "Seriously, I don't think I can this weekend."

An awkward silence fell. I should have said yes—I had no idea when I'd be able to see them again. And yet I still couldn't quite face it. Go back to that house with no Wolf in it. That *house*, drenched in memories. Fenrin seemed sanguine, but I got the distinct impression that I'd made Summer angry.

I excused myself and went to the toilet, as much to figure out what to do as anything else. I stared at myself in the mirror, trying to see what they saw. How much did my features betray of me, the real me, the coal-black and coal-bright me?

How long was I going to keep this up for?

When I got back to the table, they were muttering together, but Summer was smiling a little, and my nerves eased.

"Poured you some more coffee," said Fenrin, indicating my mug, and I took it gratefully, as it gave me something to focus on. Summer launched into a long-winded anecdote about a girl at her new school she was sure was the daughter of a famous rock star trying to go incognito, and the tension eased as the conversation changed. They talked about how strict the school was, the beautiful grounds, the tennis courts, the swimming pool, the French teacher who, according to Fenrin, defied all cultural expectations, since he was the worst dresser he'd ever seen.

They talked about new lessons, and new friends, and trying to fit in at the same time as trying to stand out, which was a problem I'd thought only lesser mortals like me grappled with. They asked me about the café, and I talked for a while about the cakes there and about Delia, who was full of stories but told them much better than I did.

We did not talk about Wolf. We did not talk about magic, and we did not reminisce about the things we had done, because all of them, I supposed, contained things we'd rather forget. Had it really gone so wrong for us that this was all we could be now?

They had come to me. I hadn't tried to go back to them. That had to count for something.

They really were funny, though. I was giggling about something stupid; I couldn't stop giggling. We'd moved on to our childhoods, and I was trying to tell them about the toys I used to have, and how for a while when I was really small, I would insist on getting only boxes of colored paper clips as my birthday and Christmas presents because I wanted to make necklaces from them, but I didn't think the story was coming out the way it should have been. I felt like my jaw might be made of chewing gum—when I opened my mouth to speak it stretched out in rubbery strings.

"Hey," I tried, and then I forgot what else I meant to say because my head was so heavy, and I leaned back, feeling sleepy.

I must have been a lot more tired than I'd thought.

I heard Summer saying, "I'm sorry."

# THIRTY-TWO

FOR A WHILE, I THOUGHT I WAS DREAMING.

The room was dark and close, but I recognized it. It was the spare bedroom on the second floor, the one I used to stay in. The rag rug on the floor. The little chest of drawers. The white walls. The bowl of devil stones on the nightstand.

I was dreaming about the Grace house again. This happened sometimes, especially nowadays.

But then my head gave a sharp throb, and my whole body felt like it was rolling, rolling. I stared at the twists in the rug, knotted flaps of color, waiting until everything made sense.

There was a smell lying heavy on the air. Flowers—that was why. Two vases of them perched on the chest of drawers. Another jam jar rammed with thick stems on the windowsill. Scattered loose all over the floor. I turned my head and it seemed to slosh gently. Looking down the length of me I could see that the same flowers had been placed all around my body, resting up against my hip and side.

This was more than a little weird.

Something dark caught my eye—something at the foot of the bed. I sat up, heart rate spiking, head surging, and I saw her. Summer, sitting on the floor, back against the wall, arms between her thighs, hands locked together, watching me.

I tried to make my brain work. This felt like something a stalker would do from some dark drama, like those grim crime shows on TV my mother always watched. But Summer didn't need to stalk me. I was all hers. Hadn't breakfast proved that? Despite everything telling me no, hadn't I let her back in again?

"How do you feel?" she said. I tried to analyze her voice. All I could hear was concern.

"Kind of like I've been punched in the face." My voice was startlingly slurry around the edges.

"I'm really sorry about that. I might have overdone it a bit. We tried to measure right, but I wasn't sure how much coffee there was in your cup. And the flowers, you know." She gestured.

What? No, I *didn't* know. What was she talking about?

She was looking at me, but I wasn't sure what it meant. I couldn't read her. It struck me suddenly that maybe I'd always found her emotions easy to tell because she didn't see any reason to hide them from me. Not me, her best friend.

Now she did.

She was becoming a stranger, a loping, frightening stranger girl with black-ringed eyes. So fast. It was happening so fast. I felt thick and sick in the throat, and maybe it wasn't just because of whatever it was they slipped me in my coffee. She opened her mouth, but the door rattled, her eyes dropped, and Fenrin walked in.

He glanced at Summer, and then his gaze settled on me.

"What the hell is going on?" I said. It seemed to take me years to get the sentence out.

Neither of them answered. There was movement behind Fenrin, and in slipped Thalia.

There they stood, all three of them, looking at me silently.

*Cut her in half and you'd see "Grace" the whole way through,* Marcus had said. *Like rock candy.*

"Well," I said. "If you wanted a reunion, you could have just asked."

"We did," said Fenrin, seriously. "You said no."

"I said not yet." I tailed off as I realized what game they had been playing with me at breakfast. Asking me to the house had been a test. The drug in my coffee was a last resort.

They all seemed to be waiting for something. What? For me to scream and rage at them? To ask them in a wobbling voice why they were doing this?

"What did you use?" I said to Summer. "To knock me out?"

"Thalia's sleeping pills," she replied, to the wall. "Sure you're all right?"

I ignored this. "Are we going to have a party, then?" I said. "It's probably a bit cold this time of year for the cove. We could do a bonfire, though, like that time in the woods."

"The fact that you can joke right now," said Thalia, her doe eyes dark, "just proves my point." She glanced at Summer, who wasn't doing much of anything.

I imagined myself rising up from the bed, striding over to Summer, and hitting her across the face. A nice big cuff that sounded like a gunshot. A cuff that neatly demonstrated her betrayal while the audience back home silently cheered me on.

"And what point is that, Thalia?" I said, drawing her name out.

"Are you hearing this?" Thalia said to Summer, her voice rising. I wasn't the only one trying to get her attention. "She acts like nothing's happened. She doesn't feel anything. She doesn't care. I told you. Don't you get it now?"

"Sure," said Summer mechanically. She was picking at her nails. It looked deliberate to me, a forced air of apathy.

"*Sure* is not going to cut it. I need to know where your loyalties lie. We both do."

Summer finally looked up, irritation lacing her voice. "For god's sake, Thalia, I'm the one who got her here. I did all the work. What do you think?"

Silence descended. I wanted to open the crack further, make some quip that would whip Thalia into a meltdown, because she looked like she was close. But my heart was hurting, distracting me.

*I miss you. You're my best friend.* Last night had been an act. A perfect plan to get me to trust Summer enough so they could kidnap me without raising any alarms. She wasn't my best friend. None of them were. It was all a lie.

I wanted to wait for the perfect moment. One beautiful, perfect moment where I could hurt them the absolute most. I wanted to find their one big weakness, nail them to the wall with it, and watch them bleed.

If only I could clear this fuzzy thickness in my head first. If only I could think properly.

"I think," said Fenrin slowly, as if he were tasting the words, "that you should tell her why she's here."

I was half-expecting Summer to bite back. But then she shrugged, shook it off. "Fine," she said. "Let's get it done." She turned away from her slouch against the wall and looked at me.

"It's the winter solstice tomorrow night," she said. "The festival of rebirth."

I felt my skin fur up in response to her words, but I held her gaze, trying to be unreadable stone like her.

"So it's the perfect time to bring Wolf back."

Except I wasn't expecting that. My pulse stuttered.

"What?" I said stupidly.

She sighed. "You heard."

"You're going to bring him back from being dead?"

"No," said Thalia. She was calm now, her arms folded. "*You* are."

I snorted a long, disbelieving piggy snort. They were prepared for my faithlessness, though; none of them even blinked.

"This is ludicrous, right?" I said. "Summer. You know this is totally *ludicrous*."

"No, it's not," said Thalia. "You killed him. So you can be the one to bring him back."

I didn't just hear that.

This wasn't funny. This wasn't real.

I needed to say something. Be shocked, and then angry. That was what innocent people were, weren't they? Shocked at the suggestion; angry that they could be thought of as capable of that. But the only thing I seemed to really want to do was laugh, hard and sharp until my belly hurt, laugh at them and me and this ridiculous, ridiculous situation.

"Thalia," I spat out, finally. My throat convulsed with a giggle. "You are officially off the rock."

"Oh," Thalia said quietly. "Did you think we wouldn't work it out?"

"Work out what, exactly?"

"Your secret."

Those two words, and all they might imply, made me want to throw up, or kill her, maybe. Maybe both.

"*What* secret?" I asked.

But she didn't want to say, and no one rushed to fill it in for her.

I shook my head. "You're insane. Wolf died in an accident. He was swept out to sea."

She sneered. "Well, it wasn't like we were expecting you to just confess." Her gaze fell on Fenrin, who was utterly silent, impassive, his arms folded. His eyes were on the far wall. Summer was watching me intently.

"Oh come *on*," I said. "What is wrong with you all? So you're telling me you think I killed Wolf? If you've known that all this time, why the hell would you wait so long to do something about it? I'd have kidnapped me and drugged me up *ages* ago."

"Well, let me tell you the rest," said Thalia. "If you refuse to bring him back, we're going to do it ourselves, with old magic. All we have to do is make a sacrifice. One life in exchange for the other."

My bones turned to ice because they knew what was coming.

She tipped her head. "You know. Yours for his."

# THIRTY-THREE

THOSE FUCKING FLOWERS.

They stank, maybe even more than when I'd first arrived. The smell filled up my lungs like soup. Made it hard to breathe. When you were concentrating on breathing, you couldn't think too well.

There was always someone outside the door to the bedroom, and they kept it locked from the outside. I could hear them shuffling, whispering to one another like they were outside a sickroom and not a prison. I tried the window, but it had been sealed shut somehow.

I'd been here a few hours already, and it was nearly nightfall. I wondered if my mother would notice that I hadn't come home. I doubted it. They had my phone—all they had to do was send her a reassuring message that looked like it was from me. I was out with friends. I'd be home late—maybe not even until tomorrow. Don't worry. And she wouldn't because she knew I wasn't with the Graces—the Graces were out of my life.

The buzzing silence crowded into my ears, and my mind ran a mile a minute but nowhere useful, just turning in circles and circles until I was dizzy. The white flowers were ghosts in the dusk light, and I imagined them crawling across the floor, up the bed, floating along my skin, laying themselves carefully on my mouth until I stopped breathing. The thick flesh petals rubbed up against one another, nestling against the floorboards as that smell rolled off them in waves.

I could hear them whispering outside the door again.

"Hey," I called.

The whispering stopped.

"Hey," I called again, desperate for them to acknowledge me. "I'm hungry. Hello?"

Silence.

A clicking as the door was unlocked and opened inward with a cautious slowness. I was sitting on the bed, my knees drawn up. I peered over their rounded tops and tried to look weak.

Fenrin came in, and his eyes found me, and my heart dropped.

We stared at each other for a moment too long. He shut the door behind him, and I heard a click as someone turned the key on the outside. I watched him look carefully around the room. Why? Checking for the booby traps I'd made from all the useful materials in here?

"We'll get you something," he said, hovering by the door. "What do you want?"

I gave him my best stare of contempt. "If you're really going to kill me tomorrow, why bother feeding me?"

He shrugged. "Summer insists."

The sound of her name hurt.

"Why aren't you trying to escape?" he asked me. "You could wait behind the door, try and get out when we open it. You might even make it."

"I don't want to leave," I snapped. "God, this is crazy. If you'd just asked me, I would have said yes, you know. We could have talked it out. You could have said, 'Hey, we're thinking of trying to resurrect Wolf, want to come?' Not all this ridiculous cloak-and-dagger shit. What do you think I'm going to *do* to you?"

He didn't answer, but neither did he come closer, as if whatever he thought I had was catching. What did they see when they looked at me now? I'd spent the last hour scanning every memory I had of us together. What had I done, what had I said, to lead them here?

The floating aftermath of the pills had worn off; I felt shaken, small, and angry scared. But there was no way I was going to let him know that. I could play games, too.

"Fen," I said.

He was sharp all over, like just being in the same room as me stung his skin.

"I don't want to dance around anymore, River." His voice was quiet. "It's time for truth, now."

Secrets and eggs.

"Because you guys are so big with truths, right?" I threw back at him.

"What do you want to know?"

"What?"

He shrugged. "What do you want to know? We'll trade. One of

my secrets for one of yours. And we get to pick each other's secret."

I was caught. This felt like a game that I didn't yet know the rules to.

"Fine," I said. "I have a question."

He leaned against the wall nearest the door. He still wouldn't come close to me. Was I so disgusting to him?

"Wolf," I said, and I was rewarded with a tiny flinch across his eyes, the fleeting flash of a fish underwater, at the sound of that name in my mouth. "You were in love with him, weren't you?"

He was silent.

I put my legs down and crossed them at the ankles, leaning back against the pillow propped behind me. "I thought this was truth time," I said.

I watched him steel himself. "Yes," he said, and his voice was impressively matter-of-fact. "I was in love with him."

The admission did something to me, a wave of embarrassment and shame all the way down to my toes. Wolf had loved him, too. He'd admitted as much to me in the garden, that he was in love with one of them. I'd just guessed the wrong one.

"Marcus told me something once," I said. "He said the Graces go in for arranged marriages."

Fenrin cocked his head.

"Promised," he replied. "That's the way they say it. It's not a marriage. It's not legally binding."

"That's . . ." I searched for a suitable word. "Really fucking weird, Fen."

He was silent.

I stared at him, the angles of his face. That snarled expression it had worn when I saw him underneath Wolf in the sand. Like nothing else on earth existed for him right then except the body he touched and the soul it belonged to.

"So let me make a guess," I said. Something I'd worked out long ago, but I wanted to see it hit home. "Wolf was promised to Thalia."

"How clever you are."

"Fen—that's crazy. So . . . what? One day someone says, 'Right, now you guys are together'? No choices?"

"I'm not discussing this with you."

I felt a surge of irritation. Apparently, I was now only worthy enough for a certain amount of truth in one go. "Fine. I mean, I've never seen two people less interested in each other. They acted more like cousins than promised, but . . . whatever. Everyone knew you and Wolf were in love, but that's cool, for the sake of *tradition*, we'll just all ignore it? So when Thalia and Wolf got together, that would be it for you two, would it? No more little trips to the beach? No frolicking in the sand?"

Fenrin's face turned hard, statue-like.

"Frolicking in the sand," he repeated, but there was no question in his voice.

I waited, puzzled.

He laughed to himself. It was not a sound of amusement. "There was actually only one time we frolicked in the sand, as you put it. Just that one time."

I knew which time he meant.

He tilted his head up, as if he wanted to contemplate the ceiling for a while. "Do you know what *I* remember from that day?"

"You said you didn't remember anything. Another lie?"

He shrugged. "I've never lied to you."

I opened my mouth in outrage, ready to give him times and dates. But nothing came.

"Everything I had to go through," he said, his body closed and tight. "The police questions, the suspicion. My own doubt. What happened, why couldn't I remember. It was torture. If I knew, then I could have moved on. I could have somehow, eventually, been okay with Wolf gone. But I didn't know. We tried everything, every charm, every spell and trick, to get my memory back. Nothing did it. But not long after your confession, I woke up from a dream. The dream was of the day he died. And suddenly, I remembered everything."

Now, finally, he looked full at me.

"It was like something had been stopping me from remembering until then. I knew exactly what had happened. Because I saw you there in the cove. *I saw what you did.*"

Hiding was a type of behavior the Graces were all particularly good at. He'd been hiding earlier, but he wasn't now. The expression on his face I was never going to forget—like he wanted to stab me and feel my flesh give under the weight of his arm.

"I guess part of it is my fault," he said. "I handled it badly that day in the grove. I should have told you I didn't like you that way, but you just completely took me by surprise. I hadn't even thought about you like that, you know?"

He paused.

"I don't think I believe that you can really bring Wolf back," he said, finally. "Even if you had the power to kill him. But it doesn't matter. In fact, I think what I want is for you to fail. Because then you die instead, and we get him back anyway."

My insides shriveled in fright.

"Fenrin, listen to me," I said, fighting panic. "Whatever it is you think you saw . . . Wolf's death was an *accident*. You of all people can't possibly believe that I can bring someone back from the dead!"

"Maybe. Maybe not. But if it doesn't work, if it really doesn't bring him back . . . well." His eyes were far away. "Your life for his. It's the right way of things. The old way of things." His gaze fell on me. "Vengeance," he finished. "An eye for an eye."

I was silent with sick horror.

How dare he turn that back on me.

How *dare* he.

Fenrin went back to the door, taking a key out from his pocket. He opened it and I watched him go, my muscles twitching just once, as if I could leap across the room and fly out of here. But I couldn't. The door was pulled shut. I heard the clicking of the lock.

I was suddenly furious, rage like gasoline fueling me. I leapt off the bed and grabbed a handful of devil stones from the bowl on the nightstand, those useless powerless stones, throwing them at the door. The noise as they bounced and scattered violently was awful, punching my ears in, but at the same time it gave me a satisfied feeling in my belly.

"Where's my *food*?" I screamed over the grinding sound of the glass rolling across the floor. "I'm hungry! You can't starve me!"

But no one came back to see me all evening, no matter how much noise I made.

# THIRTY-FOUR

I WOKE UP FROM A NIGHTMARE.

It was mostly a series of impressions. The pearly gray of dawn. Panting. Fenrin's feet, digging into the sand. The sound of the sea claiming a life in the only violent way it knew how. Violent and beautiful. It was still so beautiful even when I saw it now, and that thought filled me with shame that I found beauty in death.

There were snapshots of memories in the nightmare, things we had done together in the past. They shifted and shuffled, and they were all tainted. That first day in the thicket at school, Summer was controlling and manipulative, and we were all her baby acolytes, hanging on her every word like weak rabbits. Fenrin didn't seem happy anymore. He was cruel, tossing hearts aside like sweet wrappers, ignoring the girl he was screwing the previous week in favor of the girl he was screwing now, and her eyes, pinched with misery, watched them all the way down the corridor. At our film night they closed in on me like a pack, mocking everything I said and laughing uproariously. They poisoned my wine glass, and I threw up in front of them all, shaking and ashamed.

I crawled out of bed, covered in a light sheen of sweat, and sat on the floor under the window, the duvet wrapped around me. It was the soft pit of the night, somewhere in between two and three A.M., the time I felt most like anything could happen. The sky was clear, and the moon shined in, stirring something weird and wild in me. It was on nights like this that I used to stare out and wonder if I could just fly away, skipping across the ground like a hare, fleet and silent. Live in the woods, knowing my way perfectly, fitting into the landscape like it was made for me and me for it.

I hated myself for these thoughts because they were the thoughts of a child. But I never stopped thinking them. They weren't comforting—they made me edgy, erratic.

Earlier I'd cleared the room of flowers. I got methodical, taking each individual flower stem and shredding the petals off. Ripping them up carefully, their soft furriness squelching under my fingertips, making me squirm. I fed them through the gap under the door, taking the empty stems and poking savagely at the heap through the gap until the petal shreds scattered across the hallway.

Thalia was shouting at me to stop from outside the room. Stupid earth witch. She pretended like it hurt her when her precious plants suffered. I told her to stop playacting. She wasn't three anymore, and she needed to face reality.

She didn't believe I wanted to bring Wolf back. I could see it in her scurrying little glances, full of nervous hate. She thought she was strong, but her strength came from fear. Fear of her parents, and of her future, which just seemed to get narrower and narrower, a tunnel that shrank until she couldn't move forward anymore; stuck in a dark, suffocating place for the rest of her life.

I used to feel sorry for her, but once it turned out that she wanted to kill me, sorry was an emotion I could no longer afford.

I shifted, rearranging my knees so they didn't ache in my cross-legged position. I fancied I could feel the moonlight on my shoulders, a cold, gentle kind of touch. I knew it wasn't real, but it helped my mind to reach down and inhabit that space of make-believe that seemed to go hand in hand with magic. Believe it and it would become true.

Will. You had to will it to be so. That was what Summer used to say when we did our spellcasting. If I was a real witch, I could make the Graces set me free or believe anything about me that I wanted. But they didn't. They believed the worst of me.

It was a stupid, pointless thing, anyway, to try and make people love you. Everyone was alone. We were born alone and we died alone. Whatever we did in between was nothing but a series of attempts to stave off the darkness we knew was always waiting for us. That was weak. We should welcome the darkness in. If you knew a thing, it couldn't scare you as much. It couldn't hurt you. I knew darkness. I knew alone.

So I sat there and I willed, willed with my atoms and my molecules. But I didn't really know what I was willing. It kept changing on me. Faces slipped into each other, and the words became meaningless.

I wanted so many things, I didn't know which direction to go in.

Then the bedroom door clicked, and a sliver of black opened up wide, rushing toward me. For a second, I didn't get it—had the darkness come for me somehow? But the hinges creaked and I realized the door was opening, and there was no light from the corridor beyond spilling through. It was black and still.

Before I could even think of getting up off the floor (*and doing what?* said the voice inside me scornfully), something slipped in. The door clicked shut behind it. The key turned in the lock.

"Oh god," said a normal voice, breaking the spell.

"I'm right here."

The figure adjusted. "River? What the hell are you doing on the floor? I saw the bed empty and thought you were gone somehow."

I stared up at Summer from my seat under the window. "How would I manage that?" I said. "You've sealed the window and locked the door."

She didn't reply. I watched the figure cross toward me and bend near the bed. Warm, dim gold light flooded the room as she switched on the bedside lamp. I squinted until my eyes adjusted. She was wearing black cotton pajama bottoms and one of her many band T-shirts. Her hair was mussed, but she gave her head a tiny shake, and her hair dropped into place around the curve of her cheekbone.

"Isn't it, like, three in the morning?" I said. "What do you want?"

She ignored this and sat at the bottom of the bed, curling her feet under her. She had chipped black nail polish on her toes. She had the money for the expensive stuff, of course, but for some reason she always bought the cheap ones that lasted about a day.

I wondered why. I'd never questioned it before. I would wonder about all her motives now, forever. That was one of a long list of fallouts from what she'd done.

"I take it you didn't like the flowers," she said.

"Was I supposed to? They stank."

Summer looked at me thoughtfully. "Your reaction to them was a bit over the top, though."

"You filled the whole room with them. I couldn't even open the window. It was kind of difficult to breathe."

"Do you know why they were there?"

I settled back with a sigh, as if resigned to the interruption. "Enlighten me."

"They're a binding flower."

"Oh, not this again. What are you going to do, wrap ribbons around me while I'm asleep? Hang another little figure up in a noose?"

"More than that," she continued as if I hadn't spoken. "They're from our own garden, and Esther's been growing the bush for years, so they're pretty strong. Fen has bowls of the petals in his room. He likes the smell." Her eyes slid onto my face. "Esther makes this perfume mist with them. It's one of her bestsellers. Like a heavy vanilla, but kind of a wilder smell than vanilla. Fen wears it. Pretty much every day. In fact, that's his smell. That and sea salt."

It *was* his smell. It was a mean trick. I swallowed the sudden burst of fury I could feel blooming in my chest.

She shook her head, this funny twist of a smile on her face. "You know, until recently I was still on the fence about this whole thing. I just thought—it's not possible. It's crazy."

"And now?" I said casually, like I didn't care at all, at the same time as my heart tried its hardest to climb out of my throat. "Have you lost your mind along with the twins of evil?"

"I guess I'm waiting for you to tell me what really happened."

"So you can gaze into my eyes and see the truth?"

She shrugged. The shrug meant "sort of."

I threw up my hands helplessly. "I don't know what to say. You . . . you *drugged* me, Summer. What the hell is wrong with you? Why didn't you just, oh I don't know, *ask* me?"

"Ask?" she said. "Oh, sure. 'Hey, hey, Rivs. I'm back in your life again to ask for a teeny little favor. I know this is ludicrous because, well, if resurrection spells actually worked, we'd have a serious population problem by now, but I wondered if you fancied trying to bring Wolf back from the dead, for old times' sake, you know, could be fun?'"

"Well—"

"Also," she carried on over me, "let's look at this hypothetically. Would you ask someone's murderer to try and resurrect the person they killed?"

A hysterical laugh bubbled up out of my mouth. "I can't believe we're really having this conversation. No, hypothetically, I guess not."

"They're afraid of you," she said quietly. She wasn't laughing. "They figured you'd never do it. They thought kidnapping you was the only way."

*But why did you go along with it? Why are you doing this?*

*Summer, please, please don't be afraid of me, too. I don't think I can take it.*

"And what do you think?" I said out loud.

She ran her hands through her short hair in a tight, frustrated gesture. "I don't know, River. I thought I knew you. That's the thing that's really screwing me up about this."

"You did. You *do*."

"Do I? But you kept lying to me, so how the hell could I? No, actually, you don't lie so much as just leave really, really important things out. You never bothered to tell me, for example, that you were totally, loopy in love with Fenrin."

". . . What?"

I started to panic. Of course he'd told them. I'd thought he would, hadn't I? I'd always known he'd humiliate me like that.

She held up a hand. "Well done, by the way. I had no idea. I thought you liked me for me, not because I was a way to get close to him. I mean, it's not like it's so unusual. Most of the girlfriends I've ever had were the same. I'd just thought you were different, that's all. Shows how stupid I am, doesn't it?"

"Summer, please, that's not true. You don't understand."

"The second thing you left out," she continued, ignoring me, "is what you said to Wolf just before the wave took him."

I was mute now. Mute was my last remaining defense.

"Maybe you don't remember," she said. "But Fenrin does, now. You said to Wolf, 'If I wished you gone, and the sea just came and took you away right now, what would happen? Would he want me instead of you?'"

She was paraphrasing.

But okay.

"And the third thing you left out," said Summer, with a faint and strange smile, "is what you did to Niral."

"What?" I was mystified. "I didn't do anything to her! She bullied *me*!"

Summer hugged herself, wrapping her hands around the tops of her arms.

"It wasn't until her that I really got it," she said. "Thalia believed Fen right away. She was the one who got people to do that stupid binding crap to you in school. I tried to get them to stop. It was all so petty."

She paused, and I felt an expectant dread like falling gently push me back.

"But then there was that spell you did on Niral that day," she said. "You wanted her to stop talking shit about you, didn't you? I guess there's no time limit on these things because nothing happened at first. But she was ill, on and off, do you remember that? And then, after Wolf died, she was out of school a lot. Lou told me on the phone that she's still missing whole weeks all the time, even now. She might have to drop out."

My breath was coming up short. I didn't want to hear it.

"She keeps losing her voice," I heard Summer say.

"So?" I managed.

I could feel her eyes on me, assessing every little movement I made. "Chronic laryngitis, apparently. They have no idea what's causing it."

"She could have throat cancer or something."

"They tested for all that. I told you, they don't know what the problem is. But then, they wouldn't. They don't have hospital tests for binding spells."

"This is ridiculous," I said, urgently. "You're seeing things that aren't there. It's coincidence, that's all."

She sounded amused. "Yeah, you said that yesterday. You know, I remember telling you a long time ago that real magic wouldn't need chants, or the right clothes, or any of that point-less stuff. Real magic would be about will alone. You must have been laughing at me. You must have just sat there and thought what a colossal idiot I was. River, I wanted real magic so much to be true, sometimes I hoped so hard for it I felt like my guts were coming up. I *wanted* to believe, but I never have, not truly. Not until you."

Her pale cheeks were patched red, like she'd been slapped.

I was trying to keep my voice steady. "Are you telling me you're a fake?"

She was evasive. "I'm telling you that nothing is as black and white as that, okay? Nothing is as easy as that."

"No shit, Summer. No *shit*. Think for a second. If I truly had real magic, don't you think I could have made myself a better life than the one I have?" My voice was rising but I didn't care. Let her see my pain, for once. Let her be convinced. "I could have just magicked myself pots of money, and fixed everything wrong in my life." *I could have brought my father back.* "I could have made Fenrin love me. The love spell in the thicket—it was for him. You were right. I did like him, okay? But it didn't work, did it?"

"No," she shook her head. "It worked. He was so into you back then. He thought you were great."

"Just shut up!" I shouted at her. "No, he didn't. He loved Wolf!"

"He saw you as a baby sister, River. He told me."

"Well, that's great. That's just what I wanted when I did that spell."

"Don't you understand?" said Summer, incredulous. "He saw

you as a *sister*. Not someone to *wear* for a few weeks. Don't you get how much more that means?"

She hunched, her lips thinning.

"And you betrayed him," she went on. *"Don't you get how much more that means."*

I had nothing for that.

"I think you can undo what you did to Wolf. You can bring him back."

I felt like cradling my head in my hands. "Summer, I *can't*."

Summer's face dropped like I'd never disappointed her so much before. "Look, I'm sorry we did it this way," she said, and she sounded like she genuinely meant it. "I wanted you to *want* to help us. Just . . . River, please. We were best friends."

Yes. We were. Never to be again.

I felt only shame when I remembered how she'd made me feel. Because with the Graces I'd felt special, but with Summer I'd felt human. All the endless roaring questions I had that no one else seemed to, the relentless scratching in the core of me that made me wonder why, why, why, what is the point of us, why do we yearn when we're nothing but animals, why do I love and hate the dark things, why must I push against the life I've been handed, why can't I be normal like everyone else? Well, Summer could answer all that with just a narrowing of her eyes that meant "why would you *want* to be?"

But now it was them versus me. I'd come second best to her family. I would always come second best. Summer looked at me, and all she saw was the one thing I'd worked so hard not to be for her: a freak. A lonely, lying freak. I'd never wanted to see that look on her face, and I'd never let myself think it could come to this. But it finally had, and now that we were here, all I felt was numb.

"Summer," I said, "whatever you think I've done, whatever you think I am . . . I can't bring Wolf back. He's dead, okay? He drowned, and I saw it. And that's it. The dead stay dead."

She stared at me for a moment more.

"You're lying," she said abruptly. "God! I didn't want them to be right."

"Summer—"

She pushed herself off the bed, her bare feet landing noiselessly on the rag rug. "It's like you hate us. Like you want to punish us. You're not this person, River. You're not. But you're trying so hard to be." Her hands came up, hesitant, helpless. "And I don't see any other options left."

I watched her go with bright, wet eyes.

* * * * *

A couple of hours until dawn.

All I did was sit, staring at the wall.

I just wanted it to be over.

# THIRTY-FIVE

IN THE MORNING, I HAD A SHOWER. THEY'D LEFT TOW-els, and Esther's soaps, in the en suite bathroom. I let the water run over me and tried to think. When I was dressed, I examined the bathroom window halfheartedly, but it was tiny. I might have been able to get my head and one arm out, and I'd read in a book once that if you could do that, you could get out of even the smallest-seeming of spaces. But I was too tired to try. I just wanted to lie down and disappear into nothing.

Fenrin brought in breakfast without a word. Just unlocked the door, came in, deposited the plate of little pastries and a cup of coffee on the floor, and left. Like I was their prisoner. Like I was their pet dog.

I ate it. At first I had thought about refusing dramatically. Grinding pastry flakes into their stupid rag rug or pouring the coffee onto the bedclothes. But it would just bother me more than them—I was the one stuck in the airless room with it. It was childish, anyway. Better to keep my strength up so I could be ready.

*Ready for what?* I mocked myself. *This is not a fairy tale. This is not a hero's journey.*

*You are no hero. And no one is coming to rescue you.*

I couldn't quite believe it had only been a day since eggs in the café, and a day and a night since they had come back into my life. I felt like I had been in this room forever. I paced the length of it, over and over. I wanted, I desired, I yearned for everything to be right, and not this crazy, sickly wrong. I was half-expecting a visit from Thalia, but she stayed away. When I wasn't pacing, I was sitting, listening. The house was too quiet. I couldn't tell if someone was outside my door or not.

When the light began to fall away, Fenrin came back. He brought me meatballs this time. He put the plate on the floor and spun on his heel, leaving within seconds. He didn't even look at me. For the last hour I'd been dreaming up a plan to attack him as soon as he opened the door. It would be something, at least, some kind of defiance, however aimless. But he came in and left so quickly I hadn't even told my muscles to move me off the bed before he was turning the key in the lock on the outside.

I stared at the plate for a while, smelling faint wafts of garlic, until my stomach rumbled. The meatballs were cold from the fridge, but still amazing. There was a chalky, bitter aftertaste to them I couldn't place, and it wasn't until maybe twenty minutes later that I got a suspicion of what it might be. Because it wasn't even full dark outside, but I was suddenly so, so bone tired.

I crawled back onto the bed. I had time to think that they must have gotten the dose right this time because it didn't take so long.

* * * * *

Faces. Murmurings. I was trying to roll over, but everything was so heavy, heavy. Things were long like strings.

We were in a car, I decided. It was dark and I was on my side. I could feel someone's arms around me. How nice it was, that simple feeling.

I didn't know how long it took me to surface and understand. It was slow and fast, all at once. When I did, I knew several things.

We were at the cove.

The sound of the sea was in my ears.

The breeze was cold enough to set me shivering.

My wrists were aching. This was because they were tied behind me.

My back was against something hard. I was tied to one of the boardwalk posts.

It was a black night, and the stars were out full. The moon was half-full, a glowing chopped penny in the sky. They'd lit a fire. I was too far away from it to feel comforted. A vague sense of warmth reached my shins, but that was it.

The three of them were there, standing a little way off. Thalia had stepped forward, away from the other two, and she faced the sea, her long hair shivering in the air, the ends dancing, gently lifted and dropped, lifted and dropped.

"She's awake," Fenrin called, watching me.

"Good," Thalia replied. "We've only got an hour until midnight."

She turned toward me.

Her left hand held something loosely by her side. She was wearing a long bronze-colored skirt that stirred something vague in me, but it wasn't until I looked at Summer that I got it. They were all wearing the outfits they wore that night. The night Wolf died. They had scarves and layers and boots on, but otherwise it was the same. They'd put my coat back on me, but the air rolling off the sea cut at my cheeks. I didn't feel cold yet. Maybe I would soon, once the drugs had worn off.

"What are you doing?" I said, my words slow and thick. "You think you can bring him back with the right clothes?"

"Not us. You."

I shifted on the sand, trying to break up the gloopy feeling that had me in its grip. "Yeah, well, sorry to disappoint you, but I burned that outfit."

I'd actually given it away to charity, but if I'd had a fire handy, maybe I would have burned it. If I lived in a mansion with a real, open fireplace that we lit in winter, lounging on rugs and cushions in front of it, clutching mugs of hot chocolate. If I had that life, I could burn things in a comforting symbolic fashion, instead of walking to the charity shop on a gray Sunday morning and handing them a plastic trash bag of clothes it cost me less to buy than they'd sell it for.

"Now," said Thalia. "You bring him back."

Adrenaline swooped and dove inside me.

Thalia brought up her left arm. The firelight caught the blade of her athame quite nicely. It was as sharp as I remembered—its edge was a sliced silver gray.

Fenrin moved toward me. Before I could even think what to do, he crouched on my outstretched legs, pinning them to the sand. The weight made them buzz. Thalia crouched to my left side on her haunches, her right hand dangling between her thighs. With her left hand she held the dagger out, its point near my heart.

"Bring him back," Thalia repeated. "Or we sacrifice you for him."

I tried to pull my wrists apart, but I might as well have tried to uproot a tree with bare hands. My fingers were going numb.

"You're insane!" I shouted into her face. "I can't!"

Sucking silence. The wind lifted Thalia's hair and billowed it around her face.

"You're lying," she said calmly. And she raised the athame, pushing the tip against my chest.

"Jesus, Thalia," I managed.

"Are we really doing this?" Summer's voice, wavering with panic. "This can't be right! We can't be right about this, Thalia! There's no going back after this!"

"I know," said Thalia, and she tightened her grip.

I tried to laugh. "You're not going to do this."

"No? Why not?"

"Because it's murder, Thalia! You can't just murder someone!"

"In the laws of nature," she said, "you make your own justice. Nature doesn't care about murder if it's justified. One life for another. That's how it works."

"Yeah, sure, but back in the real world, we have these little things called the police and prison!"

Her little rosebud mouth twisted as if she was mildly concerned. "You think we'll go to prison? I'm not sure anyone will even miss you, you know. No one ever misses the villain."

I gaped at her. "The villain? I'm not the one about to stab someone through the heart!"

"Don't you get it?" said Thalia, astonished. "River . . . you're the bad guy. You're the one the good guys always try to stop. It's tragic when you die at the end, but you know, everyone agrees that it's for the best. You know that story, of course you do. You have to be stopped, for your own good. Can't you see that? Wouldn't it be better for everyone if you just went away?"

"Get off me!" I screamed, twisting and bucking. But Fenrin's weight had made my legs go numb, and all that happened was that Thalia raised the athame and waited until I stopped. The sand was freezing, numbing me. I felt the gritty pressure of it under my fingernails.

"Why are you doing this?" I said, and my voice cracked. I didn't want to be weak, sniveling and wailing, but my mind was going round in a terrified circle, an endless loop of oh god oh god oh god, shutting everything rational out.

Thalia held the athame steady and looked into my eyes, her voice absolutely sure.

"Because it's the right thing to do."

She was terrifying. I wasn't going to change her mind, whatever I said. What were you supposed to do in the face of that?

Thalia finally frayed as I did nothing but stare at her, trying with every ounce of energy I had left not to cry. "Just give him back!" she shouted, furious. "Give him back, you murderer! GIVE HIM BACK."

I don't think she meant to, when I look back on it now. She was climbing fast to hysteria, and when you're like that you don't have the best control of your body movements. But at the time, all I knew was that this cold, awful girl who had severe problems of her own and *would not listen* was screaming inches from my face, relentless, the sound pounding against my eardrums, and then I felt a red-hot wire scorch my skin and something warm pooling in the crease of my belly. Confused, I looked down and saw a spreading dark stain against the cream of my sweater.

It was blood. Blood soaking through my sweater.

The crazy bitch had actually *slashed* me.

My

Fucking

God

Rage like trying to stare at the sun, white hot, blinding. No thought. My whole self was crumbling to dust, flash fried by fury.

"No!" Summer screeched. She sounded very, very far away.

The weight left my legs. When I knew anything again, I knew to look for the source of the choking noise in front of me.

It was Thalia. Her long hair was wrapped around her neck. The wind streamed past her face in a tight, awful circle. Her hair was a rope being pulled by the air, by invisible hands. It tightened into her flesh.

She was making a horrible wheezing sound.

"No, no!" Summer was frantic. She almost fell on top of Thalia in her haste to help, hands scrabbling at the hair rope crushing her sister's throat. "Stop! STOP IT. SHE'S DYING."

Fenrin had left my legs and he was behind Thalia, trying to get his fingers in between hair and flesh. They wrestled. All I could do was stare. I couldn't move. There was nothing I could do to help. My hands were still tied, though I was guessing at that because I couldn't even feel them anymore.

I saw a hand flash out—Summer's—and grab the athame on the sand next to Thalia's thigh.

A few more awful seconds. Or maybe it wasn't even one but it felt like forever, while Thalia groaned and panted.

Then she fell forward onto her palms. There was something dark creeping down her neck like a long, thin caterpillar. Blood from where Summer scraped Thalia's skin from cutting her hair off at the base of her skull. The rope of hair slithered down the curve of her back and coiled onto the sand.

For a moment everything hung between us, suspended.

But there was no time because I heard a kind of sucking roar, and I looked toward the shoreline, and it was happening again, just like with Wolf, oh god, and I just had time to scream out:

"HOLD ON TO SOMETHING—"

The wave reached us. Everything was gone. Bubbling in my ears. I was slammed to the side as the water came crashing down. My arms, still tied, wrenched against the post, shoulders roaring with pain. I couldn't breathe. I couldn't hear.

We were drowning. We were dead.

I was almost relieved. No responsibility in death. No more consequences.

But then something pulled on me, and I slammed back against the post as the wave rolled away from us, leaving its waste behind, the toxins it no longer wanted. I huddled against the post, coughing, waiting. But it didn't come again.

Just a single, monstrous wave. As unnatural as the sky turning neon green.

I managed to raise my head, my hair hanging over my eyes like seaweed hanks. The shoreline was calm again, calm as anything. Just its little joke.

Coughing next to me. I shifted on the sopping sand, muscles seizing and freezing, and I saw three bodies.

They were all moving.

Fenrin was the first to raise himself. His face was pressed into the sand. He spat, spat again. Flopped onto his back. His skin looked gray in the dark, under the starlight. Thalia was curled into a ball. Her face was thinner without all her hair, or maybe it was the cold and the wet. Summer was on all fours, black bangs hanging down in strings over her eyes. I watched her as she looked up at me. My belly pulsed steadily. I felt no more liquid warmth on my skin, but I didn't know if it was because I'd stopped bleeding or I was just too cold to feel.

Silence. The calm sound of the sea filling the gap.

I just wanted it all to stop. I wanted to lie down and feel Summer pressed up against my back, but I'd never have that now. I couldn't bear their emotions anymore, all pouring out onto me, weighing me down, burying me. I forced myself to talk, no matter what it would cost me. It needed to come out, or maybe I'd try to kill us all again.

"I didn't mean to."

Silence.

I felt the post dig into my back, comforting. Something solid to prop up my broken self. My knees were drawn up to my face and I talked into them rather than out. But at least I was talking. I was shivering from the cold.

"I never mean to," I said. "Not really. Just for that one second.

Just a split second. But it's enough. It's always been like that. Just one second."

I was leaning my head back against the post, eyes closed.

"You know how kids will scream 'drop dead' or something when they're angry? They don't really mean it, though, not afterward. Well, for years when I was young, I thought when you wished for something bad, it happened for real, because it did. For me.

"Just before we moved here, I made my dad go away. He disappeared in the middle of the night. Didn't even pack any clothes. Left everything behind. I was mad at him—we'd had a fight about . . . this. Whatever this is that happens around me. He wanted to get me committed. To get help, he called it, but really he was too scared to deal with me anymore. That night I wished and wished he would just go away forever. And then he did. No one knows where he is. He just . . . vanished."

I found the words practically vomiting up my throat in their eagerness to be out. As if my stopper had been uncorked and my liquid secrets were spilling everywhere, staining the sand.

"Sometimes, when I was younger, I'd wish for things, and then they'd happen. Mostly they never happened at all—but sometimes, just sometimes, something would. One time I wanted this teacher in primary school to get in trouble so he'd stop picking on me in class. He got suspended two days later for fraud or something. He swore up and down that he was innocent, but he still got a criminal record. Another time, I wanted it to be sunny so I could go outside and play. We had a drought that summer. Literally just in our area—the rest of the country was fine. It was so bad our cat died. This boy felt me up at a bus stop once, and I wanted something horrible to happen to him. After he was done with me, he went to cross the road to go home, and he got run over. I never even saw a car coming. He was in a wheelchair after that. And I . . . I saw Jase surfing, and showing off, and I thought he was such a dick for what he'd said to you. And I just thought it would serve him right if he broke his leg. And with Wolf, I—" But I couldn't finish that.

They knew why that had happened.

"Maybe it was just coincidence, see. I could never be sure, not truly, absolutely sure it was me. And it was only bad things that happened around me, never good. So for a long time, I tried to think only good thoughts, just in case." I choked on each syllable as they came out, dragging their sharp edges like razor blades against my throat. "But no one can think only good thoughts. I thought I was broken. Now I just think . . . maybe I'm cursed, like you. Because it doesn't matter how sorry I am about any of it. Sorry never brings anyone back."

Thick, thick silence and the rolling sound of the sea.

"All this time. You knew what you were. You lied to us. You hurt us." Summer, thin and sopping, her eyes raised to me.

I shook all over. "But I didn't know. I didn't know for sure."

"We trusted you," said Fenrin. "I trusted you, and then you took him away from me. I loved him and you took him."

He started to cry.

We sat there, drenched and cold, silent underneath his quiet sounds. Thalia was stroking his wet hair. I made sure that I listened to him. He deserved at least that from me.

He needed a grand, evil reason why Wolf was dead, but all I had to give him was the banal truth—sometimes people died for the stupidest reasons in the world. Just for a moment, the betrayal I felt at seeing Fenrin with someone else was enough for me to want to punish him. But that wasn't the reason. It was a childish tantrum. Anyone else and they'd just be embarrassed for a while. Life would go on.

A moment was all it took. One life gone, a few others ruined. It was such a tiny thing, a moment. But it was the most powerful reality shaper there was. It was the power I seemed to have, to change moments.

I wished I could explain all this to them, all this I had inside my head. But the words didn't come. They never had. I'd been so afraid of what I could do for too long that I could no longer tell the truth to anyone, about anything. It was the best way. You built up walls and you trusted no one because you knew how untrustworthy you were yourself, so why should anyone else be any different?

If there was something wrong with you, there could be something wrong with everyone. If you were capable of such awful moments, no matter how sorry you were afterward, no matter how much you screamed and begged the universe to take it back, then maybe everyone else was, too.

I'd give anything to reverse the things I'd done, but that was the one thing I'd never been able to do. That was my tragedy. My punishment. My curse.

Summer was watching me. I didn't know what my face told her, but she started to move toward me. She still had the athame clutched in one hand as she crawled over the sand. I was so stiff and cold I felt my whole body twitch occasionally, but I couldn't get it to do anything I wanted. Kick her in the face before she stabbed that thing into my chest, for example. All I could do was watch as she disappeared behind me. It was over.

Faint tugging against my wrists. Jerk jerk jerk. Pause. Jerk jerk jerk.

"Don't," said Thalia. "Summer, don't." But the jerking didn't stop.

I didn't even realize at first when my hands came free. I tried to rub life back into them, but it was like rubbing an ice block with a brick. Summer sat back, leaning against the post next to me, her legs bent. She tipped her head back. Her lips were almost white.

"You can't bring him back, can you?" she said to me.

I was shivering. "I don't think so. I've tried every time to reverse it. It never works."

"Then it's over." Thalia stood, her arms tucked around herself. "Look, I'm really sorry about what I just did. We never meant to hurt you. We just wanted to bring it out of you."

I bit back a hysterical laugh. "Thalia, you . . . had a knife. You said you were going to kill me."

She shook her head tightly. "Because you kept lying to us. We just figured, if we threatened you, we'd bring it out of you . . . and you'd bring him back. We weren't really going to kill you. I never meant it."

But her words sounded hollow. I remembered the wild dark in her eyes as she crouched on me. I remembered the white-hot wire across my chest.

Thalia would do anything to protect her family.

She was facing me, but her eyes wouldn't meet mine. She looked so strange and thin shorn of her hair. "So if you can't bring Wolf back," she said haltingly, "then we're quits. Please just . . . promise to stay away from us. I think it's best. And we promise we'll stay away from you. Okay?"

*Okay?*

Fenrin dragged himself up to standing, but he wouldn't look at me. Thalia clutched his sopping sleeve, and she wouldn't look at me. Summer's eyes were on them and she wouldn't. Look at me.

"But . . . ," I said stupidly, and then stopped.

No, no, this was all wrong. This was my worst nightmare come true.

They were supposed to understand. They were the only ones in the world who could understand. In fact, they were supposed to *hug* me, reassure me, delight all over their faces, because they knew how to harness it. They were supposed to know how to point it and urge it and calm it and direct it like a horse. They were supposed to think it was wonderful, what I could do, and embrace me as one of them.

I was one of them.

But the fear that had stopped me from being truthful, on top of the doubt that I was even causing anything at all, was this: that they'd look at me and see the same thing my parents had.

"Wait," I said. "I know I . . . look, I should have told you from the beginning, but I was too scared, okay? All I've ever wanted was to find someone like me. I just wanted to know what I am. And I finally found you, and I . . . I thought you could help me."

"We can't help you. No one can help you." Fenrin put his arm around Thalia as he spoke.

"But . . . you can. *You* can."

Thalia's voice rose up and down, up and down the hysteria slide. "No, River, no. What you do . . . it's evil. You said it yourself. It's only bad things that happen around you. What if we fall out again? Will you kill us, too?"

Black despair crawled up my back and over my shoulders, settling over me solid and heavy, a cement cloak. "Don't," I said. "Please, please don't be afraid of me."

But they were. Oh, they were.

Summer unfolded herself. She looked like the ghost of a drowned rat. She paused, as if to say something. Above the noise of the sea, I heard Fenrin call to her, Thalia pressed to his side. He held out his hand.

For a moment, Summer stood still. Her gaze roved over my face.

Then she moved forward and slipped her hand in his.

They took the path that led them up over the dunes, and then eventually to the back of the grove. They were going home. They did not want me to come with them. They didn't want me at all.

I watched the rolling dunes swallow their shapes. They would go back to that house, dressed up with its objects that made its owners feel like they had power. Pretty, vacuous objects to display their pretty, vacuous lives. They would touch the seashells, the soft charm bags hanging from the lintels. The horseshoe over the front door for luck. They needed these things that helped them make sense of the world; otherwise it all just descended into confused, miserable chaos. I understood the comfort of that.

But I was not one of them.

That moment, when it came, was small. Just a quick, fleeting twinge of realization, there and gone. That was where the power was, wasn't it? It lay in small moments, small realizations.

*He doesn't love me.*

*She is afraid.*

*He thinks I'm crazy.*

*I'm alone.*

*I'm going to die.*

*I'm not one of you.*

*I'm not one of you.*

*I'm one of me.*

Right then, I knew what was coming. I knew what I had done. I sat on the beach and waited, watching the shoreline.

# THIRTY-SIX

IT TOOK A FEW MINUTES FOR THE SHAPE TO EMERGE.

It crawled out of the sea like a pale, jerking spider.

I thought I was full numb now, full dead inside, but not quite, not all the way, because I felt a surge of stuttering panic. Everything about this pale spider thing was wrong. It stopped, right on the tide line, its limbs braced into the sand. Then it collapsed into a heaving lump.

It reminded me of a documentary I saw once about the strange creatures that lived way down dark, in the blackest sea depths where the pressure would cave in your chest in seconds. They were translucent, with flat dish-plate eyes and needle teeth so long they could never close their mouths. If you brought them near the surface, they'd gasp and flop, blubbery lumps on their way to death.

The tide receded as the sea retreated from what it had vomited up.

I saw the lump shift, ever so gently.

I heard a sound like a long, whistling groan.

I knew what it was, but I was afraid. I was afraid of what it wasn't.

I stood up, unsteady, and forced my stiff body to walk. My chest gave a sharp ache, and then quieted, throbbing. I couldn't think about the cut Thalia had given me right now—I'd clean myself up later. The lump grew in my vision as I approached, and it stopped being a shapeless spider mass. A back appeared, the long groove down the spine. Legs. Arms. It was curled on its side. I had to walk all the way around it to find the head. Hair matted with sand and dripping. Eyes closed. It coughed, a rattling sound.

I leaned forward, my head screaming stop. Pressed my hand into its chest to roll it onto its back. The skin was cold and wet, but there was life underneath there. I could feel it.

It rolled, unresisting, and opened its eyes. They were unfocused, but they found me eventually. They latched on to my face. Confused. Blank.

I swallowed, forcing my voice out. "Hey."

The body moved. The limbs wavered.

"Hey," I tried again. I had to be calm. I had to be unmoved. Maybe it could hear fear. "Say something."

Its mouth opened, but nothing came out. Its eyes rolled away, focused on nothing. Its bare limbs twitched in the cold.

"Come on," I said. "We have to go. You're going to freeze to death. Come on. Get up. Please, you have to get up."

It took some pushing with my hands, "please" and "get up" trickling out from my mouth like a litany, but it managed to roll onto all fours. I crouched beside it, putting my shoulder under its arm, trying to lift it to standing. It dragged itself up. Its skin was cold marble against my side, and its arm weighed a ton, biting into my neck.

"We have to go," I said, and pulled forward.

It took a long time to get up to the dunes. It fell twice. The second time its arm wrenched my neck, and I was terrified it had broken me and itself. But my neck stopped flaring, and it got up again. When we reached the dunes I climbed up slowly and it followed, head hanging down, wet gritty hair plastered over its skull. Unformed—that was the word it made me think of. It looked down at its legs like it had never seen legs before. It must have been so cold, but I had nothing to give it. All I could do was get it home as quickly as I could.

When we got to the top, I put its arm over my shoulders, and my neck creaked in protest. I ignored it. A little pain was needed. A little sacrifice of mine.

It stumbled beside me. I tried to think of things to ask.

"Are you okay?"

But it never replied.

"Do you know where you are?"

It was silent. The only sounds it made were the grunts when it fell.

I didn't know how long this took.

It wasn't even that far away, but it felt like we stumble-walked together for hours and hours. The clear night helped, and the path was lit with cold, white light from the moon and the stars. It should have felt magical. But magic never felt magical, I'd come to learn. It was hard, and weary, and sometimes awful.

My clothes were still wet and my muscles ached, but at least they'd warmed up now that we'd been moving a while. We reached the Grace house. I considered going round to the back garden, but it was leaning against me so hard by this point I didn't think we could get much farther.

We made it underneath the little stone canopy that framed the front door. I pushed the body gently against the wall so it didn't fall down. It stayed. Its head almost brushed the underside of a little charm bag hanging from a nail on the wall.

I knocked on the door.

I knocked and knocked and knocked.

The door opened. It was Fenrin.

The gust of warmth from inside the house was enough to set me shivering again. They were all dry and dressed in clean clothes. Thalia looked drawn and odd without her hair.

They stared at me. I stared back.

"River, please don't come back anymore," Fenrin said to me. "Please, River. Please leave us alone, or we'll call the police."

He was trying to seem strong, but he was frightened.

If I hadn't been so weary, I think that would have irritated the shit out of me.

"I just have something for you, that's all, and then I'll go," I said through chattering teeth. I pulled on the arm of the body beside me, and it stumbled into the light spilling from the house.

Naked and trembling, it stood there.

I stepped back.

"This is my apology, okay?" I said. "I'm sorry for everything I've done. So I made it right."

I caught Summer's eye. Her jaw had dropped open. Her eyes were so wide.

The light and warmth spilling out from the house was sapping the last of my fire. The front of me strained toward it. The back of me still faced the dark. All I wanted to do was fall down and sleep.

"You said I couldn't do good things." I took in a deep breath. "But you were wrong. You were *wrong*."

"Wolf?" said Fenrin. His voice had gone unnaturally high like a child's, quavering and lost. "Wolf? Wolf?"

All he did was repeat his name.

Wolf did nothing except stand there.

I no longer had a part in this. It was up to them now. I forced myself to turn my back on them and walk up the lane. As I walked I could hear their fluttering, panicking voices like birds. The front door shut with a bang. He was inside. He was safe, with them.

I hugged my arms to me. I was so cold, and the walk back was going to take a while. At least I could get a shower at the end of it. It was this that made my legs move, over and over.

I thought of my small duplex and of how much more comforting it now felt to be going back to it. I wondered if my mother was worried that I hadn't come home yet. I'd tell her everything was fine.

I'd tell her everything was better than it had ever been before.

I'd tell her that maybe Dad didn't have to be gone forever, after all.

# THIRTY-SEVEN

IN THE NEW YEAR, I BEGIN MY THIRD TRANSFORMATION.

I have a feeling this one will stick.

I miss school assembly and am ten minutes late to my first class of the term. I walk in as our English teacher, Mr. Sutherland, is waxing lyrical on chapters ten to fifteen of *The Innocent*, which I should have read over the weekend.

He looks me up and down and tells me that bare shoulders are inappropriate attire for school, and do I have a cardigan. I tell him I'm in costume as someone who doesn't give a fuck, and I get detention for not backing down. And for the swearing.

The whole class is staring. Their attention doesn't make me want to shrink into myself anymore. I can feel eyes on my shoulders, my jagged hair. I look odd. I'm not beautiful, and I'm not cool, but I don't care. Finally, I look how I am.

There is a Grace-shaped void in this school, and I am going to fill it.

Marcus and I have been avoiding each other. It's easy when you're in different years, and he's barely been around, anyway—the seniors are all studying their lives away for their final exams.

I haven't talked to him properly since the night of the party. Part of it is embarrassment, part of it is that I just haven't been able to face him. Sometimes, with Marcus, it feels too much like looking into a mirror. I understand all the little moments that had to happen in order for him to get to this point. I understand his frustration and his obsession and his rage. Whether it's because of a curse or not, there's something special about Marcus. He knows about magic. He's been around the Graces for a long time, a lot longer than I have. Like me, he's been loved by them and like me he's been rejected by them. Now we both have to learn to live without them.

But that doesn't mean we have to do it alone.

"Why do you want to talk to me?" he says, placing his messenger bag on the table as he sits. I notice the tense set of his outline. "If it's about Thalia, I'm not interested. It's over. I haven't seen her in months. I haven't seen any of them in months. No one has, not since Wolf died."

We share a look of mutual, fleeting, complicated pain. It's gone again from his eyes just as quickly, neatly hidden. I wonder if it lingers in mine. I steel myself for what comes next.

"I'm really sorry for what happened, Marcus," I say. "Everything that happened to you. I think it's really unfair what they did. But they never suffer for it. It's always everyone around them."

He stares at me. His expression tells me that he is trying to make me out.

"What do you want?" he says.

"To show you something. And then to ask you a question."

He struggles, as if he senses a trap, but his curiosity unfurls before me.

I reach slowly into my backpack and pull out a stiff cream envelope. Inside is a rough woven card, impregnated with tiny seeds and edged in gold foil trim. It is printed in a classic, elegant script.

As soon as his eyes fall on it, my question is answered.

For a moment, he seems too confused to speak. He stares and stares at the card, deep in thought. Then he reaches into his bag and withdraws his own envelope. Without a word, he unsheathes the card inside and hands it to me. It looks just like mine.

It reads:

THE GRACE FAMILY & THE GRIGOROV FAMILY
CORDIALLY INVITE
MARCUS DAGDA
TO THE COMING-HOME PARTY OF
WOLF GRIGOROV

The date is in a week's time. The time is midnight.

I look up at Marcus.

"You got one, too," I say.

We stare at each other.

"Screw them," he says with a sudden flash of savagery. "I don't know what kind of game they're playing now, but I'm done. I never want to see them again."

It's obvious he doesn't mean it.

"Marcus," I say, and my tone turns his eyes back to mine. "Do you believe in magic?"

"Excuse me?"

"Do you believe," I say patiently, "that some people can do things others can't?"

His body is cautious. His eyes are wary. But I can feel it, the subtle shift in him. The coal-black core of him is leaning toward the coal-black core of me, hopeful.

"Yes," he replies, finally. "Are you going to treat me like I'm crazy for it?"

My smile is genuine. "No. Because I have something to tell you."

And I tell him everything.

I list them all, every single one I can think of. Every moment I've caused.

I tell him about Wolf's death.

This hurts, but it feels shamefully good, too, like digging out a black poison thorn that has been lodged in me for a long, long time. I wait to see revulsion in his face, but all I get is a confused frown.

I tell him about my father, and Niral. Anna's phone, Esther's choking fit, and her clay pots. Jase's leg.

And Wolf, again, resurrected. Here again, alive. Alive. That was me. He's alive and that was me and I'm fixed now. I'm not damaged and I'm not wrong because, finally, I can take it back.

I watch as his face shifts from utter disbelief, and then to something else.

"Well?" I say finally.

This is his test. Does he realize it?

Marcus stirs. "Well, what?"

"Do you believe me?"

His mouth opens, closes. Opens again. "Honestly?"

"Honestly."

"I don't know. I think it's the most insane thing I've ever heard."

That's fine. I know how he feels—it's taken me a lifetime to accept it myself.

"I remember that night," he says, suddenly. "The night of the party. For a second, I thought—I really did think—it was you who broke the pots. You were so angry, and they all just . . . smashed. But I was drunk. I just thought I'd made it up somehow."

I hold my breath.

His eyes rise to meet mine.

"And you're telling me Wolf is alive again." He touches the edge of his invitation. "That this, this—is real. And it's because of you."

I am silent, waiting. I will not push.

He leans back, shakes his head. Sighs.

"I don't know. I'd love to believe that it was real. It would be incredible. But I don't know."

"You don't have to know," I assure him. "Not yet. I get it. I just want your help, that's all."

I watch him recover from this latest bombshell.

"Help with what?"

"Help to understand it. You know so much more than me about this kind of thing."

He contemplates this. I wonder if he realizes all the things I don't say that I am asking of him. I'm asking for more. I'm asking for friendship. I'm asking to not be alone in this.

He realizes. His eyes are thoughtful when they come back up to rest on my face.

"I'd like that," he says. "To help."

That old glow starts to spread its wings in my chest, but I pin it before it can get too far.

One last thing.

"Suppose, in the course of things, you find out I'm for real," I say, softly. "Just suppose it's all true. Would you be afraid of me? Would you want to stop me?"

"Afraid?" He looks at me, astonished. "Hell, no. I'd think it was the most incredible gift in the world. I'd think you were *lucky*. What? Why are you grinning like that?"

"No reason," I say, shaking my head while my heart sings and sings. "No reason at all."

My gaze falls on our invitations, peeking gold at us from the table.

When I look back at Marcus, he looks back at me, and I can see what he's thinking.

"I think we should go to the party." My voice is sly.

He sighs a short, sharp sigh. "Oh christ."

But he doesn't disagree.

* * * * *

Pain is my new friend.

* * * * *

I used to think that numbness was the thing that would save me. The lack. If you didn't care, no one could hurt you, and you remained powerful. Now I'm starting to understand that pain is more powerful. Pain is what moves me. As long as I'm motivated by people's pain, I can do anything. One step at a time, stronger and stronger, feeding from pain until I can remake the world into a better place. The kind of place it should be. Who says you must accept the way things are? Anyone who ever counted for anything in the history of the human race never did.

I have a purpose in this universe, now, and I am embracing it.

I am what you become when you decide that what you are is good enough. I'm tired of trying to be less. I no longer wonder whether something like me should be allowed to exist.

I do exist. **I do exist.**

They think I'm powerful?

They haven't seen a fucking thing yet.

# ACKNOWLEDGMENTS

THE ORIGINAL FAN CLUB GETS THE FIRST SHOUT-OUT— Caitlin Lomas, Sally Felton, and Nick Coveney. I roll my eyes when you squeal at me, but secretly I'm both baffled and flattered that you continue to support me so loudly. Thank you so much. And yes, you can make badges with my face on them if you want. It's really, really weird, but I'll be down with it.

YA London Massiv—Juno Dawson, Amy Alward, Kim Curran, James Sythe, Tom Pollock, and Will Hill. May the sexy darklight of our little network never go out. Hugs.

Sam Copeland—this one was fun, wasn't it?! Thank you for keeping your cool. Apart from being possibly the most down-to-earth agent a gal could want, you're also my friend.

Alice Swan and Anne Heltzel—you're a double-team of awesome, handling author freak-outs with calm fabulousness. Without your enthusiastic championing, *The Graces* wouldn't be here. Thank you so much for taking the risk.

My family—British, French, and Greek, for being wonderful and supportive and oh-dear-god eccentric, often all at the same time. I couldn't imagine life without you. I don't *want* to imagine life without you.

Ioannis—for everything. Forever.

# ABOUT THE AUTHOR

LAURE EVE was born in Paris and currently lives in London, where she works in book publishing. She is also the author of *Fearsome Dreamer* and *The Illusionists*, both published in the UK.